JONATHAN
SANTLOFER

ANATOMY OF FEAR

HARPER

An Imprint of HarperCollins*Publishers*

This book was originally published in hardcover April 2007 by William Morrow, an Imprint of HarperCollins Publishers.

HARPER
An Imprint of HarperCollins*Publishers*
10 East 53rd Street
New York, New York 10022-5299

Copyright © 2007 by Jonathan Santlofer
ISBN: 978-0-06-088202-0

First Harper paperback printing: February 2008
First William Morrow hardcover printing: April 2007

HarperCollins ® and Harper ® are registered trademarks of Harper-Collins Publishers.

Printed in the United States of America

Visit Harper paperbacks on the World Wide Web at
www.harpercollins.com

10 9 8 7 6 5 4 3 2 1

For Joy and Doria

People are more practiced in lying with words
than with their faces.

—PAUL EKMAN, *Unmasking the Face*

PROLOGUE

This is the way he always sees it.

The man, stretched out on the concrete, blood pouring out of his head into the grooves that define the sidewalk. From somewhere beneath the body, more blood is being pumped, an amoeba-shaped pond spreading beyond the torso.

He has heard detectives describe the crime scene, and years later stole the case report so he could read what a medical examiner had written. He knows the details: one shot in the head, two in the chest. He also knows that the shot in the head came later, as the man lay bleeding though still alive, because the medical examiner had noted two things: one, that the heart had bled out, indicating that the body was still pumping blood before it shut down; and two, that there were powder burns on the man's temple, a clear indication that the assailant fired that last bullet at close range.

This is the way he sees it, often upon awakening, constantly there as he falls asleep, though more often it has kept him awake.

It has become his bedtime story and his waking nightmare for almost twenty years. It is like an artificial limb which, over time, he has learned to detach long enough so he can eat and dress, have conversations, make love, and even laugh. These are the moments when he forgets, but they are few. It is not easy to forget that you killed your father.

1

The cop led the girl to a seat. "This is Laurie McGrath," she said.

I took her in, then looked away, no more than a few seconds to register the shape of her face (oval), color of her hair (dark blond), young (no more than twenty), left eye swollen half shut, bruise the size of a perfect silver dollar on the zygomatic arch of her cheek, full lips, bottom one split and sutured.

I cleared my throat to get her attention, but did not touch her. I knew better. "Hi, Laurie. I'm Nate Rodriguez." I made sure to keep my voice soft and added a smile, though the girl did not return it. "You up to this?"

"Sure she is," said the cop, dyed red hair pulled back from a thin face, rough skin under heavy pancake makeup, ID pinned to her blouse, SCHMID.

Laurie cadged a look at me through her good eye, possibly assessing my features—dark eyes, dark hair, long bumpy nose, a mix of genetics and teenage brawls. I usually say I got the nose from my mother, Judith Epstein, formerly of Forest Hills, New York; the hair, eyes, and attitude from my father, Juan Rodriguez, NYPD Narcotics, by way of San Juan, Puerto Rico.

"Laurie is pretty sure her assailant was Latino," said

Schmid, looking away, embarrassed, as if she'd said something she shouldn't, as if I didn't know I was half Spanish. She leaned a hand on the young woman's shoulder, and I saw her flinch.

How many days had it been? I replayed the case report in my mind—*pulled into an alleyway, raped at knifepoint, beaten*—but couldn't remember. I've never been good with dates, so I looked at the girl to figure out the timing. Her bruises were fresh. It could not have been more than a day or two. You get to know these things when you've been making forensic sketches as long as I have.

"If it's okay with you, Laurie, I'm going to ask Detective Schmid to leave us alone for a few minutes." I hadn't worked with Schmid before or she'd have known I needed to be alone with the victim.

The young woman's shoulders tensed, but she nodded.

I waited until the detective left, then offered Laurie a smile, a less expansive version of what my *abuela* calls *mi sonrisa matadora*. "So, you in school?"

"Cosmetology," she said after a moment. "You know, beauty school."

"Hair or makeup?"

"Both," she said, taking a deep breath. "But I like doing makeup better."

"Must be fun," I said, thinking it was something, she was used to looking at faces and evaluating them. I asked a few more questions—the kind of cosmetics she liked to use, how long the program was, her plans—anything to keep her talking. After a while she seemed to relax a bit, glancing up at me from time to time, her facial muscles going through a series of micro-expressions—suspicion, fear, sadness—that the great psychologist/scientist Paul Ekman has dissected and codified in his *Facial Action Coding System*.

I've been obsessed with Ekman since he came and spoke to my Quantico class seven years ago, and have memorized his forty-three "action-units," the basic muscle movements the face can make that combine to create over ten thousand possible expressions. There's no way anyone can learn or identify them all, but I'm working on it.

"So, that true, what Detective Schmid said, you think the guy was Spanish?" I asked.

"I think so. His skin wasn't dark, but . . ."

"Like my coloring?"

Laurie glanced up at me, then quickly away. "Oh, no. He was much darker."

She said this as if she were giving me a compliment. I've gotten pretty used to that. Fact is, I have been aware of skin-tone racism most of my life, in particular among the people for whom it most matters, African Americans and New York Hispanics. I can't tell you how many times, after hearing my last name, a dark-skinned Latin will tell me I could pass for white, always with a little desire and resentment. If you ask me, it's totally fucked. But then, I pass for white, so what do I know?

"Sometimes it helps if you close your eyes," I said. "It's easier to visualize that way."

"I can't. When I do, he's . . . all I see."

"You know, Laurie, that's the best news I've heard all day, because if you can see him, you can describe him." I massaged my two-day growth of stubble, sat back, and let that sink in. "You think you can do that—close your eyes and try to let it in just for a minute?"

She nodded, her bad eye closing, the other flickering a few times before it shut. When it did, she sucked in a quick breath, almost a gasp.

"You see him," I said, and knew she had. "I know this is difficult, but hold on to him. Think of this: You've got *him* now." I paused to give her a minute, let my fingers flit over the surface of my high-end drawing paper, Arches hot press, which I cut down to eleven-by-fourteen inches so it fits easily inside a case file, heavyweight so I can erase without tearing it, and one-hundred-percent rag, which makes it archival. I like the idea that my sketches will last, and I'm superstitious enough to believe that if I use good materials the drawings might turn out better. I gripped my Ebony pencil in one hand, a gray blob of kneaded eraser in the other.

"So, let's start with something simple, okay? The shape of his face. Try to see it like a geometric shape—round, square—"

"Oval," she said, squeezing her eyes shut, "with a pointy chin."

"Fantastic," I said, my pencil already moving on the paper, anatomical names—*mandible, maxilla, lacrimal*—automatically clicking off in my mind, words I'd learned in anatomy class that I might use with an ME but never with a subject. I started, as I always do, with a general template, a sort of guide for myself.

It wasn't anything, but I knew there was an image there, waiting. I think of a sketch the way Michelangelo thought about a slab of marble—that the figure was inside and he just had to chip away at the rock to release it. I'm no Michelangelo, but I try to keep that concept in my head while I'm drawing, and without the tricks. I've tried them all— Smith & Wesson's Identi-KIT, PHOTO-FIT, MEMOPIX, even the hot new computer program FACES—but they're not for me. To my mind, moving stock features around on a computer screen leaves something out. Soul, maybe.

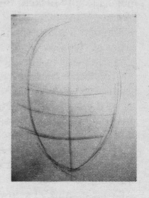

I don't know. But I get something from scratching a pencil on paper that works for me.

At Quantico, I studied all the greats in the field of forensic art, memorized the guidelines in the *Composite Art Manual,* and that, coupled with psychology courses and Ekman's theories, have made me pretty good at reading faces and creating them.

Laurie had her eyes tightly shut, obviously concentrating on the face in her mind.

I needed her to describe it and have learned it's better to come at it obliquely rather than asking a direct question.

"So what kinds of makeup do you use in class?"

"Oh, all kinds. Almay, because it's hypoallergenic; MAC; Great Lash by Maybelline is the old standby mascara, but I like Lancôme's Hypnose, even though it's really expensive."

I zeroed in on the mascara, moved her to eyeliner, then to her attacker's eyes.

"They were in shadow, but . . . I think it was that he had a heavy brow, you know what I mean, like it came to a V."

"His eyebrows, you mean? Like a unibrow?"

"More like his brow was just . . . thick and heavy. This is going to sound stupid, but—"

"Nothing is stupid."

"Well, you know the way Leo, Leonardo DiCaprio, the way his brow comes to a V above his nose?"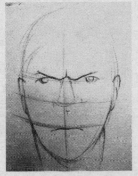

I pictured the young movie idol, could see his face, and quickly got that aspect of it down on paper.

"That's great," I said.

I'd always been able to draw. When I was in junior high I designed personalized tattoos for all my friends, one for myself too, which I glanced at now, regretting I'd ever done it. For weeks after, I'd worn long-sleeved shirts though it was a hot New York summer and I was sweltering. I was trying to hide it from my mother, but she eventually saw it and threw a fit. *Didn't I know that tattooing was against our religion?* I asked her if I'd missed something, like when she got to be so Jewish?

"So, anything else about DiCaprio's forehead?"

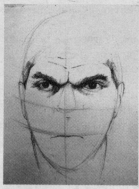

"Just the V, only cruder, and a lot meaner."

I sketched in the heavy brow and dark eyes.

I asked Laurie to move down his face, to his nose, and got her to describe it.

"Thick," she said. "Wide . . . and the nostrils were—what's the word?—flaring?" She added a few details about the nose and eyes, then came back to the brow and the V, and soon her words slipped inside my head like strokes of paint, and I was really starting to see him too.

Laurie's eyes suddenly flipped open. "I'm not sure I—I keep thinking . . . why me? What did I do to deserve this?"

"You didn't do anything." I tried to sound convincing, though part of me was thinking, well, maybe you or your mother or your brother or your ancestors pissed off Iku, or someone hadn't made the correct offering to Chango, which annoyed the hell out of me because I could not believe how this stuff was ingrained in me.

"I—I don't think I can do this."

"Listen to me, Laurie." I tried to hold her in my gaze. "You can do this. I know you can. This guy is scum, an animal, and we don't want him to hurt anyone else, right? You *can* do this."

There were tears running down her cheeks, so I took a gamble, reached out and touched her hand. She flinched, then tightened her grip.

I let her hold on to my hand but after a minute said, "I'm going to need that hand back."

Laurie almost smiled, let go, and closed her eyes again.

"Any scars?" I asked.

"No, I don't think so." She opened her eyes, and the tears started again.

"Stay with me, Laurie. Think of it this way: You conjure his image and give it to me. I record it on paper, and you can forget it.

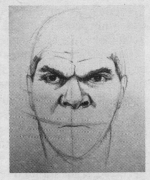

He's gone, erased. It's a shamanistic sort of thing. You know what I'm saying?"

"Like you're a witch doctor?"

I had to smile at the label, something I'd heard tossed around incorrectly most of my life. "Yeah, I guess. Sort of."

Laurie closed her eyes and I closed mine, and for a moment I thought I could see the face in her mind. From time to time it happened, an inexplicable transference.

When I opened my eyes I went back to work.

Now Laurie started talking, really getting into it, emphasizing the pointy chin, the flared nose, and something new: full lips. "Thick and pouty," she said.

"That's great. How old would you say?"

"Thirty? Maybe a little older."

She continued to talk and I kept drawing. Twenty or thirty minutes passed.

"I'm going to need you to look at this."

I waited a second before I turned it around.

That sound again, air sucked into her lungs, a stifled gasp.

I didn't say anything, just waited, chewing on the back end of my pencil, a bad habit I couldn't kick.

"It looks like him, but . . . the chin is wrong."

Defense attorneys often argue that you cannot depend on a victim or eyewitness for identification, but plenty of people have damn good visual memories. Over the years I'd made hundreds of sketches from witnesses and victims, and more than half of them have resulted in an arrest and conviction, so I beg to differ with the suits.

Laurie was staring at the drawing and I saw something change in her eyes, a bit of excitement now mixing in with the dread, something I'd seen lots of times.

"There's something else," she said. "Something missing, but I don't know what."

"Hold on a sec." I reached for my stack of cards: images I had collected over the seven years I'd been doing this job, from newspapers, books, and paintings, cut out and laminated, all sorts of faces, all races, mostly men. I sorted through them, selected a group, and spread them onto the table. "Anything in these?"

Laurie ran her tongue over her sore lip and shook her head.

I tried another group. "What about these?"

"No, but . . . wait. That's it! His chin! It wasn't that it was pointy. It was that he had a, you know, a goatee, like that guy there, in that picture."

I quickly sketched it in. "What about a mustache?"

"Yes. No. More like he hadn't shaved in a while." She looked up and glanced at my cheeks. "Like you—stubble, you know, only it was fuller on his chin, like I said, and pointy."

I reworked the drawing for a minute, then turned it back for her to see.

Laurie let out a startled gasp.

"It's like him?"

"Yes," she said. "But wait—he was wearing a hat!"

"What kind? A cap or—"

"Yes, a cap, a woolen one."

We were really into it now, our minds connecting.

"It was . . . rough. It rubbed against—" She shook her head back and forth as if trying physically to dislodge the memory.

"Stay with me, Laurie."

"Yes," she said, "yes. The hat—it was one of those knit caps, you know, that you just pull on. It covered the top of his head, and—" Her eyes were tight slits of concentration. "It just covered the tops of his ears."

I sketched it in and turned the pad around.

"Jesus," she whispered, blinking, as if she wanted to look and not look at the same time. "It's . . . him."

"Is there anything else you can remember about his face, anything that I should change?"

She shook her head no, holding her breath.

I touched her hand again. "He's on paper now, remember? Not in your head."

She looked at me, good eye narrowed to match the bruised one. "He'll always be in my head."

"Try closing your eyes."

"What's the point?"

"Maybe he won't be there."

I could see she was scared to try.

"C'mon," I said, without pushing too hard.

She took a deep breath and closed her eyes. "I still see him."

"But he's fading, right?"

"Maybe," she said. "Maybe he is."

"And soon he'll be gone." I hoped my face was not betraying the lie. No way he'd ever leave her. Certain pictures remain etched on the brain. I knew that to be a fact, but I didn't say it. I told her she'd done a great job, that she'd be okay.

When she left I stayed behind, got lost in the drawing for a while, added shading, blending areas with soft cardboard stumps or my fingertips, attempting to give the face more dimension and life, then I sat back and assessed it.

It wasn't bad, not exactly art with a capital A. Not science, either. It was sort of like me: not quite a cop, not quite an artist, more like I was swimming around the periphery of each.

I took the sketch into a hallway, sprayed it with fixative so it wouldn't smudge, and dropped it onto Detective Schmid's desk.

Afterward, I stopped into the men's room, washed the graphite off my hands, splashed my face with cold water, and felt a chill. It was one of those bad feelings you can't explain until the bad thing happens and then you think: *Was that it?*

2

The room, a windowless cell of his own design, is like his mind, focused to the point of obsession, shut down to everything and anything other than this moment, the only sound his pencil scratching against paper hard and fast, flecks of graphite catching in the fine blond hairs of his muscled forearms, until lines become forms and imagery takes shape— the bodies everywhere, strewn across the pavement like broken marionettes, arms and legs at impossible angles.

But how to depict cries and groans?

He stops to consider the question.

Shattered bodies, cracked sidewalks, exploding cars he can replicate. But cries? He doesn't think so. Of course the sound track always comes later. True Dolby surround-sound. The real thing.

He stares at the drawing, pale blue eyes riveted.

No, he is getting ahead of himself. This one is for later.

He exchanges the drawing for a folder, puffs at imaginary specks of dust, begins to skim notes of timed entrances and exits until his visual memory is triggered and he sees the man coming out of the brownstone in split-second fragments.

Yes, this is what he is after, what he needs to do now.

He swipes his gloved fingers across a clean page in the sketch pad and sets to work.

One fragment. Then another.

But the picture is incomplete, the rest of it stuck in a synapse.
Damn.

He paces across the room, drops to the floor, does a quick set of push ups, and now, now,

with his heart pumping fast and breath coming in one tiny explosion after another, he sees more of it, bits and pieces that he hurries to get down on paper before they are lost.

But still they remain fragments.

Why can't it ever be born in its entirety?

Must he always get lost to find his way? He tries to locate the part of himself that knows this is simply how it is, that his mind works like some fucked-up computer gathering bits of data that will eventually coalesce.

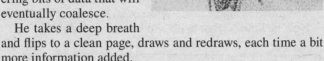

He takes a deep breath and flips to a clean page, draws and redraws, each time a bit more information added.

Yes, that's it, there it is.

The one picture is finished; the relic no longer headless, he sets it aside. He is halfway there, one part of the process complete.

But another image is already pressing against his frontal lobe demanding attention.

Pencils sharpened quickly, electric impulses from his brain telegraphing tiny muscles in his hand to make specific and nonspecific strokes, another enigmatic drawing begins.

But what is it?

His cognitive power to recognize has not yet caught up to his hand.

Trust it. You have been here before.

The pencil starts up again like an extension of his hand, a simple repetitive mark-making machine, stroke after stroke until finally . . . there it is.

He sits back, gloves stained with graphite, adrenaline pumping in his veins, and surveys his work.

The drawings have made sense of it.

Now he knows what to do and how he will do it.

3

"**F**or Christ's sake, keep those people back."

Badge out in front of her, Terri Russo made her way past the uniforms who were trying to maintain order on the Brooklyn street. It was dark, but the combination of yellow street lamps and flashing red beacons bathed the crowd of fifty or sixty people, all angling for a better view, in an eerie orange glow.

Damn it, thought Terri. Didn't they know better? Perhaps the line between real life and entertainment had finally become so blurred, people just thought it was another reality show.

She stopped a moment, her eyes on the crowd. *He could be here.*

Her pivotal case had been one of those—a creep who just couldn't help himself, had to be there, right under the uniforms' and detectives' collective noses, watching them clean up his ugly mess. She'd spotted him from a police sketch, followed him without stopping to think, without calling for backup, which some would call foolish—and did—particularly as she'd taken a bullet to her right shoulder. Worth it, if you asked Terri; it was the collar that had catapulted her into her current position, heading up an NYPD

Homicide Resource Division out of Midtown North. Hell, she ought to thank the little creep.

"What have we got?" she asked the Brooklyn detective, though she already knew. It was the reason she'd been called—the drawing pinned to the dead man, same as the guy who'd been stabbed in midtown Manhattan.

Stabbed, she thought, *not shot.* That didn't make sense.

The Brooklyn detective's eyes did a slow dance over Terri's breasts beneath her tight jean jacket, then back up to her face, her dark hair pulled into a ponytail that made her look about eighteen, though she'd be thirty-one in a week.

He handed her the dead man's wallet. "African American male, shot between six and six-thirty," he said, stifling a yawn. "Couple of witnesses confirmed the attack, heard the shots, but didn't see the shooter. Vic's name is Harrison Stone, lives just there." He pointed to a four-story brownstone. "Wife's already made a positive ID, arrived on the scene about the same time the patrol cars did, approximately ten minutes after the shooting." He angled his head toward a group of detec-  tives, a couple of uniforms, a blond woman crying. "The wife," he said, maybe sneering, Terri wasn't sure.

She noticed one of the crime scene crew removing the sketch from the dead man, about to bag it.

"Over here," she said, pulling on gloves.

Chief of Department Perry Denton arrived at the scene as if he was expecting a red carpet, klieg lights, and Joan Rivers to ask: *Who are you wearing?* He wasn't a big man, but carried himself as if he was. He stuck an unlit cigar between his teeth and surveyed the scene.

Terri thought it was funny that people assumed she'd fucked Denton to get where she was. The truth, if it had been up to Denton she would never have gotten the promotion, not when she'd abruptly ended their affair less than a month after it had started. But that had been over a year ago, when Denton was still heading up Narcotics. How was she to know he'd end up being her boss?

The chief of department took the sketch from her hand, his arm, accidentally-on-purpose, brushing against her chest.

Terri wondered if his wife knew he fucked anything that didn't have a dick. She turned and headed in the opposite direction. She introduced herself to the dead man's wife, a glacial beauty who reminded her of that fifties actress Grace Kelly, though right now the woman's pale blue eyes were red-rimmed, cheeks streaked with mascara. Terri said she was sorry.

"Why . . . Harrison? It . . . it makes no sense. Can you tell me . . . why?" She stared into Terri's face, waiting for an answer.

"Maybe you can help us figure that out," Terri said softly.

The woman shook her head, blond page-boy hair swirling like a skirt around her sculpted jawline.

Denton signaled Terri over with a crook of his finger and the kind of smile that had caused all the trouble in the first place. He moved in close as he talked, lemony aftershave she remembered commingling with the smell of cigar. There were another detective and a couple of CS techies flanking him, just enough audience. He waved the sketch. "I want the lab to go over this like they were going through a murdered whore's pubic hair, you got that?"

Terri flipped open a small notepad and spoke while she

wrote, "Like . . . a . . . murdered . . . whore's . . . pubic . . . hair. Got it."

"Funny," said Denton. He locked his hand on to her shoulder and kneaded it through her jacket.

She slid out of his grip, her shoulder throbbing. It was the exact spot where she'd been shot. Had Denton realized that? She knew the answer. It hadn't taken her long to discover the man was a sadist.

He whispered in her ear, "Need a ride back to the city?"

It had been almost a year and she had no intention of changing her mind. *I'd rather swim,* she thought. "Got my car," she said, trying to keep the attitude out of her voice. She had to be careful. The man could make her life miserable. Of course she could do the same for his. "I should hang out awhile," she said. "See what the immediate canvass produces." This was her second chance and she did not want to blow it.

"Right," said Denton. "You just do that."

4

"**N**ate is Spanish the way Madonna is Jewish."

My friend Julio grinned at his wife, both junior partners at a downtown law firm where they each argued they were the token, Jessica the woman, he the Latino; their baby asleep in a nearby bassinette while we ate dinner ordered in from the local Chinese restaurant.

"*Cálmate*," I said.

The truth was sometimes I didn't know who I was—my Grandma Rose's *tatelleh* or my *Abuela* Dolores's *chacho*.

Hector Lavoe's *La Voz*, the voice, was playing in the background, but only because I'd brought the newly reissued CD of the Puerto Rican salsa singer's groundbreaking 1975 album with me. Otherwise it would have been Mozart or Beethoven, which I still couldn't get used to hearing in Julio's house.

I looked around at the leather couch, Persian rugs and antiques, two floors of a brownstone on Ninety-fourth between Fifth and Madison. Ironic, I thought, Julio living the good life only minutes away from the mean streets of El Barrio where he'd grown up.

"This place is too good for you, man."

Julio made a fist, tapped his heart, and slid into the street talk of his youth. "Don' worry, brothuh, even though I'm at the top, you still my main-mellow man, *mi pana*."

Jess rolled her eyes. "Must you guys always act like teenagers when you get together?"

"Yo, *mira,* I think so." Julio winked at me.

We'd been buddies forever. Julio's aunt lived in the same tenement as my grandmother and he'd hang out there because it was better than the peeling paint and roaches of the project where he lived with his single mom, who worked day and night to keep a roof over their heads. We met one day in the stairwell, Julio hiding out so his aunt wouldn't see and tell his mother that her son was smoking dope at age eleven, and he gave me a toke, my first. When I recovered from the coughing fit we started talking, bonding over the music of Prince and Carlos Santana. From that day on we were brothers.

After that I started going uptown all the time. El Barrio was an ugly ghetto, but compared to where I lived—the Penn South apartments on Eighth Avenue and Twenty-fourth, which was filled with old people and had about as much life as a funeral parlor—it was exciting. My parents didn't like it, but I told them I was in search of my Spanish heritage. Of course that was bullshit. What Julio and I were searching for was alcohol and drugs—and we found them.

Julio would buy weed off the local salesman, some guy who hung around his junior high, then we'd get stoned and go lie around my grandmother's apartment watching TV, playing Nintendo, and laughing. She was always asking *"¿Qué es tan chistoso?"* which would make us laugh even harder.

Julio asked if I was okay and I nodded, but a piece of my past had started to play and I couldn't stop it. I was back in my parents' apartment on Eighth Avenue and Twenty-fourth Street, reliving that night, seeing it all—my room with its posters of Che and Santana, but mostly the look on my father's face.

It was inevitable that he would find out. Maybe I even wanted him to. I thought I was cool and dangerous, bringing shit home with me, grass and crack pipes, not bothering to hide them well. Ironic, you might say, me discovering drugs and my father being a narc with the NYPD. When he found the stash he went ballistic.

Don't you know what I do for a living? Don't you know every week I find kids like you dead, OD'd? What's wrong with you?

He went on like that for a long time, face bright red, veins in his forehead standing out in high relief. He wouldn't stop until I told him where I'd bought my stuff, then he stormed out in search of the guy who was turning his son into a junkie. I was scared shitless. I called Julio, told him to warn the dealer, and asked him to meet me uptown.

I came back to the moment, rubbing my temple.

"Headache, *pana*?"

"It's nothing."

I'd started getting headaches after things went bad. The doctors couldn't find anything wrong with me, so my mother sent me to a shrink. He told me it was displaced anger or guilt and I told him to shove it and never went back. But it wasn't anger or guilt that was giving me a headache right now. It was a combination of my past and the nonspecific dread I'd felt earlier in the day that was still with me. I couldn't shake either one of them.

Julio started talking about a lawsuit he was working on, and got all excited; Julio, the big real estate lawyer, it still surprised me.

"Hey, remember when we used to say you'd be a musician and I'd do your CD covers?"

"That was a long time ago," said Julio.

"You mean you wouldn't swap your career for Marc Anthony's?"

"*¡Nipa-tanto!* Not even for that gorgeous wife of his,

JLo." He looked at his wife. "Who's got nothing on Jess. And for your information, I love my job." He smiled, zygomatic major muscles flexing his cheeks to the corners of his lips, muscles tightening around the eyes that accompanied a genuine smile, which was impossible to fake. It was true: He loved his job and loved his wife.

"And what about your dream of becoming an artist?"

"I *am* an artist," I said.

"Yeah, *mira*, a cop artist," he said, but smiled. "Jess, have I ever told you Nate was top of his class at the academy, got every award, special this, special that?"

"Yeah, I think you told her about a dozen times." I looked at Jess and sighed. "Do not believe everything your husband says. Let me correct that. Do not believe *anything* your husband says."

It was simple, why I gave up actual police work after six months on the street. I couldn't take it. Period. I couldn't take the sour coffee or the sour pimps or the sour prostitutes or the petty thieves or anything else. I hadn't gone into it for the right reasons, and when it didn't reward me by assuaging my guilt, I folded. End of story.

The baby started to fuss and I lifted him out of the bassinette and cooed him into silence.

"Yo, *pana*, you missed your calling. You should have been a wet nurse."

"Be quiet," said Jessica. "You're a natural father, Nate."

Julio's eyebrows slanted up, his mouth down, "action-units" that suggested sadness or anxiety, and I wondered why.

Jess leaned across the table. "Nate, there's this great girl at the office, Olivia—"

"Olivia? For Nate? No way."

"Why not? She's pretty, and—"

"She's all wrong. Not Nate's type."

"What's Nate's type?"

"Not Olivia."

"Hey, guys," I said. "I'm still in the room, remember?"

"*¿Y qué?* Who cares?" said Julio, and laughed.

They went on like that, discussing this woman or that one as a possible match for me because when you're single, couples feel it is their duty to get you married. I just listened while the baby fell asleep against my chest.

At the end of the night Julio was still wearing that sad-anxious expression and I wanted to ask him what was wrong, but he got me in a bear hug before I could.

5

The call from Detective Terri Russo had been a surprise. There was something she wanted to show me. A drawing, I guessed. Or one she wanted me to make. She hadn't been clear, but what else could it be? I crossed a path between the maze of buildings that made up Manhattan's Police Plaza, rubbed a hand across my chin, and thought maybe I should have shaved.

The sky was a bright cobalt blue that only New York City gets in winter, but I was sick of the cold and looking forward to the spring that you never believe will come in March. I dug my hands deeper into the pockets of my old leather jacket. It wasn't really warm enough, but I didn't own an overcoat and had been wearing the jacket for so many years it felt like a second skin.

I glanced up past the buildings that made up Police Plaza to the place where the World Trade Center had stood. On the day of the attack I had been down here working on a sketch with a witness to a bank robbery when we heard the first plane hit. We came outside and saw the flames and smoke, and like so many others who had come out on the street thought it had been some horrible freak accident. But when the second plane hit twenty minutes later, there was no mistaking it. From where we stood, I could see the bodies leaping and falling. It was so unreal I thought I had to be dreaming, it had to be a nightmare, that Jesus or Chango had gone insane, that I was in hell.

About a week after the attack I read a piece in the *New York Times* by a psychiatrist who said denial was a necessary part of human existence and I took refuge in that, and understood what he meant because I'd practiced it from a fairly early age and had, apparently, become very good at it.

So now I focused on a handful of crocuses that had bravely pushed up through a light dusting of snow in the center of the walkway, and took them as a hopeful sign that spring would come and that all was right with the world, that Inle had gone to work healing, as my grandmother would say. I wanted to believe that someone was thinking about healing, but even now, more than five years after the towers had come down, I could not stop worrying about landmarks exploding, poison gas in the subway, or an avian flu pandemic. I started chewing a cuticle, a habit I developed after I'd quit smoking for the third time.

I thought about my first and only meeting with Detective Russo over a year ago, as I emptied my pockets to go through the metal detector. Good-looking but tough, at least that's how she'd seemed when I'd handed over the police sketch I'd done for her, which had led to her capturing a perp, which in turn led to her promotion, or so I'd heard. She never told me. It wasn't like I was expecting a gift-wrapped thank-you, but a call wouldn't have killed her.

The door was ajar and Russo was pacing back and forth. I caught a few glimpses of her tight jeans and black tee. She was letting her hair down, combing her fingers through it, and it reminded me of a pastel by Degas, one of the artist's *Bathers*. She was cinching her hair into a ponytail when I tugged the door open.

Detective Terri Russo was even better looking than I remembered, high forehead, straight nose, her full lips reminiscent of the actress Angelina Jolie.

"Sorry to drag you all the way downtown." Her voice was deeper than I remembered, tinted with an outer-borough accent I couldn't quite place, maybe Brooklyn or Queens. "But the lab isn't finished with these." She indicated some sketches laid out on the desk that had already caught my attention. "Homicide Analysis has looked them over and Forensics too, but there are more tests and full workups to come." She was talking in a rush, obviously worked up. "I asked you here because I need a good set of eyes on these. Maybe you can see something in them neither the lab nor the technicians can."

I waited, but she didn't add any details.

"So what do you think?"

"They're not bad."

"I wasn't looking for a review. I want to know if you think they were made by the same person."

"Well, that's not what you asked, and I'm not a mind reader."

"Really? I'd heard just the opposite. You've got a reputation." A small grin passed over her lips, but didn't set up camp. "So, is it?"

"The same artist?"

"Yes." She was rapping her fingernails against the edge of the desk.

"Okay if I take them out of the bags?"

She nodded and handed me a pair of gloves. I put them on, slid the drawings out, and came in for a closer look.

"The mark-making technique looks the same in both drawings, one just a bit looser than the other," I said. "Drawing is like handwriting." I took another minute going from one sketch to the other, while Detective Russo kept up the annoying fingernail tapping.

"You could take something for that," I said.

"For what?"

"Your nerves."

Russo's upper lip registered just a bit of disgust at my comment, so I guessed she didn't think it was funny. I said I was sorry and went on to tell her a bit more about the pencil strokes I was looking at, pointing out how they both used the same sort of angled stroke.

Russo was leaning in close, her perfume, something fresh and herbal, filling the air between us.

"My guess is that it is the same guy, and that he's right-handed." I knew this because I was right-handed and laid my strokes down in a similar way, but did not tell her because it

was a bit creepy to think I had anything in common with whoever had made these drawings.

"Lab says they're made with graphite."

"Aka pencil. And a fairly soft one. Could be a standard number-two pencil, though probably softer, a three or four." I gave her a little tutorial on pencils, hard versus soft, taking them out of my pencil box and displaying them as I did, ending with my personal favorite, the Ebony.

"Looks like a beaver chewed it," she said.

"Bad habit," I said, resisting an impulse to make a crude beaver joke, which I knew would not be appreciated.

"What else can you tell me about the drawings?"

I looked again. "I'd say he's making them fast, and with a certain amount of assurance. He might have had some training, maybe art school, some drawing or design classes."

Russo was listening intently, brows knit, a slight squint, like she was cataloging the information, maybe cataloging me too.

"The lab will no doubt be seeing if the paper is the same. And while they're at it maybe you'll get lucky and the guy will turn out to be a secretor and have left you a little DNA from sweaty palms."

"Sounds like you've been hanging around the NYPD too long."

"I went through the academy."

"Really?"

"Yeah, but I chose forensic art over the street."

"Didn't want to get your hands dirty?"

"Just the opposite." I tugged off the gloves and displayed my hands, the graphite and charcoal always there, no matter how many times I washed them, under the nail beds, and my slightly chewed cuticles.

"I didn't mean that as an insult," she said. "Unfortunately, prelims say there are no fluids—other than the two vics' blood—on either drawing." She looked directly at me. "Anything you can tell me about the unsub from the drawings themselves?"

She'd switched into cop lingo, *vic* for victim, *unsub* for unknown subject. On some level she had started treating me like a cop. I took it as a good sign.

"You mean like, does he hate his mother or torture animals?"

"Not quite, but—"

"I get your drift. Analyze the artist through his art."

"Something like that."

"Hope nobody ever does that about me."

"Why? What would they find?"

"I don't know . . . that I have an obsession with rapists and murderers because that's all I ever draw?"

She arched a brow. "So what about this guy?"

I told her I wasn't a psychiatrist, but from the look of the drawings I'd guess whoever made them was neat, compulsive, and very definite, the latter because I couldn't detect any erasing. "It's just my initial read, and it's possible someone could make totally tight-ass drawings and be a mess in real life." I knew that for a fact: My own drawings were even tighter than this guy's and if anyone saw the mess in my apartment they'd never guess I could make them. "You might want to send them to Quantico for a psyche profile."

"We've got it under control," she said, but I could see she was bullshitting when she said it because the exact opposite flashed across her face.

People don't realize our faces are controlled by a totally separate, involuntary system of muscle movements that reveal what we're really feeling. They listen to what's being said when they want the truth. Me, I watch what's happening on the face.

Like right now, Russo was practicing what's called neutralizing, trying to freeze her face. But there was something going on around her mouth, the first place to look for facial leakage, her orbicularis oris muscle being used for what is commonly referred to as lip sucking, a dead giveaway for anxiety. My guess was Terri Russo was worried that if she didn't get something soon, the G, which is how the cops referred to the FBI, would be taking over the case.

"So why do you think this guy makes drawings of his vics?" she asked.

"Don't know. The only thing that drawing his victims proves is that he's stalked them, right? He'd have to, to be able to draw them."

"Yes, but my question is why make them in the first place?"

"Could be his signature? Maybe he wants everyone to *know* it's his work?"

Russo angled another look at me. Maybe she was thinking I was smarter than she'd expected, not just a drop-out cop with a flair for drawing who'd forgotten to shave.

"You should have been a shrink, Rodriguez."

I told her that the shrink stuff had been part of my college and forensic art training, but didn't bother to tell her that my mother was a psychiatric social worker and I'd grown up around it too. "No way," I said. "I couldn't take people complaining all day."

She glanced from me to the drawings, then back at me. There was something going on in her mind. I could see it from the dozens of fleeting micro-expressions that were passing over her face, none of them staying quite long enough for me to read.

"By the way, I owe you a thank-you," she said. "I should have called about that sketch you made for my department, but I got busy, you know how it is."

"Sure," I said.

"It was an amazing resemblance. I knew the guy right away. How do you do it—I mean, capture that kind of likeness?"

"What can I say? I'm a trained professional."

"No, seriously."

"I don't know. It's something I could always do, draw from memory. I used to practice as a kid, do portraits of my friends when they weren't around; athletes and movie stars too." Something about her question made me start back on a cuticle.

"Right, but those are faces you'd be familiar with, that you'd seen. I mean, how can you draw someone you've *never* seen?"

"It's mostly the training, but . . . sometimes, when I make a connection, things just come to me, and I see them."

"Like what things?"

I glanced at my cuticle. It was bleeding. I shoved my hand into my pocket. "I don't know, not exactly. It's some sort of . . . transference."

"What do you mean by that?"

"Like between a shrink and a patient—you know, the Freudian thing? But maybe that's the wrong word. If you ask one of the geeks who use computer programs, the ones that move noses and lips around instead of pencil on paper, I don't know what they'd say, but I'm guessing they'd think it was more science than intuition."

"But you don't think so?"

"I guess I'm just a dinosaur, but I like my pencils and paper, and I like the time it takes to get acquainted with a subject, to hear what they're saying, to look at them." I looked at Terri Russo, her good bone structure, smooth skin across her frontal eminence, the beautifully arched brows over her supraorbital, the nice sharp angle of her mandible, and smiled.

"What's so funny?"

"Nothing. Sometimes I forget I'm not working."

"But you *are* working." She raised her brow for a second. "So you can draw just about anything."

"Is this a test?"

"You don't have to get defensive, Rodriguez."

"Nate."

"Okay. Nate. It was just a question."

"Yeah, I guess I can draw just about anything."

"See," she said. "That wasn't so hard. I was asking because we haven't yet come up with a witness to either of these murders, but if we do, you'd obviously be the man to call."

I nodded.

"Right." She glanced up, the muscles around her mouth

pinching her lips. She was deciding whether or not to ask a question. "And . . . what if we never get a witness?"

"Excuse me?"

"I was just wondering if you might be able to make a sketch."

"You mean without a witness?"

"Yes."

"I'm not a psychic or a witch doctor."

"No, of course not." She scanned my face a moment, and once again I could see her weighing a question. "But what about the transference thing?"

"Well, yes, but I need someone to have it with."

"Right," she said. "Of course."

6

The images have begun to appear, just a few repeated fragments, but enough to record.

A new sheet of paper, a few more fragments drawn, but still they refuse to coalesce.

Relax.

A long deep breath, eyes closed, trying to imagine what he will do and how they will die. But still the images resist, fragments doing a jitterbug in and around his optic nerve, not quite ready to make the journey from brain to eye to paper.

He pushes away from the table with a hissing sigh, gazes at the pictures he has affixed to his walls for inspiration, and the fragments in his mind start up again.

The puzzle pieces have begun to take on meaning, each one adding to the whole: a stroke, a shape, an abstract blob, coming together to tell him what he needs to know. He sets one against another, fleshing out the picture, time passing, more and more fragments committed to paper, the image finally harvested.

He sits back, eyes closed, and pictures the event: collecting his gear, changing his clothes, riding the subway, stalking his prey.

7

Terri Russo turned toward the commotion, two cops dragging a guy into the booking room.

"Get the fuck off me, assholes!"

"Who's the asshole, huh?" said one of the cops, face bright red. He elbowed the cuffed man in the ribs while the other cop slammed him into a metal chair and cuffed him to it—a good thing, as the guy was bucking like one of those kiddy rides they used to have in front of dime stores and supermarkets.

Detective Jenny Schmid of Sex Crimes made her way across the room to greet the detectives and their prey.

"This the piece of shit?" she asked.

The red-faced cop said, "No question. We got a call, a break-in, and look who we find." He handed Schmid a paper with a picture on it.

"You read him his rights?" asked Schmid, leaning over the guy, who was huffing like a horse after a run, his nostrils flaring. She held the picture up.

Terri glanced from the police sketch in the detective's hand to the guy cuffed to the chair.

Schmid dangled the sketch in front of the perp's face. "Looks like you fucking posed for this."

The other cops in the room stopped writing up reports and

turned toward the show, practically twitching in their chairs, waiting for an excuse to take a potshot at the perp. And they might have if some office type in khakis and a button-down shirt hadn't come in with a big carton of folders, which he plopped onto a desk so he could get a good look too.

Schmid peered at him over the top of her glasses. "And you are?"

"Office of Public Info," he said. "Just delivering some stuff for Detective Towers."

"Well, deliver it," she said. "And go."

The guy lifted the box, but leaned over to peek at the drawing at the same time. "Wow," he said. "That's really good."

"Thanks *so* much for your expert opinion," said Schmid, who aimed a finger at the door.

The guy narrowed his eyes at her, then sighed and left, balancing the carton in one hand like a waiter with a tray.

Terri cleared her throat.

Schmid acknowledged her with a slight turn of her head and another look of annoyance.

"That sketch," Terri asked. "Who made it?"

Schmid sighed as if Terri had asked her to donate a kidney, but handed it over before going back to her suspect.

Terri flipped it over, noted the date, time, name of the witness, and the sketch artist, Nathan Rodriguez. She looked back and forth between the sketch and its living embodiment cuffed to the chair, the resemblance dead-on. Rodriguez had a gift, no question.

How did he do it? She could not imagine. But then, all Rodriguez had needed was one look at her unsub's drawings to know they were made by the same man, one who was right-handed—and the lab had confirmed it. The sketches had come from the same kind of sketch pad, the glue that had held them in place still detectable along the edge of each. It was something, a connection, though nothing a DA could take to court. If they were lucky they might find something on the drawings other than the vics' blood, though so far there was nothing.

But it was the same MO, the unsub had a signature, a ritual. Something else Rodriguez had been right about. She'd fed that info—two vics, two drawings—into VICAP, the Violent Criminal Apprehension Program, but there'd been no match.

A serial killer. Something no one wanted to say aloud. Not yet. Terri knew what it meant: that the feds would be all over it, and soon. Serial killers were their thing. Though in the last few years those particular bad boys had ceded a little bit of their numero uno status to terrorists, which the bureau was not quite as good at capturing or deterring, not that there was any way to deter serial killers unless the government opted for sterilizing all potentially abusive parents, for a start, which Terri thought was a damn good idea. Of course there was still that unexplainable part, the "evil gene" so many scientists were talking about these days. Score one for nature versus nurture, thought Terri. No doubt that cheered the parents of the Jeffrey Dahmers of the world.

"You saving that picture for framing?" Schmid asked.

"Sorry," said Terri. She handed it back to the detective and cut out of the booking room, thinking about Nate Rodriguez and his special gifts. She wasn't sure how he was going to help her, but she was working on it.

8

The odor hit me in the face the minute I entered the apartment and I froze, worried, until I realized it wasn't that kind of smell. I knew that smell, had had the misfortune my very first week on the beat to find two bodies in the final stage, the putrefaction stage, in an abandoned crack house where they had obviously OD'd. I'll never forget it.

I called out, *"¡Uela!"* and followed the odor's trail down the dim hallway. It revealed itself in the kitchen, a large pot bubbling away on the stove, steam rising from it. I leaned over it holding my breath. *Weeds.* My *abuela* had been wasting her social security check at the local *botánica,* nothing unusual about that. She's a true believer, a practicing *santera,* a sort of neighborhood priestess. People flock to her for answers and guidance. I think it's because she's kind and understanding and has a gift for making people feel good about themselves, but she sees it as her calling, and she's devoted.

I went into the living room, which was decorated with bright purple curtains; a pink afghan throw on the couch; a mix of bold prints on the pillow covers; walls covered with drawings I'd made over the years, a few pictures of saints mixed in, and the eight-by-ten glossy of my father, a graduation photo from the police academy just above a white-clothed table tucked into a corner, the *bóveda,* a shrine to the dead. I'd seen it hundreds of times in various forms. Right now it held a dozen glasses and goblets filled with water, and I knew what it meant: My grandmother was asking something of her ancestors.

I took a step into the hall and heard voices from behind the closed door of the *cuarto de los santos,* the room of the saints, where my *abuela* held her consultations.

I knew better than to disturb her, though I thought it was nonsense; and occasionally dangerous, when someone should have been in a doctor's office rather than the back room of a railroad tenement in Spanish Harlem, but it was impossible to convince my grandmother of that.

The door opened, the woman beside my grandmother looked up, startled when she saw me, gasped and crossed herself. Not a surprise. Many of the followers of Santeria remained Catholics. It didn't seem to matter they were practicing a religion that bastardized the faith by renaming the saints, the *orishas,* after African gods to whom they prayed for guidance, forgiveness, even wrath and punishment for others, or that Santeria had been condemned by the church.

I had tried to explain the contradiction to my grandmother, as well as the origin—that Santeria was a consequence of forcing Roman Catholicism on Africans brought to the Caribbean by slave traders—but she would never listen. She went to church regularly and did not see any conflict. As a kid she had me memorize the names and powers of the individual *orishas* even while she was dragging me to church every Sunday. Between my maternal Jewish grandmother telling me about the deadly Passover plagues while stuffing me with latkes, and my *abuela*'s heavy-duty mix of Christianity and Santeria, it pretty much explained my becoming an agnostic. But my *abuela* loved Jesus as passionately as she loved Olodumare, the supreme being, and I'd long ago given up trying to convince her otherwise because I loved her.

"Nato, pensé que te había oído."

Of course she'd heard me come in, she always did.

She turned to her customer, whispered something in Spanish, handed over candles with garish images of saints, and explained when to light them.

"Did you charge her for those candles?" I asked after the woman had left.

My grandmother planted her hands on her hips and narrowed her dark eyes. "I do not steal from ones in need and pain."

"I know that, *uela*. But you can't spend all your money on other people."

"*Cálmate,*" she said, a nice way of telling me to shut up, then got a tender grip on my face with both hands. At five feet tall, the top of my grandmother's head just cleared my shoulders. "*Ven, estoy cocinando.*"

"Yeah, I know you're cooking, but what, the cat?"

"*Ay, qué chistoso.*" She shook a finger at me, but smiled. "Why you never shave, Nato?"

Nato, her favorite among several nicknames for me; *neno, nenito,* the others. Nathan was impossible for her to say with its *th* sound, plus she'd never liked the name. She brought this up to my mother at least once a month, and I gave her credit for never quitting. Lately, she'd been lobbying for Anthony or Manuel. At my thirty-third birthday this past January she'd presented me with a wallet with the letter A stamped on it. "What's with the A?" I'd asked. "In case you decide on Anthony," she'd said. You had to give it to her. My mother almost *plotzed,* which was my Jewish grandmother's favorite word or saying: *I could plotz,* she'd say, or *I'm plotzing.* My two grandmothers adored each other, though I don't know if they ever understood what the other one was saying, which is maybe why they adored each other. Occasionally my *abuela* used the word *plotz,* and it always made me laugh.

We headed into the kitchen and she asked me again why I didn't shave and I said it was because I didn't like to look at my face. She called me a *mentiroso,* a liar, and waved a hand at me, the bangle and beaded bracelets at her wrist clanging out a tune.

I glanced at the pot on the stove. "Cooking up one of your potions for a client, a *riego,* right?"

"You think you know everything, *chacho.*" Another nickname, this one generic, *boy,* to put me in my place.

"And of course you're paying for it."

"¿Qué importa?" she said.

"It matters because I don't like to see you wasting your money."

"It would be better if you worried a little about yourself, *Nato.* The way you stay in your apartment, alone, or at work, making pictures of those *diablos.* It's time you found a girl, *una mujer,* to start making babies."

"Oh, brother."

"Do not oh brother with me, *chacho.* Find a nice girl, it's time." She took my face in her hands again. *"Oye, guapo."* She was playing at being exasperated, but still called me handsome. My grandmother thinks I look like Fernando Lamas and every other good-looking Spanish actor that ever existed. Last week she added Ricky Martin to the list. I do not look like any of them.

For a moment her face clouded, and I saw something behind the good-natured scolding. I glanced back at the boiling pot, the *riego,* knew that it was used to sprinkle around an apartment to chase away evil spirits.

"¿Qué pasa, uela? ¿Pasa algo?"

"I had a dream," she said.

"One of your visions?"

She nodded.

"A bad one?"

Another shrug and wave of the bangle-bracelet hand.

"You want me to draw it?"

I'd been drawing her visions for half my life—mostly Chagall-like fantasies with clouds, wild plants, Latin crosses, and the occasional dancing animal. But there had been bad visions too, dark and brooding ones filled with omens that even as a boy had chilled me. My grandmother hadn't kept those. I suspected she had burned them, offered them up to one of the *orishas* as some form of sacrifice.

"It is not clear," she said.

"Maybe if you describe it, it will get clearer."

"Later," she said. "First, eat. Yesterday I cooked *bacalaitos,* just for you."

I could practically taste the fried, doughy cod fritters. "Good. For a minute there I was afraid you were going to feed me that foul-smelling *ebo.*"

"*Chacho*, do not make fun of the *ebo*—of the sacrifice. It is not good to offend the *orishas.*" My grandmother got serious, wheeled around and plucked a small blue bottle from a shelf crowded with dozens of others. She whisked off the top, mumbled something under her breath, tapped some liquid onto her fingers, and flicked it at me. *"Muy bien. Un poco de agua santa."*

I just stood there, accepting the sprinkling of holy water. There was no point in fighting her.

"Sit." My grandmother turned the flame off the *riego,* got the cod fritters from the fridge, heated up a portion that was way too big, and presented the platter. I ate most of it while she nattered on about this poor soul and that one, and how people should be happier and kinder and why the man at the fish counter was a sneaky one trying to sell old fish, then asked again why I had no new girl in my life, and I had a brief flash of Terri Russo running her fingers through her hair. I told my grandmother I just wasn't lucky with women and she suggested I make an offering to Oshun, the *orisha* of love, to which I sighed and she sighed too.

I refused a second portion, and my grandmother cleared the plate. She had stopped making small talk and I could see she was ready. She beckoned me to follow. *"Ven p'aca."* She started singing an old song, a favorite of hers, but without the usual lilt.

"Ten Cuidado con el Corazón . . ."

I knew the song well. Please be careful, it began, a warning that things can always change or go wrong.

In the living room I retrieved the pad and pencils I kept

at her apartment, took a seat on the couch, and opened to a clean sheet of paper.

"A room," she said, crowding beside me on the couch to watch and direct.

"Just a room?"

"Oye, nene, pon atención." The usual playfulness was gone from her voice. She rested one of her jeweled hands on her heart and closed her eyes. "A room," she repeated, and began to fill in the details, the picture in her head transferring to mine, then onto paper.

My grandmother was always my best witness, her descriptions perfect. Or maybe it was just that we were in tune after so many years of practice. She gave my drawing a glance, and said, *"Muy bien."* She enjoyed the process of seeing her vision take shape and come to life.

She turned her attention to another detail.

"Y una ventana," she said, and went on to describe it.

She leaned over the pad. *"Bien hecho,"* she said, and though she was still not smiling I could see that something was being lifted from her. Maybe that's what it had always

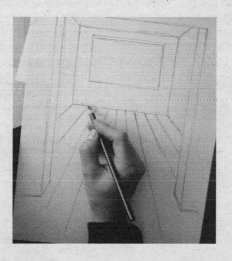

been about—her telling, me drawing—the transference easing some of her anxiety. What I had been trying to describe to Terri Russo.

My grandmother took a deep breath. *"Otra cosa,"* she said. "You will have to change something. *Aqui.*" She pointed to the paper and explained what it was she wanted me to add.

I'd gotten into it, I always did, adding details, blending with my fingertips.

"Bueno," she said, then sat back and crossed herself. "But . . . *está mal.*"

"What's bad? My drawing?"

"No, *neno.* The room."

"It doesn't seem so bad, *uela.*"

She raised a jeweled hand to stop me from talking. "There is a man in the room—or the spirit of a man. Chango has sent a warning. I cannot see him, but . . . maybe you can."

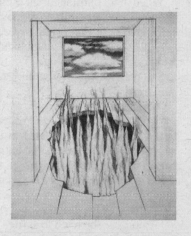

"You want me to draw a man you haven't seen?"

My grandmother looked at me as if believing I could, but lifted a finger to my lips. *"Escucha,"* she said.

I stopped talking and did as she asked, listened.

"Hay más," she said, and explained it.

I went back to the drawing and tried to capture what she described.

"It looks like hell," I said. "Your vision. Not my drawing." I laughed, but my grandmother did not. She crossed herself. "There is something else in that room. *¿Cómo se dice? Un diseño.* In front of the window, a circle . . . And inside the circle," she went on, "*un diseño,* another one . . . I had it in my head, but . . . it is gone."

"Close your eyes and let it come, *uela.*"

After a moment she said, *"¡Lo veo!"* and told me what to draw.

When I was finished she smiled because I had done a good job, but her smile faded fast.

"The *ashe* in that room, *no es bueno.*"

Ashe: the basic building block of everything according to Santeria.

She reached for my hand. "Nato," she said. *"Tengo más que decir."*

"What is it, *uela*?"

"You, *neno,*" she said. "You are in that room. Not now, but . . . sometime. It is hard to explain." She let go of my hand, crossed the room, and gathered up seashells scattered between the goblets of water on the *bóveda.* "I will read the shells and figure out exactly what sort of *ebo* will keep you safe. *No te preocupes.*"

"I'm not worried, *uela.*"

"Nato . . ." She tried to smile. "Make your *abuela* happy." She plucked a large purple candle off the table and handed it to me. "Take this and burn it in your apartment. For me, for your *abuela.*"

"It doesn't work if you don't believe, does it?"

"There are forces stronger than you, Nato. *Por favor, toma la uela.*"

She handed the candle to me, and I took it.

9

"**B**ut we have theater tickets, Perry, you know that." His wife whined in the singsong Indian accent that he once found so adorable.

"Take one of your girlfriends, baby." He pulled her to him, locking his fingers firmly behind her back, their faces inches apart.

"You smell like a cigar." She managed to get one of her hands to his chest and tried to push him back. "And don't call me baby."

They'd met at the UN, some party for the delegate to Botswana. He'd come with the woman he'd been seeing at the time, a leggy blonde, secretary to the delegate from Botswana, but the moment he'd met Urvishi he'd forgotten about the blonde. Urvishi was a translator, and the most beautiful woman he'd ever seen. But that had been seven years ago. And who was it who said that no matter how beautiful the woman, somewhere there was a man who was tired of fucking her? Wise man, thought Perry Denton.

"You used to like it, bay-bee." He grinned and tightened his grip, then let her go and took a step back. "Look, baby, you're the lucky one. You get to go to the theater. Me, I'm stuck in another damn meeting with the mayor."

"You spend more time with the mayor than you do with me." She pouted like a little girl.

"You have any idea the kind of pressure that comes with my job, baby?"

"I think you like your important meetings."

Denton's hands clenched into fists and twitched at his sides, but the wife of the chief of department could not be seen in public with a black eye. *Too bad,* he thought.

His wife seemed to read his mind. "I'm sorry," she said.

"Sure you are, baby." He phoned in a smile. "Enjoy the play—and don't wait up."

"No driver tonight, Chief?" The doorman, a young Irish kid who Denton thought looked like half the rookies in the academy, tipped his cap.

"Just going for a walk."

"Can I call you a cab, sir?"

"Hard to take a walk in a taxi," said Denton, lighting up a cigar as he headed toward the corner.

The subway car was half empty, the evening rush long over. At Ninety-sixth Street most of the white people got off.

Denton brushed a few hairs—blond, definitely not his wife's—off the lapel of his cashmere jacket and stared at his reflection in the smudged windows that looked out on nothing but darkness. He adjusted his sunglasses and glanced around to see if anyone recognized him. There were only a few people in the car and no one looked his way.

The subway roared into the station and Denton got off. This was the last time he would meet Vallie up in the fucking Bronx. He had made the decision. Vallie had forced his hand.

*   *   *

Terri looked past the drawing in her gloved hand to the victim sprawled on the pavement just a few feet away: life imitating art.

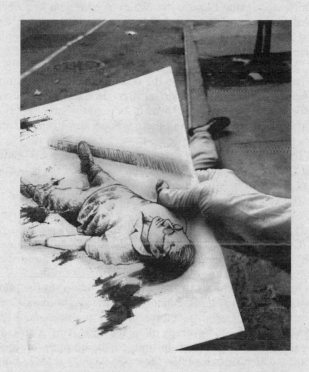

She handed the drawing back to Crime Scene. "Not for public consumption," she said. She did a slow three-sixty of the quiet street, the four- and five-story brownstones, mixed with taller apartment buildings, and tried to reconstruct the crime.

Had the shooter approached the vic, shot him point-blank, or had the shots been fired from a distance?

"Any witnesses?" she asked one of her detectives, Vinnie Dugan, a pug-nosed Irishman who'd expected to get Terri's job and hadn't gotten it. He'd been going through the crowd, which wasn't that big, maybe twenty people who had been awakened by police sirens at 2:00 A.M. Had it been earlier, and a different neighborhood, this sort of spectacle would have been SRO.

"Nada," said Dugan. "And no one heard the shots."

But someone had to have the heard shots! Terri took another look at the quiet residential street. Had the shooter used a silencer? And if so, why? Was it some sort of paid hit? But that didn't make sense. And there was another drawing, another fucking drawing.

Terri tapped a CS tech. "Have you checked the vic's shirt for anything that could have gotten on it when the drawing was pinned onto him?"

The guy looked insulted by the question. "Of course."

"And you've got the pin, right?"

He displayed a plastic bag, the pin inside.

The medical examiner swabbed the dead man's forehead with a Q-tip and zipped it into a bag. "The lab will do further tests for GSR, but right now I'm saying there's residue."

Terri studied the victim's position and turned to the photographer. "Can you get a shot of the vic from both east and west? Full-body shots. Pictures of the street too—and the crowd." She turned to survey them, the outer fringes already breaking down, people returning to the comfort of their homes, which surprised her. Most people did not leave until the body had been bagged and taken away, the best part of the show. She figured things weren't moving fast enough for them, no close-ups, no snappy dialogue. She signaled to Dugan.

"Who's doing the canvass?"

"Detectives from the Twenty-third," he said. "It's their beat, remember?"

"And part of *our* investigation," said Terri. "Take a uniform and start on the north side of the block." She gestured to her other men. "O'Connell, you and Perez can work the south."

"People up here don't like being awakened in the middle of the night," said Perez.

"Like I give a shit?" Terri sighed. "Look, guys, I know it's late. I'd like to be home in bed as much as you. Tell you what, finish up here, meet me at the station, and I'll treat you to breakfast."

"As long as it's a real one," said O'Connell. "None of that Egg McMuffin crap."

"You got it." Terri watched them walk away. Maybe they wouldn't be calling her bitch behind her back, which she knew they'd been doing her first few months on the job. She wondered where Denton was. Off screwing one of his interns, her best guess. He'd be pissed that he had missed a photo op. The press had just arrived, TV reporters hooking up mikes, film crews angling for shots as CS finished up and EMT finally bagged the body.

She glanced over at the man who had discovered the body, a young guy who had been to a bachelor party, reeling a bit as if his feet were glued to the ground and his body tugged by opposing magnets. He hadn't seen anyone, just the body. He'd probably tripped over it.

One decent witness, was that too much to ask? Someone who had seen something, who could sit down with Rodriguez and let him do his transference thing, his magic.

Terri's adrenaline was starting to ebb, replaced by an empty sinking feeling.

Hell, it would have to be real magic if they did not have a witness. After all, Rodriguez could not make up a face from thin air.

10

Perry Denton's office had the look of an important man, leather and brass, a wall of books that Terri knew he'd never more than glanced at. He'd had it redecorated when he assumed the job because, he'd told Terri, the chief of department had to set the right tone.

"So where were you last night?"

"Busy," said Denton. "Is that why you're here, to ask me where I was? I don't have time to run to every crime scene, Russo, that's not my job."

"Sorry, I was simply asking. I thought . . ." She let it go, glanced at the *Post* and *News* on Denton's desk. The murder had made both morning editions. A man shot dead on the Upper East Side was the sort of story that made New Yorkers uncomfortable. They didn't notice if someone was gunned down in Harlem, but this sort of thing didn't happen in their neighborhoods, and when it did, they wanted answers.

The PD had managed to keep the victim's name out of the papers, and, more important, the drawing. If the press got hold of that piece of information, it would be a field day. And it was only a matter of time before some eager reporter sniffed it out. They always did. Terri knew it. Denton knew it too.

She turned the *Post* around to read it and Denton stopped her, his hand on top of hers.

"Is there a reason you're here, Russo?"

She slipped her hand out from his and laid the sketch on his desk.

"What's this?"

"A sketch by one of your men, a freelancer, a cop. Nate Rodriguez."

"Yeah, I know who he is. Sketch artist. So what?"

"So the perp was caught. Detectives say they picked him up by the sketch alone."

"Meaning what? That it was a good sketch?"

"More than a good sketch. A *great* sketch. 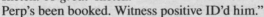 Perp's been booked. Witness positive ID'd him."

"So it was a great sketch." Denton looked perplexed.

"Well, Rodriguez is an asset, a good cop."

"What's your point, Russo?"

"Rodriguez is being underused."

Denton grinned. "Meaning you have an idea about how he should be used, that it?"

"Yes." Terri took a deep breath. "I'd like to take him with me, let him talk to a few people around each of these vics, the ones found with the drawings—"

"Rodriguez? On the street? You shitting me?"

"No."

"Wait a minute." Denton leered. "What is it? You sweet on the guy?"

"*Sweet on the guy?* You been reading romance novels, Perry? But for the record, no, I'm not sweet on him. I think he can help with the investigation, that's all. He's a cop with a special talent."

"A cop who spent what, three days on the job?"

Terri tried to collect her thoughts. She'd done her homework, stayed up late reading the files: Rodriguez's college and police academy records, references from his stay at Quantico, all excellent. "He was top of his class, aced every course, Crime Scenes, Elements of Proof, Interviews and Interrogations, Communications—"

"I know the course work, Russo. So what?"

"There are letters in his file from over a dozen academy instructors, all testifying to the guy's talent. Before the academy there was Hunter College, double major in psychology and art." She put a hand up to keep Denton from interrupting. "And of course there's the Quantico forensic art course, which included profiling, more psychology, more interview techniques, plus commendations from every Quantico instructor."

"But the guy's got no street creds, and—"

"I'm not asking him to shoot anyone. I just want him to do what he does, *draw.* You ever look at the stats on his success rate? One of two of his drawings has resulted in an arrest."

"I'm impressed," said Denton, voice flat.

"You should be. Half the PDs in the States call him in to do freelance work for them, Seattle, L.A., next week the Boston PD. We're lucky to have him." She paused to let that sink in. "Maybe he can come up with a sketch, a composite of our unsub."

"But nobody's seen our unsub; remember that part, Russo?"

"All I'm asking is to let me take Rodriguez to meet a few of the witnesses who—"

"—didn't see anything." Denton shook his head. Did he need this petty shit, now of all times? "Bet you didn't take this up with your department chief because you knew he'd turn you down."

"No, I didn't because I'm asking *you,* Perry."

"Forget it."

"Look—"

"No, you look." Denton pointed his finger at her like a gun.

"I've got a city to take care of, and people to answer to. I've got a reputation to protect, you understand that, Russo?"

"Oh, yes. I understand all about protecting your reputation." She didn't have to spell it out and didn't want to say what Denton already knew—that she could do him some real damage, though it would probably end both of their careers. She let it hang in the air a moment before she went back to Rodriguez. "The guy's got a talent for getting people to talk, for drawing the pictures they have in their heads."

"But nobody's seen anything. Do I have to say it again?"

"Maybe someone saw something and they don't even know it. I've seen what Rodriguez can do with a witness and a sketch. I'm just saying maybe he can add something."

"So bring in whoever you can dig up and let Rodriguez work with them at the station."

"I want him to talk to the witnesses on their own turf and I want him to get a feel for the scenes—the places where our unsub has struck."

Denton stared down at his shoes. He seemed to be thinking about something else, but Terri didn't know what.

"Hey, the G is going to be all over this any minute," she said. "Wouldn't you rather take care of it in-house? Isn't that what we'd all like?"

"You think Rodriguez is our ticket to scooping the G? Because if that's it, you're too late. The G is already in. FO's have already been assigned. Manhattan FBI wants everything we've got, case and lab reports, everything."

"Shit."

"It's a done deal, Russo. Like so many things." Denton gave her a leering, knowing smile.

"When does this go into action?"

"Now." Denton sighed. "What the fuck, Russo. Let them have it if they want it. It can be *their* problem, not *ours*."

That last case Terri had worked with the feds started playing in her head, but she wasn't about to quit. "So what about Rodriguez?"

"Isn't that a moot point?"

"Are they sending in a profiler?"

"We're on a waiting list."

"That could be weeks."

"Your point?"

"Rodriguez has a profiler's mind."

"But again, not the creds."

"He's Quantico-trained."

"In fucking portrait painting."

"Give me a break, okay, Perry? Let Rodriguez come with me, talk to a few people, do some drawings. If nothing pans out we haven't lost anything."

Denton decided to let her have her new toy, but didn't feel like saying it yet. He was enjoying the fact that he had the power, that he could make her wait.

"Rodriguez has been around the PD for seven years, assisted on hundreds of homicides, rapes, and robberies— more than most cops ever get to work."

"Making *drawings,* Russo."

"And that's all I want him to do. But I want him with me on the street to do it. Jesus, Perry, are you going to make me beg?"

Denton almost said yes, but he was getting tired of the game and had bigger things to worry about. "Okay, if you want this guy so bad." He took a few steps closer and aimed a finger at her. "But anything fucks up, Russo, I'm holding you responsible. It'll be your ass on the line, remember that."

11

Terri Russo had called. She wanted me on the case. Just like that.

My grandmother would not agree that the call had come out of nowhere. She believed that everything happened for a reason. She would say that the spirit of the dead had brought Russo to me; that I had been beckoned by someone's *ori*.

I looked around, a bit sorry it had beckoned me here of all places, to the morgue.

The smell of formaldehyde was leeching through my mask, the Vicks VapoRub smeared on my nostrils not quite doing the job. *If I'm smelling death, am I also breathing it in?* I wasn't sure I wanted to know the answer to that.

The coroner, a tired-looking guy with streaks of blood and viscera across his smock, said, "Vic never knew what hit him. Bullet went straight into the medulla oblongata and came out the other side."

Russo was beside me. "Thought it would be good for you to see the real thing to compare it to the drawing," she said.

I looked at the victim, a Latino man between thirty-five and forty. She handed me a bagged drawing.

"Can you confirm this was made by the same guy?"

"It looks it, but I'd like to see the others along with it to be sure."

"Right," she said. "I've got copies of everything in my office."

I looked from the drawing to the corpse. "It's a decent likeness, which means the unsub stalked him, earmarked him for death. But why?"

"Well, that's the big question," said Russo.

"Any witnesses?"

"Not that we know of. But I'd like you to talk to all the people who last saw any of the vics, or had contact with them. Maybe they saw something and didn't realize it."

"And you want me to draw a sketch from their descriptions, that it?"

"You think you can?"

"I can try."

I could see Russo smile even behind her mask. She checked

her watch. "I've got a meeting, but you can start with this vic's wife." She handed me an address and phone number.

"The guy's hardly cold."

"That's why I want you to speak to her now—while every-thing is still fresh in her mind."

The woman who opened the door was probably in her mid-thirties, but at the moment it was hard to tell, her face strained and pale, eyes red-rimmed.

I showed her my temporary shield. She sighed deeply and let me in. She lived only a few blocks south of Julio and Jess, Eighty-sixth and Park, primo Manhattan real estate.

"I'm sorry for your loss," I said. "I'd like to help."

She looked up at me, incredulous. "And how are you go-ing to do that?"

"By finding the man who did this."

She led me into an art-filled living room, Warhol *Brillo Box* on the floor, cool minimal Robert Mangold painting on one wall, Catherine Murphy landscape, Chuck Close portrait on another. An eclectic, expensive mix.

"Amazing art collection," I said.

"That was Roberto's realm, but I enjoyed it." She man-aged a slight smile. "He started collecting in the eighties, after the Wall Street boom."

"He was a trader?"

"Oh, no," she said, as if insulted. "He had his own fund."

"He obviously did well.

She sighed again. "Yes."

I got her talking about the art, and she said her husband had recently bought the Warhol at auction, which I knew meant he'd paid well over a million. After a while I asked, "Tell me what happened the night he was killed."

"You mean *last* night?"

I said I was sorry again, but the sooner we knew, the faster we could do something about it.

"There's not much to tell. Roberto was keyed up, so he decided to go out for the paper. I told him it was silly. We get the *Times* and the *Journal* delivered every morning, but when Roberto has his mind set, it's useless to fight him." She welled up with tears. "If only he'd listened to me."

"Don't blame yourself for something that isn't your fault, Mrs. Acosta."

"Cambell. I use my maiden name."

"Sorry, Ms. Cambell. But you need to put the blame where it belongs, on the man who did this."

"That's very kind," she said, and seemed more eager to talk. We went through the events of the past night: Her husband had gone to a store on Lex for the *Wall Street Journal* and hadn't made it back; she hadn't seen the shooting and couldn't imagine there was a reason for anyone to kill him. "I've been through this with the police. Roberto had no enemies."

I opened my pad and explained what I did. That same look of incredulity passed over her features, but I convinced her to sit down and close her eyes. Then I asked her to think back over the past week.

"Has there been anyone hanging around that looked suspicious? Anyone. A delivery boy who seemed weird?"

"No, I, I don't think so, but . . ." A moment passed. "There was this one man; I saw him twice. He wasn't doing anything, just standing on the corner of Park Avenue, which was odd, just standing there and looking over at the building."

"Was he black or white?"

"He was definitely white, but he was across the street, so I didn't see him close up. He was staring at the lobby entrance when Roberto and I came out. I mentioned him to Roberto, but he didn't pay attention. I kissed my husband good-bye and . . ." She stopped and dabbed her eyes with a tissue. "I'm sorry."

"What happened after that?"

"Nothing. Roberto left for work, and when I looked across the street, the man was gone."

"And that was it?"

"Well, no. I wouldn't have thought about him again except he was there the next day. And it's Park Avenue. People just don't hang out on Park Avenue. I wondered if he was a Realtor scouting our building. But he didn't look like a Realtor."

"Why is that?"

"I don't know. It was just . . . a feeling. Maybe it was the baseball cap."

"Anything else you noticed about him?"

"He had on a long coat. But the impression I have of him is from the back. He turned away after I looked over at him, and the coat sort of billowed out at the bottom, from the wind."

I started drawing.

"Oh, God." She put a hand to her mouth. "Do you think I actually saw the man who—"

I didn't let her go there. "What else did you see?" I asked, and went back to the drawing.

She looked at my sketch. "Yes. That's it, the general impression I got."

"What about his face?"

She shook her head. "It's a blank. He was across the street, and I didn't really see it."

"But you said he was white."

"Yes. I'm pretty sure about that. Though . . . his face was in shadow."

"Was he tall or short?"

"He might have been tall, it's hard to say."

"Was there anything you can compare him to, something in the street that might tell you more about him physically, why you thought he was tall?"

She closed her eyes again. "Well . . . he was leaning against a street lamp and his head was not that far from the plaque that tells you when you can and can't park. That was it! Why he seemed tall."

"That's great."

"If only—" She broke off and started crying.

I tried to console her, to get her back into the drawing, but her housekeeper came in and gave me a dirty look, and that was it.

12

I went back home, got a beer out of the fridge, opened my pad onto my work table, and looked at what I'd done. It wasn't much yet. Nothing I could show Russo, and I didn't want to disappoint her.

It got me thinking about my last girlfriend, the one who told me she didn't know me any better after six months of dating than she did after our first, and said good-bye.

I looked around my spare apartment, at the furniture I'd inherited and never improved upon, the once white walls that had yellowed. I usually liked the fact that other than the superintendent I was the only resident in a building filled with small factories and offices, but right now it just felt lonely. Five years ago I'd taken over the lease from a painter with artist-in-residence status, which meant the city

allowed you to live in a place other human beings thought uninhabitable. Any minute I was going to start feeling sorry for myself, so I went back to the sketch I'd made of the man in the coat, and added a little more tone.

But the face was still blank, and nothing was coming to me.

I got another beer, set my iPod into its docking station, and listened to some music—Marianne Faithful, Lucinda Williams, and Tim Hardin, a singer I'd recently discovered who had OD'd in the seventies—real suicide material.

I looked back at my sketch, but another image snaked its way into my psyche.

I knew what it was—a variation on an image that had been in my mind for years.

I finished the beer, switched my iPod to an upbeat playlist of Reggaeton, Spanish rap over Jamaican dance hall with a little salsa thrown in, Daddy Yankee rapping *"A ella le Gusta la Gasolina"*—she loves gasoline—a double entendre if ever there was one, but the music didn't work to distract me. My father was in my head, and I knew he was not going to quit anytime soon.

My father: who had been Superman, Batman, and every other Marvel and DC superhero to me. I thought about the good times—my father teaching me how to swing a bat and rhapsodizing about his hero, Roberto Clemente, the first Puerto Rican major league ballplayer; night games at Yankee Stadium and Shea, trips to the Planetarium. He'd initiated my love of music and he took me to a hundred movies, and when my tough-hombre dad cried during *The Incredible Journey*—a cornball movie about a lost dog and cat that I will never forget—I knew it was okay for me to cry too.

I pictured him when I was a little kid and he'd worn the uniform, standard blue, and then, when I was twelve, how he'd exchanged it for the narc's costume of jeans and heavy bling.

Bits and pieces of those years started playing in my head: skipping school, taking the subway uptown to meet Julio in the middle of the day, smoking pot and snorting coke in alleyways and abandoned buildings, and there I was, back to the night my father found the drugs.

After he stormed out of the apartment I went to meet Julio, both of us edgy and eager to get stoned. El Barrio was stifling that night, everyone out on the streets, old men on milk crates playing dominoes; hydrants open, kids playing in the water; boom boxes blasting salsa music, men and women dancing. It was beautiful, the grit and garbage of the slum veiled by the darkness, moonlight painting the sweat on the dancers' skin and the sprays of water silver.

Julio and I wandered the streets, sharing a few joints and a bottle of rum. We ended up in a movie theater and stared at the screen, but all I could see was my father's face, and him yelling at me. Sometime around 3:00 A.M., I sobered up enough to realize I was going to have to face him. I begged Julio to come home with me as a buffer, but he wouldn't do it.

That night was washing over me like a wave that knocks you down and drags you under. I drank another beer and turned the music way up, a raunchy number by some Puerto Rican duo, lots of drums and percussion. I managed to exchange the memory for the case, and worried I might not be up to it, that I hadn't worked a homicide before.

Then I realized I had worked hundreds of homicides, just differently. I went to the closet and pushed stuff around till I found it, the Smith & Wesson NYPD-issued .38 Special heavy-barrel revolver. I hadn't touched it since I left active police work, though I had kept up the permit. I got my hand around the stainless-steel grip. It felt good, but I remembered why I'd exchanged it for a pencil.

I went back to my work table and started a new drawing.

I had no idea why or where this was coming from, but stayed with it.

When I looked at it I shuddered. What the hell was *this*?

Maybe I was a little drunk. But the drawing made me feel sober.

I thought about my father again, how he had always encouraged my art. He'd take my best drawings to the station and tape them inside his locker. He was proud of me, of my talent. The night he'd found my drugs, he had not only berated me but reminded me that I was special, that I'd been given a gift, and one day, he prayed, I would stop wasting my life and put it to use.

I wished he were here so I could tell him I had done what he asked. But sometimes you don't get a second chance.

13

I was back at Midtown North with Terri Russo standing over me. I showed her the sketches.

She came in close and looked at the ones of the eye. "What the hell is this?"

"That's what I asked myself. I don't know. I might have been a little drunk."

"Oh, great."

"It was just a few beers. But I wasn't drunk when I drew the others."

"The guy in the coat?"

"Right. It's not much, but—"

"You got this from Acosta's wife?"

I explained about the man on the corner.

"It's something," she said. "I'll make copies. Cops can show it around to the neighbors. Maybe it'll jog someone's memory." She spread copies of all the crime scene sketches across her desk.

"I want to be sure it's the same guy doing all the drawings. Last time you told me that the guy was right-handed, neat, and compulsive. Now there are three drawings, so I thought you might see something more."

"You have any aspirin?"

She rummaged through her bag, came up with Excedrin,

handed me a bottle of Poland Spring. "You're not a drunk, are you?"

"This is the result of three beers. I'm half Jewish; what more can I say?"

She laughed.

I washed down the pills and looked at the drawings. "Okay. Yeah, there's the same mark-making, same angled stroke, same confident drawing style. There's some talent here too. These are hard poses to draw, particularly the two with all that perspective. There's a famous painting of Christ laid out in this kind of perspective, by an Italian Renaissance artist, Mantegna."

"Is this the art history lesson?"

"It came into my mind because there's something religious about these drawings, like the victims have been crucified."

"You think it's got any significance?"

"Maybe he sees his victims as martyrs, or himself as one. Or it could be he's just showing off, you know, how good he is at drawing—and murder." I looked from one to another

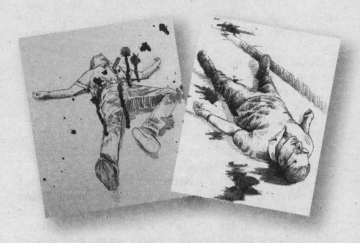

and a thought came to me. "It's like he imagined their deaths ahead of time."

"Well, they're premeditated, of course."

"Yes. But it's more than that. It's like he *sees* how he'll kill them by drawing it first, like he's visualized the murder ahead of time." I tapped the drawing of the black man from Brooklyn. "Here, a guy taking a bullet to the chest. He's drawn it, then carried it out. Maybe it's his process, his ritual."

Terri nodded. "But it doesn't tell us *why* he selected these victims. And it can't be random."

"What do we know about the victims' backgrounds?"

"Vic number one was a college senior, twenty-one, going to get his car parked in a lot three blocks from the bar where he'd been with friends."

"And the friends didn't see anything? No one following them?"

"They were at the bar when he was killed. According to their statements they didn't see a thing."

"And the second?"

"Harrison Stone. Came out of the subway, walked four

blocks, boom, shot dead. There was an elderly couple down the street, but they didn't see it happen. Woman says she saw someone hovering over the body, but had no idea what was going on till they got closer, and by then whoever was leaning over him was gone."

"Any description?"

"Male." She frowned.

"And her companion, he see anything?"

"He's blind. Literally."

"What about traffic? Maybe a cabdriver saw something?"

"Dead-end street. Virtually no traffic."

"You said the victim walked four blocks. So the unsub could have shot him earlier, but waited. So he must have known about the dead-end street." I closed my eyes and tried to picture it, but couldn't. "I should go to the scene. And I want to talk to the woman who saw the man leaning over the body. She might have a picture in her mind that she doesn't even know is there."

Terri's face brightened. Clearly, this was what she wanted from me.

"I've just got to do some paperwork," she said. "Give me an hour and we can go to Brooklyn together."

I liked the idea of that.

"Afterward you can talk to the college kid's roommate. It's a long shot. He wasn't on the scene, but he was there just before it went down." Russo looked into my eyes. "We've got three dead men, Rodriguez. Someone had to have seen something."

Terri closed the door behind Nate and glanced down at the sketches he'd made—the man in the long coat, the scary close-up of the eye. Maybe the Brooklyn witness could add more. One thing for sure: She'd been right about Rodriguez. And now, with the G looking over her shoulder, she needed all the help she could get.

She thought back to the meeting earlier that morning,

Agent Monica Collins throwing around terms like *methodology* and *victimology* like she had invented them, asking Terri if she understood. She just smiled, said, "Yes, I think I've got it, but thanks so much for asking." *Bitch*. Why was it women were always so shitty to one another? Wasn't there supposed to be some sort of sisterhood? Not so she ever noticed. At least with the men it was right out there, grabbing your ass or ignoring you. The women, they were all smiles while they cut you off at the knees.

Denton had run the meeting, acting like he actually knew something about the case, though it had been Terri who'd briefed him, written everything in simple prose he could regurgitate. He hadn't thanked her, not that she expected he would. He was too busy charming Agent Collins, smiling at her with that sexy grin of his, flirting with the bureau, not the woman, though poor Agent Collins didn't seem to know that. *Poor Agent Collins, my ass*.

For now, the G team was collecting data and feeding it back to Quantico. Nobody had said anything about the NYPD quitting the investigation, not yet. Three different precincts involved, and now the G. What a mess. The feds wanted full reports and full cooperation. No doubt full credit too.

Terri glanced at the crime scene drawings she'd laid out for Rodriguez. Three men—one black, one Hispanic, one white. If it hadn't been for the college kid, the white guy, she would be thinking racial angle, but this didn't make any sense. So what was it that was nagging at the back of her mind?

14

Perry Denton popped a five-milligram Valium into his mouth and washed it down with decaf. It wasn't that he needed it—he could quit at any time—it relaxed him, that's all, and these days he needed to relax. He picked up the phone after the sixth annoying ring.

"What time will you be home, Perry?"

"Why?"

"Because we have guests, remember?"

No, he did not remember. And hadn't he specifically told his secretary to screen his calls, especially his wife's?

This morning's meeting with the feds was still on his mind. He was glad they were taking the case, and before the media got hold of the fact that it was a fucking serial killer and there was a media sideshow that *he* would have to deal with to calm the city's residents.

"I'll be home when I get home, baby. I've got a lot of shit to deal with."

Damn. His job was supposed to be administrative, to oversee the workings of the various NYPD departments; he was not responsible for every fucking psycho who decided to snuff a few blacks and Hispanics. And couldn't the guy have killed them in the neighborhoods where that sort of thing was acceptable? The college kid was the real problem, from a wealthy family who would be making a lot of noise if they didn't get some answers, and soon. Denton couldn't decide whom he disliked more, rich people or poor people.

"What time are you coming home, Perry?" His wife's singsong voice cut into his thoughts. "It's embarrassing, always having to make excuses for you."

"So don't make them." He slammed the receiver into its cradle and shouted, "Denise!"

His office door opened and a heavyset woman stood in the frame.

"Where were you? Aren't you supposed to answer my phone, screen my calls?"

"Yes, sir, but I was down the hall copying those documents you'd asked for."

Denton sighed, extended his hand and took the papers. Damn it, did he have to do everything himself? He waited till the woman left his office, then found the number he'd written on a Post-it, and stared at it. It was risky, but less risky than his current situation. And he'd already set the wheels in motion, put half the money in an off-shore account. Now he had to buy another crap cell phone and make the final call.

Monica Collins had spent the night going over everything—case reports, background checks, autopsy results, ballistics, crime scene pictures. She was feeling a mix of excitement and anxiety, the result of too many unanswered questions and three cups of coffee. She had forwarded everything to her associates back at Behavioral Science, but knew BSS moved slowly, particularly these days with the "Oakland Sniper" getting all the attention from the media and priority from the bureau. Six killings in six months. Last she heard, the agent who'd been supervising that case had been transferred to somewhere in Washington State, and not one of the scenic parts.

Well, that was not going to happen to her. Not after six

years of undergrad and postgrad work, then recruited by the bureau only to sit behind a desk for eight years while her college girlfriends got married and had babies. She had finally gotten out from behind that Quantico desk and she was going to stay out. She looked around her temporary quarters at Manhattan FBI and liked what she saw. She liked the city too. And she liked New York's Chief of Department Perry Denton, the kind of man who rarely, if ever, paid any attention to her. Maybe it was just the case, but she thought she'd detected something a bit more from him.

She glanced up at the bulletin board and the crime scene photos of the three victims she had tacked to it along with copies of the drawings that had been pinned to their dead bodies.

Serial killers had always held a fascination for her, particularly the handsome ones like Ted Bundy and Jeffrey Dahmer, the idea that one could be seduced to their death both terrifying and thrilling. Bundy had been her favorite until she had read about the kid who called himself Tony the Tiger from the Color Blind case two years ago. She'd paid him a visit—strictly for observational and educational purposes—at a state hospital for the criminally insane. She'd never forget it, his almost girlish good looks, blue eyes cold and gorgeous, the seductive, unsettling smile. Thinking about him now brought a chill, and another emotion she did not want to consider.

Collins looked back at the crime scene pictures and wondered about this unsub. All they had surmised so far was that the guy lived somewhere in the geographic vicinity, had experience handling weapons, and could draw.

She had her two full-time field officers, Richardson and Archer, combing through the tax records of every former soldier living in the tri-state area, anyone who held a job in commercial art, design, or architecture, as well as students and professors at the local art schools. Maybe something would pop up, though that was not the way it usually happened, and she knew it.

Damn it, she needed a break.

She wished she could get someone from BSS to give her a psyche profile, but these days Homeland Security was sucking up the bureau's dollars and she had been told to make do with her two full-time FOs. For now, Quantico was strictly for analysis and backup unless the unsub escalated, and she expected to capture him before that happened.

She didn't know what she could expect from the NYPD, particularly Detective Russo, who had fucked up a case a few years back. She'd read the file. Of course if the detective gave her any trouble it would be easy enough to bring up the past and blame her all over again.

Collins sat back and crossed her legs. They were still, she thought, her best asset. She decided she'd wear a skirt to her next meeting with Chief Denton.

15

"**I** didn't see nothing." The old lady, Mrs. Adele Rubenstein, reminded me of my Grandma Rose. She pursed her lips together and cherry red lipstick snaked its way into whistle lines like sidewalks cracking in an earthquake. "The police, they already asked, and I told them. I didn't see a thing." She glanced up at Terri Russo. "You don't even wear a uniform."

"I already explained that, ma'am. I'm a detective. We don't wear uniforms."

The old lady shrugged and made another face. Russo was getting nowhere.

"This is important to the investigation, ma'am. Anything—"

"I told you, there's nothing. I was a block away and my eyesight isn't what it used to be. I saw a man leaning over a man, and that's it. I can't tell you anything else. You want I should make it up?" She folded her arms across her chest.

I stepped between Russo and the old woman and offered up my best "nice Jewish boy" smile.

"Tell you what, Mrs. R, you mind if I call you that?"

The old lady shrugged and I could see that my smile hadn't quite done it. I'd have to drag out the big guns. "My mother," I said, "Judith *Epstein,* always says—"

"Epstein?"

"Yes," I said. "From Forest Hills. My father was Spanish, but my mother's a hundred percent Jewish."

Adele Rubenstein looked at me for the first time. "You understand that makes *you* Jewish. Your father—" She waved an arthritic hand. "He doesn't matter. The line is through the mother. You're Jewish, and that's that."

"Of course. I know that."

."So, you had a bar mitzvah?"

"Huge affair, relatives, friends, friends of friends, the whole *mishpucheh*." I figured if I was lying I might as well give myself a big party, the whole nine yards. "We had a chopped-liver mold like you wouldn't believe. Like a piece of art. It was a sin to eat it."

"And your father, he didn't mind?"

"Oh, my father . . ." I went for the home run. "He converted."

"Call me Adele," she said, her face one big smile.

Russo gave me a look.

"Adele," I said. "Let's make this fun. You tell me everything you can remember and I'll draw it. I do this with my grandmother all the time." I didn't bother to tell her it was with my Spanish grandmother because I knew she'd assume I meant my Jewish one. My *abuela* would be the same way. She considered me a hundred-percent Spanish. "And call me Nathan."

"A beautiful name."

"Yeah," I said. "My grandmother loves it. So, here's what I want you to do, Adele. First, get comfortable, sit back and take a deep breath."

Adele Rubenstein inhaled deeply and sagged into her plastic-covered couch.

We were in the living room of the brownstone she and her husband, Sam, the blind man, had been living in since 1950, and it looked it. Danish-modern coffee table, chipped; faded, overstuffed ultra-suede armchairs; a Formica dinette set with red vinyl-covered chairs.

"Okay, Nathan," she said. "I'm ready."

I opened my pad. "So you were on the street—"

"With Sam. It was our evening *shpatzir,* a walk. It's good for Sam, the fresh air. The man is a hermit. He'd sit home and watch TV all day if I didn't make him go out. I say to him, 'Sam, you're blind, what can you be watching?' It doesn't matter to him, he says, he likes to listen. He watches the old shows, which he remembers from before he went blind, *kaynahorah.* He says he can picture them, but I'm not so sure. His favorite is that one about the men in the war camp, *Hogan's* something or other. To think they made a show about such a thing." She shook her head and I took it as my chance to break in.

"So you said you saw a man leaning over the victim, the man who was shot."

"Oh, such a terrible thing. Right there, on the street, in our neighborhood." Her voice dropped to a whisper. "The man who was shot, he was colored, but a nice man. I'd seen him before and he always smiled and said hello. And good-looking, you shouldn't know from it, like Sidney Poitier. You know Sidney Poitier? He's before your time. A wonderful actor. He won the Oscar. *Lilies of the . . . Valley,* the movie was called, or something like that. The first colored man to win. I know they don't like that term, *colored.* But I don't understand it. When I was growing up I had plenty of friends who were colored, and they didn't mind being called colored. They ate in my house, everything. To my mother a person was a person. You know what I'm saying, Nathan?"

"Yes. I know exactly what you mean." I took a deep breath. This was not going to be so easy.

Russo was smiling, enjoying herself a little at my expense.

"Close your eyes and try to picture exactly what you saw. I'll ask you questions and you try to answer with two or three words. You think you can do that, Adele?"

"Why not?"

"Good. First question. Did you hear anything? A shot, maybe?"

"I don't think so, but this is Brooklyn, and the traffic, I don't have to tell you, it keeps me up half the night. I said to Sam just the other day, Sam—"

"Just a few words, Adele, remember?"

"Oh, of course. No shot. I didn't hear a shot. Is that short enough, Nathan?"

"Perfect. So the first thing you saw was one man leaning over another, is that right?"

"Not exactly. He wasn't leaning. He was just standing there. And I said to Sam, 'Sam, I think someone is hurt.' "

"Why did you say that?"

"Nathan, forgive me. This will be more than two words, but it was obvious. There was a man lying on the ground and he wasn't moving. What would you say?"

"You're right, Adele. So, the man who was standing, was he a big man?"

"It's hard to say." Adele pursed her lips. "He had on a coat, a long coat."

I glanced over at Terri and we exchanged a look. "That's great." I went back to the sketch I'd made after talking with the last victim's wife and asked her to picture what she'd seen.

"We were walking, like I said, and I looked down the street and I saw them. I couldn't understand it," she said. "One man standing while the other one is lying on the ground, not moving. But then, when we got closer and I saw . . ." She clasped a hand to her cheek and rocked her head. "*Oy vey iz mir.* Terrible. That poor man. I could see he was dead. He was just lying there. Awful. A *shondah*. And his poor wife. I saw her later, when the police came. Awful."

She stopped and I tried to see it too, images starting to come together in my mind. "You mentioned the man's wife; how did you know it was his wife?

"Because the police were questioning me and she was there being questioned too, poor thing." Adele Rubenstein leaned toward me and whispered, "They were one of those mixed marriages. Very common these days. Me, personally, I have nothing against it, but what about the children? It can't be easy for them."

I didn't bother to remind her that she was talking to a half-breed because she'd already accepted me as one of the flock. But it struck me that no one had mentioned that pertinent piece of information—that the black victim had a white wife. I glanced over at Terri, then at Adele. "So let's go back to what you saw?"

"What else could there be?"

"You never know, Adele." I patted her arm and asked her to close her eyes, which she did. "As you got closer, did the standing man see you?"

"He . . ." She was squinting, looking inward and reliving it, the pars orbitalis muscles of her cheeks flicking under her loose flesh, an anxious grimace setting in.

"Just relax, Adele. I'm right here with you. You're safe. Now, think back to the standing man."

"One minute he was there, the next—" She shook her head.

"It's okay." I touched her arm again. "Stay with the picture in your mind, a man standing over the dead man. Trust it, Adele."

She let out a breath and her facial muscles relaxed with it.

"Now tell me, did you see his face?"

"Yes. No. I saw something, but . . . I'm not seeing it now."

"Take your time."

And she did. Two full minutes passed, me staring at Adele

Rubenstein's wrinkled *punim,* as my Grandma Rose would call it.

"Adele, are you with me?"

She nodded.

"Remember, you're perfectly safe now, but I need you to go back to that street. You're taking a walk. Sam is by your side. You look down the street and you see the two men—"

"Yes . . ."

"You're getting closer now. The standing man looks up and sees you coming—and you see him." I saw her expression change, no longer afraid, her incisivi labii muscles puckering her lips with determination. "His face," I said. "You can see it, I know you can."

"Yes! I see it! He was colored. Just like the dead man! No, wait, wait. That wasn't it. He wasn't colored at all. I'm wrong. I'm dead wrong. I see it now. He was wearing a mask!"

"Tell me about the mask."

"It was a knit one, not like on Halloween, but the kind you can pull down over your face, with the holes in it."

"A ski mask?"

"That's it exactly! He had on a ski mask."

"Totally covering his face?"

"Total."

I spent a minute adding that to my drawing.

"Have a look at this, okay?" I turned my pad around.

"Oy vey." Adele Rubenstein shivered and rubbed her arms. "Goose bumps. I've got goose bumps. You're a regular Houdini, you know that, Nathan? It's like a photograph, you made." She pointed an arthritic finger at my sketch. "That's the man. That's the man I saw."

* * *

Terri and I were out on the street heading to the spot where the victim had been slain.

"Sorry if I stepped on your toes in there. I just thought—"

"No, it was okay. You were good, the way you drew it out of her. It's like you've got your own kind of interrogation technique."

"It sort of evolved over the years. I've been dealing with witnesses for a long time."

"Well, it worked." She smiled. "I'm just sorry I missed your bar mitzvah. I do a damn good *hora*."

"Too bad I missed it too. Never had one. My mother's totally assimilated, and my father—"

"Juan the Just."

I stopped and turned toward her. "You know about my father?"

"Only what I've read. That was his nickname, right?"

"What the cops called him, but I didn't find out until—"

"Yeah, I know. Sorry about that. Must have been tough, losing your dad so young."

I didn't want to talk about it and turned the conversation around. "What about you?"

"What about me?" she said, her outer borough accent going a bit harsh.

"I hear your father's a cop too."

Her eyebrows pulled together and the corners of her mouth turned down, a combination sad-disgust face, a *blend,* as Ekman would call it. "He's retired, but still alive, if you call staring at the TV all day alive. Maybe he should come and watch with Sam the blind man."

"I hear the feds are coming in."

She nodded, the disgust factor lifting her upper lip. "That's right."

"So, we wasting our time?"

"The case is a *collaboration,*" she said, disgust in her voice matching her face. "And I'm still working it. By the way, there's a total media blackout around this."

"Isn't it a little late for that? All three murders have been on page one."

"All three *unrelated* murders. Get it? Nobody but Holly-wood likes a serial killer."

"The media is going to get it from somewhere. They always do."

"Just not from us, okay?"

"Wouldn't tell my mother."

"You've got a mother, Rodriguez?" Russo smiled. "By the way, and you're going to love this. The G has given the case a code name. They're calling it—and the unsub—are you ready?—the Sketch Artist."

"You're kidding me."

"Afraid not. The G loves their code names."

"The newspapers are going to love it too."

"*When* they get it," she said.

We had reached the corner where Harrison Stone had been shot and killed. I glanced at the warehouse that ended the street in a dead end, then down at the concrete. I could make out a few places where it was stained darker, possibly from blood, and a shadow slid across my unconscious.

"You mind if I try and draw something?"

"That's why you're here. You want me to take a walk, or—?"

"Just give me a few minutes."

I watched Terri walk toward the corner, her gait determined, but with a slight swaying of her hips, sexy without trying. Then I stopped looking and opened my pad.

I drew for about ten or fifteen minutes.

It was the same shadowy figure in the long coat and ski mask. Something more of the face had materialized, though I couldn't be sure I wasn't inventing it. Maybe I'd allowed the witch doctor concept to go to my head.

Terri leaned in for a look. "Wow, you're fast, Rodriguez."

"You have to be in my line of work. No agonizing over perfection allowed if you want to get something on paper

before it fades from the witness's memory. "Could be I'm seeing what the witnesses planted in my head."

"Well, I didn't hear Adele Rubenstein say anything about the unsub's eyes. Did Acosta's wife?"

"No. But there was the other eye I drew. It's in my mind, but . . ." I didn't know where it had come from, and I said so.

"Could be that transference thing you talk about."

"Could be. But it's just an eye. Not enough for an ID."

"Maybe not," said Terri, looking up at me. "But it's a start."

16

He pores over the newspaper looking for some mention of his early work. But there is nothing. All they write about is the new one, the dead man on the Upper East Side. He cuts the story out, pins it above his desk, reaches for a pencil, still staring at the article, no longer reading it, the muscles around his eyes beginning to ache, type blurring. Then a picture starts to swirl in his mind like an eddy gathering force and he needs to draw it, to capture it on paper.

It's just a fragment, but he recognizes it.

The big one, he thinks. *Soon.*

He prints the word PATIENCE below his drawing and puts it aside, but his hand has begun to tremble as a memory slithers into his unconscious and hangs there, a web ready to snare him.

No way he will allow it.

He drops to the floor, balancing on fingertips and boot tips.

Up, down. Up, down. Up, down.

His own private hell, fueling him like hot coals.

Up, down. Up, down.

The sweat has begun to drip from his forehead and gather under his armpits.

Up, down. Up, down. Up, down.

Faster now, blood pumping, fingers aching, arm muscles quivering, breath expelled like gunshots.

Up, down. Up, down.

The demons are breaking up the way his drawings come together, fragmenting, dissolving.

Up, down. Up, down. Up, down. Up, down.

There they go, gone. Dust.

His arms give out. He rolls onto his side, drawing in breath after breath, then slowly pulls himself up and regards his fragmented drawing, recognizes it as just a portion of his opus, his major work, the pieces not quite there yet. In the back of his mind there are mini-explosions like Fourth of July fireworks, gorgeous, thrilling, and he knows in time the drawing will come together and he will make it real.

17

Terri had to head back to Midtown North for another meeting with the feds but dropped me at the NYU campus.

I spent what felt like a worthless half hour with the roommate of the murdered college kid, Dan Rice. He and Rice had gone to a bar for a couple of beers before Rice went to get the car he kept in a midtown garage. He was planning to drive out and see his parents, but never made it. The roommate didn't see anything. No man in a long coat or ski mask. The only thing I learned, which I hadn't known before, was that Rice was from a wealthy Greenwich, Connecticut, family, but I didn't think that was enough reason to kill him. He suggested I speak to Rice's girlfriend.

"Was she with him?" I asked.

"No, but maybe she could tell you something."

I told the kid he'd make a good cop and he smiled.

I cut across the campus, showed my badge to a guard in the dormitory, and took the elevator to the third floor. I was still thinking about Harrison Stone, the man shot in Brooklyn, when Beverly Majors opened the door.

She was a beauty, but that wasn't the important part. The important part was that she was black. Harrison Stone's wife was white. The same was true for Acosta, a Latino.

Interracial couples? Had the PD put it together too?

I asked Beverly Majors how long she had known Rice and she said about year.

"Did you mostly stay in or go out?"

"We just liked to hang out." She shrugged, trying to act cool, but she had started to chew her lip and blink a lot; what people do when they're trying not to cry. "I'd meet him downstairs in Washington Square." She pointed out the window. "See that bench? We had lunch there like once a week. Sometimes, when we had time, we'd go up to Central Park and take a long walk."

Washington Square. Central Park. Places to be seen.

But why had the killer gone for Rice and not her?

I couldn't figure that out.

I asked her if it was all right if I sketched her and she shrugged again. It wasn't just that she was beautiful. I just felt a need to draw her.

"I don't look *that* good," she said when I stopped.

"Sure you do."

"You going to do anything with it?"

"You want it?"

She shrugged again, but I could see she did, so I tore it out of the pad and handed it to her. I didn't think I needed it. I had just needed the process.

The process. Drawing. The way to capture a subject.

It made me think about the unsub, the fact that he drew his victims before he killed them. Was it his way of capturing them?

Beverly Majors said "Thanks" and offered up a wan smile. She had stopped chewing her lip and seemed a little more relaxed. Maybe I had established some sort of rapport with her.

I brought her back to the night Rice had been killed and asked her to try and picture it.

She took a deep breath. "It was raining. I remember because I'd worn suede shoes and they got ruined. Oh, God, that sounds awful. I don't care about the shoes. It's just something I remember. I stepped into one of those greasy puddles, you know, in the curb, when gasoline or something mixes with the water?" She swallowed and I could see she was fighting tears.

I asked her to close her eyes and think about the crowd that had assembled once the cops were there.

"Did you notice anyone? Someone who stood out, someone you might have seen earlier in the evening, or anytime before?"

"I don't think I ever looked at the crowd. I was just staring down into the puddles. I didn't want to see what was going on." A tear cut down her cheek.

"I know this is hard, but—"

"It's okay. I, I don't even know how I feel. I mean . . . I can't locate my emotions. Does that sound weird?"

I shook my head.

"I don't know if Dan and I even had a future, but now . . ." She took another breath. "Dan was from a rich family and I grew up in a project. I can't imagine what his parents would have thought if their only son brought home a black girl—and Dan never did. Bring me home, I mean."

She was so charming and beautiful, it was hard to imagine anyone not falling for her, but I'd witnessed enough to know that prejudice lay just below the top layer of almost everyone's skin, regardless of their color. Some hid it better than others, and some tried to overcome it. But it was pretty much here to stay and I guessed Beverly Majors knew that as well as I did.

I asked her a few questions that she couldn't answer, but seeing her had told me something important.

I went downstairs and sat on the bench she'd pointed out from her dorm window. It was near the north end of the square, just a few feet from the arch and out in the open. Anyone could have seen them. Obviously someone had.

I called Russo right away and told her. The minute I did she said, "Interracial couples! Jesus! That's what I've been trying to get at. The racial angle. I knew it had to be there."

18

Agent Richardson handed Monica Collins a printout two inches thick, then took a seat at the conference table beside his fellow field officer, Mike Archer. "Active and inactive soldiers in the tri-state area," he said.

Collins fingered the stack of paper. "How is it broken down?"

"Military divisions—army, navy, National Guard, active and inactive; New York, New Jersey, everything highlighted by color. Blue is anyone over the age of fifty, so not worth looking at. Yellow are active, but out of state or overseas, also eliminated. Green is active, full-time, which would leave little time for a homicide hobby. Orange are your badly wounded and handicapped, obviously not our man. Red are your psyche discharges, which I'm thinking are priority. Twelve hundred and sixteen of them. National Guard are purple."

Collins acknowledged his work with a slight nod of approval, then slid the mass of paper back toward him. "Like you said, start with the psyche discharges. And see if anyone's got a police record or done time."

She turned her attention to Archer, who had an equally impressive tome in front of him.

"Current list of every art student and art teacher in New

York," he said, patting the papers. "Borough schools included, like Pratt Institute in Brooklyn, Queens College, and a place called P.S. 1 in Long Island City, which has an artists-in-residence program. I'm having a couple of Quantico interns go through everything. Off the bat we eliminated the girls. Don't see our Sketch Artist as a woman."

Collins nodded. Though she knew all about Aileen Wuornos, the serial killer about whom they'd made that movie *Monster,* and had read about others, women serial killers were still a rarity. "Stick to the men, particularly upperclassmen and teachers."

"Right," said Archer.

"This is all fine," said Collins. "But it's just a start."

She spent the next twenty minutes going over each of the murders, the confusing issue of the three vics' being of different racial backgrounds, which was uncommon, and the fact that the killing method had varied.

Archer displayed a photograph of the knife that had killed the college student, Rice, a detail of where the blade met the handle, the words WEAPON OF CHOICE clearly etched into the steel. "It's a small mail-order company," he said. "They advertise in the back of magazines like *Soldier of Fortune.* Problem is they stopped making this particular kind of knife six years ago and their files only go back five, or so they say. Even so, they were not happy to give up their client list, but I've got it." He waved a fax. "Quantico ran the addresses. Ninety percent of these yokels have their weapons sent to PO boxes."

"No surprise there," said Collins. "Did you check out the ownership of the PO boxes?"

Archer nodded. "Got about a fifty percent return. The other fifty rented boxes under John Smith, paid for the month their weapon was being shipped, and that was it, gone. Paid cash, of course." He sighed. "Interns are checking out the fifty percent that are checkable."

"Maybe we'll get lucky," said Collins, but she had a feeling their unsub was too smart for that. If he'd bought the knife by mail order with intent to do damage, he'd have covered his ass. Still, it was something to do. She'd report what they had found and what they were doing to her superiors at Quantico. They liked reports and paper and at least she had plenty of that. She was scheduled for an audiovisual hookup in a couple of hours, which did not thrill her; the idea that there were a whole bunch of agents in a room watching her made her nervous.

She glanced at her watch. "Locals will be here soon for the meeting. Let's see what they have to offer." She looked from Archer to Richardson. "This meeting is strictly informational. There's no need to give them what we've got."

19

Terri left the meeting with Dugan, Perez, O'Connell, and a headache. The bulk of the agenda had been how to manage the media. According to Denton, by way of the mayor, by way of the FBI, they still wanted a total blackout. No serial killer. No racial angle. Any crime that had to do with race, even hinted at being a hate crime, was incendiary. But trying to keep a story like this out of the press these days?

As if, thought Terri.

The work was to remain divided between the three precincts, each assigned to handle one of the three murders, thereby dispelling the notion that they were in any way related, though in actuality they would be tripling efforts and pooling information.

To Terri's mind this baroque process would undoubtedly slow down the investigation. She had worked enough cases to know that the number of bodies working on it did not necessarily mean success, particularly if the bodies would be working out of different precincts and under separate commands. It seemed to her a guarantee for confusion, but there was nothing she could do about it. Her crew was on the Harrison Stone murder, the black man shot in Brooklyn, which was further complicated by the fact that the Brooklyn division still had official jurisdiction, another way to allay suspicion that the cases were connected. She wasn't sure why the feds had not completely taken over, her best guess being they were short on manpower and wanted the NYPD to do the legwork.

Collins and her field officers had arrived late and tried to act like they knew nothing and everything all at once. Terri could see they were fishing but not sharing.

For now, she was just happy to be out of the meeting. She leaned toward one of her detectives. "You're related to Cole in the Twenty-third, aren't you?"

"Yeah, he's married to my sister, a good guy," said O'Connell. "You want me to keep up with what they're getting on the Acosta case, that it?"

"We're supposed to share information, right?"

"I hear you."

"You can tell Cole we'll share too."

"So what did you make of *Lewinsky*?" asked Dugan.

"Who?"

"The case agent, Monica, as in . . . 'Lewinsky.' "

Terri cracked up. She needed the laugh and appreciated it. "Nice," she said. "It's Lewinsky from now on."

"What do you say we chip in and buy her a blue dress?" O'Connell said.

"With a big fat *stain* on it," Perez added.

All three men laughed and Terri joined them, enjoying the joke at Collins's expense. A rarity. The men working under Terri had rarely shared anything with her except their resentment.

Nothing like a common enemy, she thought.

"The G has more than they're letting on, but that's nothing new." She dropped her voice to a whisper so her men had to move in close. "But so do we, and let's keep that between us."

Terri had asked me to join her crew after their meeting with the feds. We were on the third floor of Midtown North, a conference room between Terri's office and Department Command. It had a view looking west over Fifty-fourth Street with a quarter inch of the Hudson River visible between a couple of high-rise buildings. I was feeling a little uncomfortable, Dugan and Perez eyeing me, their faces saying: *What the fuck is he doing here?* Perez, in particular, maybe because he was Puerto Rican and saw me as some sort of competition for the Latino seat, which was absurd, but what could I say? O'Connell was friendly, but he seemed a little drunk. When Terri had finished her recap of the meeting with the FBI, Perez finally came out and said it: "So what's Rodriguez doing?"

"Making a sketch," she said.

"How can he make a sketch if we don't got any witnesses?"

"Some of the witnesses saw more than they think. Rodriguez is trying to piece something together." She looked over, gave me a slight smile, and I returned it.

The detectives were all on last-name or nickname basis. Dugan was alternately "Duggie" or "Howser," Perez was "Pretzel," and O'Connell was "Prince." I had no idea why they called him that. Maybe he was a fan of the *Purple Rain* pop star. None of the guys had a nickname for Russo. She was just Russo, though they probably had plenty behind her back. I could only imagine what they were calling me.

Terri reviewed the cases, stopping to ask her men for their opinions, a smart move. I'd seen enough to know that guys on the force didn't much like taking orders from a woman, particularly one younger than they. She had this way of tilting her head and squinting when any of her men were talking, as if she was really listening. It could have been an act, but I didn't think so. I was really starting to like her; respect her too. And there was another factor: She was sexy as hell in her tight black jeans and white blouse open at the neck, thin gold chain resting against her olive skin. I thought about doing some sketches of her while she walked back and forth, but was afraid I'd start imagining her naked and the way my drawings had been spontaneously creating themselves these days, I couldn't chance it.

"Is there anything you'd like to add?"

It took me a second to realize Terri was talking to me. I cleared my throat and reiterated what I thought was a major point. "You've got a killer who's making portraits of his victims, so it's obvious he stalked them and chose them for a reason."

Perez looked up at me with a sneer. "Yeah, I think we know the reason—the racial angle we're not allowed to talk about because it *upsets* people."

"There's that," I said. "But I was thinking more about the stalking angle—that the guy had to have watched his victims for some time to be able to draw them."

"How about telling us something we don't know?" said Perez. "You spent, what, three days on the street? Too tough for you out there?"

There were smiles teasing O'Connell's and Dugan's lips. Their resentment didn't surprise me.

"Six months," I said. "And you're right, I don't have the street experience, and I'm not going to pretend I do. But I went through the academy, just like you, Perez. And I spent some time in Washington."

"Ooh, Washington." Perez shook his hand like I was hot stuff, and I let him have his fun. For a minute.

"I've put seven years into the job. How long have you been on the force?" I asked the question knowing the answer: he'd only been working five years.

"What's that got to do with the fucking price of tea in China?"

Terri laid her hand on his arm. "This isn't productive."

"Productive, my ass."

"Exactly," said Terri. "So just make nice, okay?"

Perez opened his mouth as if he was about to say something, but stopped.

I could have said more too, but Terri was right, it wasn't productive. Still, I wasn't going to apologize for my lack of street creds. I'd made hundreds of drawings and probably interviewed as many witnesses as he had.

"The unsub's drawings are obviously his signature," I said. "And he takes his time." I was reminded of what had just happened between me and Beverly Majors. "Could be that in the act of drawing his victims the unsub is creating some sort of bond with them."

"Not that they know of," said Perez.

"No. Of course not. But that doesn't matter. Not to him. The relationship is in his mind. It's the way visual people think, in pictures. It's a way to see the world and make sense of it."

"Visual people? You mean crazy people," said O'Connell.

"In this case, yes."

"So, you're suggesting he draws the vics to make a bond with them; but why?" asked Terri.

"Could be his way to see them more clearly, to remember them and chart them. He must see the couples out in public and become fixated on them, the way these guys often do; then he draws them."

"Why not take their picture?" asked Dugan.

"Because when he draws them he can put them into the poses and positions *he* wants, imagine them the way *he* wants to see them. Drawing them is all about *his* vision of them."

O'Connell and Dugan nodded. Perez didn't, but I could see he was listening to what I said.

We kicked that around a few minutes, and the guys seemed to forget I was an outsider, and I had a chance to observe them the way I had Russo.

O'Connell's face was puffy but slack, probably a result of his constantly hitting a thermos of coffee laced with booze, a tried-and-true muscle relaxant. Perez was the opposite—face taut, upper lip frozen into a permanent sneer. I'd heard he was divorced with two small girls he never saw, which might have accounted for part of the anger. Dugan's face, drooping upper eyelids and a slightly down-turned mouth, suggested sadness. They were wearing the job on their faces. I looked back at Russo. Her face was all about worry—eyes fixed, brow wrinkled. It reminded me of the way my mother looked whenever my father was late coming home.

"So why kill Rice and not his black girlfriend?" Dugan asked.

"Right," said O'Connell. "If he's motivated by race, wouldn't killing the black girl make more sense?"

"Maybe he doesn't kill girls," said Terri. "Maybe he's got some sort of standard, like it's not right to kill women and children."

"A killer with moral standards?" said Dugan.

"They're all governed by something," said Terri.

"Still, seems to me that if he was trying to make a point, it'd be easier to either kill the black girl or just choose another black or Spanish guy," said Perez.

"But that's because you're trying to make sense of it," I said. "We don't know what making sense means to this guy. David Berkowitz was taking orders from a *dog*."

"Ahhooo!" O'Connell put down his thermos and howled.

We all laughed a minute, then Terri got quiet. "I've spoken to Monteverdi in Hate Crimes. They're going through all the active files, see if they can come up with someone who has any art or design background."

"I thought this wasn't a hate crime," said Perez.

"Well, not publicly," said Terri.

20

Terri was going through what seemed like endless micro-
fiche provided by Hate Crimes, active files of individuals
and organizations.

The phone rang and it was O'Connell. He'd just heard
from his brother-in-law in the Twenty-third, who had just
heard from someone who worked in the Fifth.

A body. Down by the old Hudson piers. And a drawing.

The PD had erected a ten-by-twelve tent between the river
and the West Side Highway, a hundred yards north of the
Chelsea Piers sports complex where a new building had
been going up. Outside the tent, there were pilings driven
into the earth where they were still clearing out boulders
and flattening the ground. All work had stopped, derricks
idling, a string of workmen sitting on their hard hats. There
were a dozen police vehicles, an EMT, and a Crime Scene
van. Cars were slowing on the highway to see what was going on, though uniforms waved to keep them moving.

Terri had called and asked me to meet her here. I showed
my temporary badge to a uniform at the entrance to the tent.
A CS tech handed me gloves, mask, and disposable bootees.

Inside, Crime Scene was combing every inch of ground like ants at a picnic. The terrain looked as if a minor earthquake had struck, slabs of concrete from the original pier upended by the construction. There was a smell of newly uncovered dirt spiked with something rotten. Behind my mask I was trying not to breathe. The same CS tech who'd given me the paraphernalia at the entrance offered up a Vicks. I lifted my mask and rubbed it below my nose.

I spotted Terri and the ME huddled with her men and some cops I didn't know across the tent peering over a concrete slab about eight feet long and three feet wide. It was doing a *Titanic* impersonation, jutting out of the ground at an acute angle.

At first it looked as if the girl were alive, though I knew it couldn't be possible from the condition of her body. But her face seemed to be moving, eyes blinking. I looked close, immediately sorry. It was maggots. Crawling in and around her eye sockets.

I closed my eyes too late, the image already imprinting on my retina.

"Body must have rolled under the rock after the attack," said one of the detectives.

"Or the slab was used to hide her," said another.

"It kept her nice and cool," said the ME. "That, and being so close to the river."

"How long has she been here?" Terri asked.

The ME leaned in, kissing distance from the corpse. "I'd guess weeks, maybe even a month or two. Hard to say, the way the body's been sheltered. It's all ice under the concrete, like she was in cold storage." He plucked up a squiggling maggot with a pair of tweezers and dropped it in a bag. "Lab will tell you more once these babies are tested."

The photographer's strobe flashed, illuminating the girl's hair like a halo.

The ME lifted her mini with a pencil. "Doesn't appear to be a sexual attack. Underwear's intact, and there's no bruising on the inner thighs." He moved to the torn fabric of her tank top. "Can't tell how many stab wounds until we get her back and hose her down." He indicated slight bruising on her inner arm. "And she's a user."

"Probably a pros," said Perez. "In this neck of the woods."

"Any ID?" Perez asked CS.

"Nada. Just some cash, which her attacker didn't bother to take."

Terri caught my eye and nodded toward a makeshift evidence table. I knew what she wanted me to see, the drawing.

"It was beside the body, half under her," she said. "And you hear what the ME said? Could be weeks, maybe a month; it's an old kill."

"Yeah, I heard. And this sort of wrecks your moral-standards theory."

Her eyes, above the mask, looked puzzled for a moment.

"You know, the part about him not killing girls."

* * *

Monica Collins arrived at the scene just as the NYPD Crime Scene van pulled out. She had her shield out in front of her, field agents flanking her like sentinels, and enough attitude to fill the tent.

"Why wasn't I informed about this?" She snapped on a pair of gloves.

One of the detectives from the local Fifth Precinct who had never met her must have missed her FBI shield because he said, "Sorry, but I don't got your number. Is it listed?"

Collins asked for his name and badge number.

Terri stepped in. "No one knew if this is related to the case yet, Agent Collins."

Collins wheeled around. "What part of 'full cooperation' do you not understand, Detective Russo?"

"No one wanted to waste your time if it wasn't related."

Collins didn't respond. She headed toward the concrete slab that hid the body. She hadn't put on her mask yet and I was sure she'd be sorry.

Everyone stopped to watch as she reeled back from the corpse, hand across her nose and mouth.

"Hope she chokes," O'Connell whispered.

Collins tried to look cool though her face was a bit green. "Where's the drawing?"

"Lab took it for testing," said Terri.

"Already?"

"They're efficient."

Collins's eyes narrowed above the mask she had finally gotten in place. "Did the sketch look like the others?"

"Not my area of expertise," said Terri. "Plus, it was a mess. Torn up and stained. Hard to tell if it had anything to do with the vic. Could be a coincidence that it was found near the body. Might have blown onto her or been dug up by the construction."

I wasn't sure if Terri was trying intentionally to piss off the agent or not. Everything she said was true, but Collins was steaming. She looked past Terri and caught my eye. "You," she said. "Sketch artist. Did it look like the vic?"

"You saw the vic's face, Agent Collins. Nothing much left to compare it to." I was pretty proud of my answer and could see by the slight smile in Terri's eyes that she was too.

Collins's eyes narrowed to slits. "I'll be speaking with Quantico officials, bringing them up to speed on these events." She looked over at Terri, then turned and left.

"You're going to have to play ball with them eventually," I said to Terri.

"Gee, thanks for telling me that, Rodriguez." She turned to her men. "You hear that, guys? Rodriguez here says we are going to have to play ball with G."

I put up my hands in defense. It just seemed to me that she was asking for trouble, and maybe I had been too.

"Hey, I know," said Perez. "Why don't you draw a picture of 'Lewinsky' and we can frame it for her, like a gift."

"I'd make a drawing of *you,* Perez, but I draw *faces,* not *assholes.*"

Perez's arm snapped back, ready to let me have it, but O'Connell grabbed him. "Easy there, Pretzel. Rocky here didn't mean no harm, did you, Rocky?"

Rocky?

"It was a joke," I said to Perez.

"Pendejo," said Perez.

I was ready to call him a fool too, plus a few other choice names, but Terri told everyone to relax. Then she looked up at me, a smile ticking at the corners of her lips. "Rocky?" she said. "Hmmm . . . don't know about that."

21

Terri had half the department going through Missing Persons and within a few hours they'd come up with three viable candidates for the Hudson Pier Jane Doe. After that, it didn't take long to match the dental records to a nineteen-year-old runaway named Carolyn Spivack, who had priors for possession and prostitution.

An hour later we were in the basement of a housing project on West Twentieth: dung-colored walls, cracked linoleum tiles, flickering fluorescent lights. It was a teen shelter for runaways, unwed mothers, and junkies, and the last-known address for Carolyn Spivack. Terri had asked me along in case there was a drawing to be made.

We knew what we were looking for, but didn't expect to find it so quickly.

"I can't believe it," said Maurice Reed, the guy who ran the shelter. "Carolyn had totally straightened herself out." He eased himself into a hard-backed chair. "She just wanted to help others who had been in her position. She'd been working here for eight months. She was . . . a beautiful human being."

It was Reed who had reported her missing, his name on the

missing persons report, though that did not clear him of suspicion. It was a well-known fact that killers often reported their crimes, particularly when they were close to the victim.

"Do her parents know?" he asked.

"Her parents are on their way from Cincinnati to claim the body," said Terri.

Reed blinked a few times, and swallowed. It looked to me as if he was fighting tears.

"How did Carolyn come to the shelter?" Terri asked.

"Like most. She sort of just washed up, you know, broke and broken, at our door." He sighed. "Nicky brought her in."

"Nicky?"

"A former street hustler, but he's cool now. He'll be here in a little while if you want to talk to him."

Terri didn't soft-pedal her next question: "There were track marks on her arm. You know about that?"

"They had to be old ones. Carolyn was clean. I'm sure of it. She was here every day. I managed to get her on staff with a small salary I wheedled out of social services. She had to go for drug testing every week. I'm telling you, she was clean." He exhaled a deep sigh. "Carolyn was great with people, particularly the girls who'd gone through the same stuff she had."

A dozen micro-expressions—all of them sad—passed across the man's face.

"You know where she lived?" Terri asked.

"I wouldn't know that."

"You said she was here every day," said Terri. "And she never told you where she lived?"

Reed's facial muscles went from sad to scared, mouth open, eyes wary, and I started to sketch him.

"What are you doing?"

"It's just . . . what I do. I'm a sketch artist."

"Wait a minute. You don't think I could have—"

"No one said anything about you being a suspect, Mr. Reed. It's what Rodriguez does to keep his hands busy."

It worked. Reed got nervous.

"Now that I think about it," he said. "She must have been at the Alfred Court, over on Sixteenth, between Eighth and Ninth. It's the last of its kind, a rooming house. Pretty funky, but it serves its purpose."

"You sound like you know it pretty well, Mr. Reed."

"Well, we put some of the runaways up there; the state pays for it."

"You ever been inside Carolyn's room?"

Reed's eyelids flickered and he looked away. "No."

He was lying. But I'd pretty much surmised what was going on the minute we'd stepped into the shelter and met Reed, and I was sure Terri had too. It fit the profile. What we had been looking for that had made Carolyn Spivack a target. I roughed in a bit more of his face, though he kept looking down or turning away.

"It's easy enough to check on that, Mr. Reed." Terri needed to hear him say it, and I knew what was coming when she reached into her tote. She brought out a CS photo of the victim—a close-up of the young woman's destroyed face—and held it in front of Reed.

"Jesus Christ!" Reed gasped and looked away. "Why the hell are you showing me that?"

"Mr. Reed." Terri kept the photo right in front of him. "I need to know about your relationship to the victim. I need to know it now or I will assume you are hiding something."

"No way. You have it all wrong. You don't know what you're saying." He caught his breath and there were tears in his eyes. "Carolyn and I—we were—she was living with me."

"So you were a couple."

"It just sort of . . . happened, you know, after she came here."

Terri lowered the photo. "Go on."

Reed cadged a peek at my drawing and frowned. "I was so afraid she'd slipped up, gone back on drugs. Why she'd disappeared, I mean. I never thought . . ."

"Why didn't you say you were a couple in the first place?"

"This is a city job, and with me being in charge, and . . . Carolyn was a lot younger."

I took Reed to be about forty. Carolyn Spivack had been nineteen.

"So you kept your relationship a secret," I said. "Here, at the center, I mean?"

"Well, we didn't advertise, and folks here, they got their own stuff to deal with."

"But you could have been seen together."

"Well, sure."

"Where? I mean, outside of the shelter."

"We liked to take long walks, along the Hudson mostly. We'd just head west and follow the footpath either downtown or up. Didn't matter. We talked a lot, about why she'd left home. She was trying to come to terms with her journey, you know, running away from home, the drugs, and what had happened to her."

A perfect opportunity to be seen, I thought, the footpath along the river always crowded with walkers, runners, and tourists.

"That's where she was found," Terri said. "Down by the river. Just where the two of you would take your walks. Quite a coincidence, Mr. Reed."

"It was where we liked to walk. That's all."

I watched Reed's face closely to see if he was controlling his expression, *modulating* it, as Ekman calls it. *Acting,* as I call it. But he didn't seem to be. His words and expressions were in sync.

"You have any idea what she was doing there?" Terri asked.

Reed pinched the ridge of his nose. "She used to go there to talk to the kids who sold themselves along the waterfront, offer to help them get clean. She didn't want them to suffer like she had."

"She was dressed like a hooker," said Terri.

"Oh, please, my niece, who's seven, wears tank tops and

short shorts. She wants to look like Beyoncé." He shook his head.

I stopped sketching, was about to close my pad, but Reed asked to see it.

"What are you going to do with it?"

Terri waited, holding the moment. "We'll just . . . keep it on file."

We hung around till Nicky showed up. He turned out to be a pale skinny kid with blue-black hair and gold hoops through his lower lip. He wasn't big and didn't look strong, and his face registered genuine shock and sadness when he heard about Carolyn. He told us he'd spent a couple of years prostituting himself after his father threw him out of the house because he was gay.

I asked him, and Reed too, if they'd seen anyone hanging around the shelter who looked suspicious. Nicky laughed and said everyone around the shelter looked suspicious.

I showed them my sketches of the man in the long coat and ski mask and they drew a blank.

"So what's this all about?" asked Reed. "Was Carolyn's murder part of something bigger?"

Terri said no a bit too fast, then told them they'd have to give official statements, and that was it; we were out of there.

"**A**nother interracial couple," said Terri as we got into her Crown Victoria. "And by the way, sketching Reed was a good idea, got him talking."

"Power of the pencil," I said.

"I've got to bring the team up to speed," said Terri. "And yes, the G too, in case you're worried."

"Hey, it's not *my* job I was worried about."

"Thanks for caring, Rodriguez."

"I do care. And what happened to Rocky?"

She pushed her hair back behind her ear, which was loose today. "Didn't sit right with me. I kept seeing Sylvester Stallone." She edged the car out into the traffic, and got serious. "I know I have to work with the bureau. And it's fine. Well, it's not fine, but it's the way it is. I just don't like giving it away. I've worked too hard for this. If I have to play with the G, then I'm going to make them see I can be just as good as they are."

"Who said you weren't?"

"No one is as good as they are. Just ask them."

I'd been to Quantico, and I thought they *were* good, but I'd been around the police longer and knew they were good too. "Does it have to be a game of who is better?"

"Believe it," she said. "Maybe it's about proving myself, and undoing some old damage.

Old damage. Something I knew all about.

"Agent Collins seems very determined."

"I know all about determined women, believe me."

I believed her.

"And it's not like I'm trying to fuck her over. I just want a chance to play in the same arena, not get pushed out, you know?"

We came to a light. She stopped and turned toward me. "There's going to be another briefing, Nate, and I'd like you to be there to talk about the unsub's drawings."

Ah, I was Nate again. I was listening.

"They need to hear they are definitely made by the same hand."

"But you already told them that and the lab's confirmed the paper, right?"

"But you're the expert. I'd like them to hear it straight

from the horse's mouth so it's undeniable. Maybe we can cut through some of the crap. And it will be good for Denton to see how valuable you are."

Now I got it. What she meant was that it would be good for Denton to see how valuable *she* was, how smart she'd been to bring me in. But I didn't mind proving my worth.

2 2

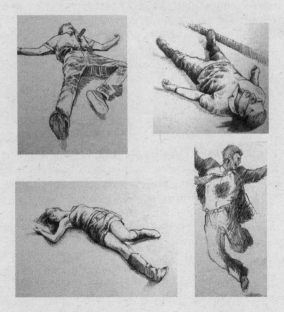

Over the past seven years I'd sat with hundreds of witnesses and victims making sketches, and I usually felt calm. But as I stood in front of a darkened briefing room, my hands were sweating. I had laid fresh copies of the sketches into four overhead projectors, the pictures now enlarged and cast onto the front wall.

"I've had the computer lab clean these up, remove all bloodstains and dirt so you can really see them," I said. "And this may be the first time you're seeing them all together." I went from one sketch to another, pointing out similarities, how the drawings had been built up with a repeated side stroke that indicated the man was right-handed, his loose but sure handling of the images, the quality of the graphite—all of it adding up to my consensus that they were all drawn by the same person.

I was recounting this to Chief of Department Perry Denton, Chief of Operations Mickey Rauder, Special Agent Monica Collins, her two field officers, Archer and Richardson, a stenographer sent over from FBI Manhattan, division heads from the precincts working on the homicides, and of course Terri Russo and her team.

In the middle of it I noticed something I had missed before in the drawing of Carolyn Spivack, but didn't stop to point it out. I just wanted to finish. Public speaking was not my thing.

When I sat down, Denton took over. He was a handsome guy, but a little too slick in his designer suit and shiny tassel loafers. His major emphasis was keeping the lid on the serial-killer aspect for as long as possible. The murders, though still getting attention, had fallen off page one, the drawings that connected them still unknown to the press. Denton reported that the PR Department had let it slip that Carolyn Spivack was a druggie and a hooker so her story didn't get much play in the media, which must have made her parents really happy.

"Once the link is made in the press, we'll have every crazy in the city calling in to use up their free Verizon minutes," said Denton, "and we don't have the manpower to log in all the calls." He glanced at Terri, and I saw her stiffen, though I didn't know why.

After that, both Denton and Collins attempted to make it clear it was their organization helping the other. Collins mentioned she was in constant communication with her

Quantico superiors, and Denton brought up the fact that he spoke to the mayor several times a day. But there was something other than crime-fighting politics going on, if I was reading the body language correctly. Granted, faces were my specialty, but if Agent Collins had hiked her skirt up any higher or gotten her legs any closer, Denton could have performed cunnilingus on her by simply sticking his tongue out, which, personally, I'd have found a lot more entertaining.

Denton ceded the floor to Mickey Rauder, who addressed the division heads about individual strategy. Rauder was an older guy, face like a basset hound, amiable, and on a first-name basis with everyone, asking one department head how his wife's operation had gone, congratulating another on his kid's college scholarship. He seemed like the real deal, and he wrapped things up quickly.

I was glad the meeting was finally over, but it wasn't for Terri. She insisted I go up and meet Denton. I think she wanted to show me off like I was a new blouse or something.

"I told you Rodriguez could add something," she said to him.

"Yes," said Denton, wearing an artificial smile, zygomatic major muscles stuck in neutral. "Nice job, Rodriguez. More proof we are looking for one man—just what we need, huh?" He forced a laugh. "But glad to have you on board."

I said, "Thanks," eager to get going, but Terri wasn't.

"And he's started a sketch," she said.

"Really?" said Denton. "I'd like to see that, but how is it possible?"

"Rodriguez has a gift. He can see inside people's heads."

"No shit," said Denton.

"Not really," I said. "I just do my job."

"He's being modest."

Terri was throwing me in Denton's face and I was starting to get an idea why.

Denton looped his thumbs into his pant pockets and

rocked back on his heels. "So what is it, Rodriguez, you read minds or something?"

"No, sir. Just faces."

"Really? So what's my face telling you right now?"

A couple of micro-expressions flashed over Denton's features, ending with the telltale asymmetry of someone who has something to hide: a smile in direct contrast to a fixed glare, upper eyelids raised against a lowered brow, which almost always suggests the first phase of suppressed anger.

That you're pissed about something—Me? Terri?—but trying to conceal it.

But I couldn't say that, so I just returned his artificial smile.

Denton leaned into Terri in a way that made me think he was marking his property—*this gal is mine, sort of thing.* "Well?" he said.

"I would say that your expression is one of a successful and self-satisfied man."

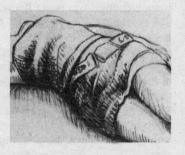

"Is that so?"

"Yes, sir."

We stared at each other a moment, then Denton turned away from me and asked Terri to follow. I watched the door close behind them, then flipped on the overhead projectors to look at the drawing of Carolyn Spivack.

I played with the projector's lens to enlarge it as much as possible.

What is it?

I slipped the picture out

of the projector and remembered where I had seen it. But it didn't make any sense.

Out in the hall Denton was nowhere in sight. Chief of Operations Mickey Rauder was talking to Terri, and he signaled me over.

"Nice work," he said. "Your old man would have been proud."

The sentence stopped me cold, though I could see he was waiting for me to respond. "You knew my father?"

"Yes, we were in the same division, Narcotics, way back when." He squinted at me. "You look like him."

Did I? I had never allowed myself to think so.

"Juan Rodriguez was a good man."

I nodded, unable to locate my voice.

"Guess I'm one of the few cops who decided to stay way past when most cops retire, but it paid off. Here I am chief of operations. Some days I can hardly believe it, but if you stay in long enough you never know."

I managed to say, "Uh-huh," looked past the man's basset-hound wrinkles to see he was younger than I'd originally thought, mid-fifties, like my father would have been.

"I think your old man would have stayed too." He squinted at me again. "Can't get over how much you look like him."

I nodded again, hoping he would just stop talking.

But he wouldn't quit. "I was thinking back there in the briefing room how your father would bring your drawings into the station and hang 'em up. He was so damn proud of you."

Mickey Rauder waited for me to say something, but when I didn't he slapped me on the back, said he hoped to see me around, to keep up the good work, and left me standing there with tears burning behind my lids and my heart in my throat.

"**Y**ou okay?" Terri asked.

"Yeah, fine."

"Good. There are a few things I want to go over with you."

"Later," I said, and took off.

I headed out of the precinct with a picture of my father so strong in my mind that he could have been walking right beside me.

23

I shuttled crosstown from Times Square to Grand Central, then waited on the subway platform for the number 6 train. It seemed to be taking forever. I kept looking down the tunnel, impatient, highlights of Mickey Rauder's conversation reverberating in my head.

You look like your old man . . . He was so damn proud of you . . .

When the train finally pulled into the station I was so lost in reflection, it startled me.

I gripped an overhead bar and stared at an ad for whiter, brighter, teeth without seeing it, the drawing of Carolyn Spivack shimmering in my brain.

What I was thinking did not seem possible, but I was going to check it out.

My grandmother was waiting at her front door as I came out of the fifth-floor stairwell. I was puffing for breath.

"The elevator, *está roto*?"

I shook my head, took a few deep breaths. "No, I, uh, just wanted the exercise."

She gave me a look. *"¿Qué te pasa?"*

"Nada, uela. Everything's fine."

"*Estás mintiendo.* I see it in your eyes."

My grandmother read faces better than I did.

"I just need to see something." I leaned down to kiss her cheek.

She laid her hand on my arm. "*¿Cuál es el problema?*"

"There's no trouble, *uela*. I just need to get my drawing pad."

She planted her hands firmly on her hips. "You don't have another at home?"

"I just want to see something, is that okay with you, officer?"

"*Oye, chacho.*" She waved a hand. "You are such a *mentiroso.*"

She headed to the small hallway closet where I kept my pad and pencils, but I beat her to it, grabbed my pad, and hugged it to my chest. I wanted to look in private.

She pursed her lips and narrowed her eyes. "You will have something to eat." It was not a question.

I went into the living room and sat down on the couch. My hands were shaking as I opened the pad to the last drawing I had made, the one of my grandmother's vision.

I took out the copy of the sketch found at Carolyn Spivack's crime scene and an enlargement of the symbol on her belt that I'd made after I'd seen it projected on the briefing room wall.

I had not been wrong. But how was it possible? It had to be some totally weird coincidence—the same symbol in the CS drawing and in my grandmother's vision.

My grandmother called out from the kitchen: *"¿Quieres algo de tomar, cerveza?"*

I knew she just wanted to see what I was up to, but I said yes.

A minute later she was handing me a Corona.

She leaned over the couch. "What is so *importante* about this drawing pad?"

I had already closed it and hidden the copies of the crime scene drawings.

"I just wanted to check something."

"¿Qué?"

"Since when are you a detective?"

"Siempre."

"Always is right." I had to smile. "Okay." I opened the pad.

She looked at the drawing and crossed herself. "I told you, the *ashe* in that room is no good."

"Yeah, I remember that. But what does the symbol mean?"

"Yo no sé. It just appeared to me." She sat down beside me. *"¿Por qué?"*

I could never hide my feelings from her. I wasn't sure I wanted to put too much stock in her visions, but this was undeniable.

I was suddenly thinking back to the day before my father died. I'd been up on the roof of the building, Julio and I smoking a joint, listening to salsa music coming from open windows. When we came back into the apartment, there were lit candles everywhere and glasses filled with water at the *bóveda*. When I asked my grandmother why, she had waved me off.

I didn't want to stir up old grief, but had to ask. "The day before *papi* died you lit candles and filled the *bóveda* glasses. Why?"

"Hace mucho tiempo."

"Sí, it's a long time ago, *uela,* but I need to know."

"Why you want to know now?"

I looked at her and waited.

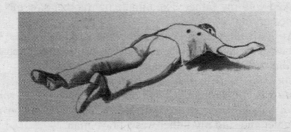

She took a deep breath. "I had a vision," she said. "The night before . . . before it happen." She described the vision, and I saw it.

It was all I needed to bring me back to that night twenty years ago.

I had begged Julio to come home with me, even kidded him. "Yo, *mira,* you're supposed to be my bodyguard, *mi pana,* right?" But he wouldn't do it.

When I got out of the subway at Twenty-third and Eighth, the streets were deserted; no music in the air, no hydrants spraying diamonds into the gutter. Just a drunk collapsed in front of a deli, and steam rising off the pavement.

I headed up the two short blocks to Penn South. There were only a few windows lit, and I didn't have to count the floors to know that it was my apartment, my parents waiting up for me. My mother had been at work when the shit had gone down between me and my father. By now, she had to know.

I chewed a piece of Dentyne to mask the booze and dope.

The apartment complex was quiet, the lobby empty. When I got off the elevator I could see light under the apartment door.

I knew I was in for it. I took a couple of deep breaths and opened the door.

There were two men standing there, detectives who worked with my father. The minute my mother saw me she started crying.

At first I thought the cops had come looking for me, but that wasn't it. She asked them to tell me. She couldn't speak.

Your father's been shot, said one of the cops.

Looks like a drug bust gone bad, said the other.

Must have happened spontaneously, something going down that he tried to stop. The cop laid his hand on my shoulder and said my father was a brave man.

I had to ask. And they told me.

Two shots in the chest. One in the head.

But only I knew what had happened—that it had been my fault.

I never told my mother. How do you tell your mother that you killed your father, her husband?

I forced the memory out of my head and listened to my grandmother.

She said that after she had the vision she'd sought out the gods. She should have warned him, but knew that her son, a nonbeliever, would have scoffed at the warning.

"Still," she said, "I should have tried. *Es un arrepentimiento.*" There were tears in her dark eyes.

I wanted to tell her that it had been my fault, not hers, but couldn't find the words.

She patted my hand and started talking about the *egun,* the dead, and how they interact with the living. We all have a specific number of days on earth, she told me, and those who are killed before that allotted time hang around as ghosts until their time is up, until their souls, their *ori,* can rest.

I wondered if my father's *ori* was looking for me.

She tapped my drawing and her face grew dark. "There is something in that room, *algo malo*." She looked up at me. "And now you are here to see it again. *Por qué?*"

"It's nothing, *uela,* like I said."

"Nato, *por favor,* do not lie to your *abuela*."

"It has to do with a case at the police station, that's all. It doesn't concern me, not personally."

My grandmother's face showed me I was wrong. "You must stay away from this case, Nato. *Es muy peligroso para tí*."

"*Sí*, it is dangerous, *uela,* but not for me."

She shook her head. "I see *you*, Nato, in that room."

Now I was listening. "What else do you see?"

She leaned back into the couch and closed her eyes. "I see you in that room with a man."

"What sort of man?"

"*No lo veo*. It has been too long since I had the vision, but I still . . . feel him. *Entiendes?*"

I told her I understood, and to relax, and her shoulders sloped a little, the muscles in her face eased. After a minute she said, "*Las llamas,* the flames, remember? In the room?"

I turned back to the sketch I had made.

"What about the man?" I asked.

She squeezed her eyes shut. "I see a dark face. *Un hombre en máscara.*"

A man in a mask. I shivered.

"There are—*¿cómo se dice?*—holes for his eyes and nose, his mouth too." She was pointing out the features on her face with her eyes closed. "I can see the eyes, light eyes, *con una mirada fría.*"

I found the sketch I'd made and asked her to look at it.

"*Madre mía.*" She crossed herself and mumbled something under her breath about Chango.

"Is there anything else?" I asked, feeling like I was

in some paranormal thriller like *The Omen*, things I had always claimed I did not believe in but were now impossible to deny.

"The eyes," she said, describing them while I made another drawing.

I showed her what I'd drawn.

She took a deep breath and crossed herself again. "*Sí,* those are the eyes."

But how could my grandmother, up in Spanish Harlem, have any idea about the man we were hunting?

She suddenly grasped my wrist. *"Nato, ten cuidado."*

"Sure," I said. "Of course. I'm a careful guy, a born coward, a *cobarde*." I tacked on a fake smile.

"Don't be a wise man," she said, meaning a wise guy, which made me smile; and she shook a finger at me. "Do not make fun, *chacho*. I have seen you in that room. I do not know what it means, but . . ." She got up and crossed the room to the *bóveda*.

I looked back at the symbol my grandmother had described, which I had drawn from her vision, the almost identical symbol on Carolyn Spivack's belt, and it gave me another chill.

My grandmother scooped up seashells from the *bóveda*. She was humming to herself while she moved the shells from hand to hand, *"Ten Cuidado con el Corazón . . ."* That favorite song of hers, a love song that came with a warning: *Be careful*.

24

I folded myself into a hard-backed chair opposite Terri's desk. I'd done some research and needed to tell her, but there was a question stuck in my mind since she'd pushed me into Denton's face.

"So what's up between you and Denton?"

"What do you mean?"

"It seemed to me that there was some history between you two."

Terri's eyes flashed. "I have no history with that man."

That was essentially a declaration that she *did* have a history with "that man." I remembered a lecturer at Quantico saying that people became impersonal when they wanted to distance themselves from something and it's usually because they are hiding something or lying. It was like Bill Clinton saying, "I did not have sex with *that woman.*" I remembered hearing that and thinking, *Oh, Bill, you so did.* Which, by the way, was fine by me. If the president of the United States can't get a blow job, who can? Though, perhaps he should not have gotten it in the Oval Office, from his intern.

"So you've got no history with *that man.* Fine."

She tried to neutralize her face while maintaining eye contact. People tend to think if they make eye contact you will believe them.

Terri let out a held breath. "Oh, fuck, what the hell do I care if you know I once had a five-minute fling with that son of a bitch? So what? It was before he was chief. Ancient history."

"Oh, ancient history. Sorry, I guess you thought I was asking about modern history."

"Screw you, Rodriguez."

"I was kidding. What are you getting so pissed off about?"

"You were not kidding. And I'm pissed because you're condemning me for something that was a mistake and meant nothing, and is over, and by the way, is none of your fucking business."

I put up my hands. "Sorry. And I'm not condemning you."

"I see it in your smug little face, Rodriguez. And why the hell do I care—why the hell do *you* care—who I've slept with?"

"I don't."

"Fuck you don't."

I thought about that: Why *did* I care who she slept with?

"Have I answered your question sufficiently, Rodriguez?"

"Sorry," I said again, and laid the images I'd brought with me out in front of her, which I knew would change the subject.

"What am I looking at?"

"It's from the drawing of Carolyn Spivack. I made an enlargement of what was drawn on her belt." I didn't bother to tell her how I'd come to recognize it from my grandmother's vision because I didn't want her to think I was crazy.

"Okay. But what is it?"

"I did a little research, Googled everything from Egyptian hieroglyphics to the Rosetta Stone until I finally found it."

"And?"

"That's the cover of *The White Man's Bible*. It's like the white supremacists' handbook."

"Is it in any of the other drawings?"

"Not that I could find." I slid a stack of pages over to her. "I pulled these excerpts off the Internet. *The White Man's Bible* preaches violence against blacks, Jews, and race traitors—which is anyone who defends them."

"Or marries them, or hangs out with them, that it?"

"Bull's-eye. Boyfriends like Daniel Rice and girlfriends like Carolyn Spivack."

"Race traitors," said Terri, shaking her head. "Has a really nasty ring to it. But it makes sense of why the unsub sometimes chooses the white partners."

"To show us that they're just as guilty. Maybe guiltier, in his eyes. I wonder what that makes me, a Jew and Latino—a doubleheader, right?"

"Don't kid about that."

"Who says I'm kidding?" I picked at my cuticles.

"I've got to get this to Hate Crimes. Maybe they can identify a specific group that reads this crap."

"My take is they *all* read it."

Terri sucked on her lower lip while I made a mess of my fingernails.

"There has to be something Hate Crimes can tell us: the local groups, maybe a few addresses."

"These days they stay in touch through the Internet. It's a lot safer. Which means it's not just local. Check this out." I handed her another sheet of my online research, a list.

"There's a whole lot of them out there—the KKK, Christian Identity, Youth Scene, Aryan Nation, Soldiers of War, World Church of the Creator, which is your basic ecumenical come-one come-all assemblage for Neo-Nazi skinheads and white supremacists. Some statistics say there are as few as twenty thousand in the U.S., but the analysts who keep track of these groups . . ." I shook my head. "They put the number at about half a million—and growing."

"Jesus," she said.

"Don't know what they'd make of him, probably wouldn't go for the long hair and preaching love for thy fellow man."

"So we're looking for a fanatic." Terri rapped her finger-nails along the edge of her desk. "I hate to say it, but clearly the G can add to this. I'm sure they have reams of info on these groups and files on all the leaders. I've got to show them. It totally confirms what we thought about the hate crime angle."

"And tells us something about the man who added the symbol to his drawing."

"Like?"

"Like on some level he wants people to know it's him. He was telling us something intentionally, right? I'd say he's bragging."

I could see Terri considering that. She stopped rapping her nails and touched my hand. "This is good work, Rodri-guez. Thanks." She let her hand rest on mine a moment, then she gathered all the papers together and stood up.

"I'm going to see Monteverdi and Bransky in Hate Crimes. And don't worry, after that, I'll go visit my new best friend, Agent Monica Collins."

25

Perry Denton smoothed his hair back the way men who are aware of their appearance always do and headed into the Bronx tenement. The first-floor stairwell was lit by a dim red bulb, the one on the second floor burned out. He gripped the railing with a gloved hand as he made his way up to three, thinking this was the last time he'd be visiting Joe Vallie in this hellhole.

Vallie was sitting at the table in his kitchenette, an alcove off the living room with a stove, a half-size fridge, and a naked lightbulb that made the pockmarks on his face look like craters.

Denton didn't feel one bit sorry for him. He'd brought this upon himself, no matter what he thought. It wasn't his fault that Vallie had lost his job and pension, even if Vallie thought it was.

"You're late."

"You're lucky I got here."

"No, *you're* lucky you got here," said Vallie. "Such a busy man."

Denton ignored the sarcasm. "This is the last of it, Joe." He placed the stack of bills onto the table. "I can't keep doing this."

"Sure you can, Perry. Way I see it, you're sitting on top of the world." He slurped some coffee out of a cracked mug. There was a pot on the stove, but he didn't offer any to Denton.

Pitiful mess, thought Denton. But he was way past feeling sorry for Joe Vallie. It made him sick to think that his ex-partner would do this to him. And enough was enough. "This is the last time, Joe, I mean it."

"I heard you the first time." He fingered the wad. "But I got expenses, you know that."

"Yeah, I heard you were sick. How come you didn't tell me?"

"Guess I didn't think you cared."

Oh, I care. When he'd heard Vallie had cancer, all he could think was, *Maybe he'll die.*

"Guess you're hoping I'll die."

"Something like that." Denton laughed. "Just kidding."

"No you're not. But don't get your hopes up, I'm in remission."

"Yeah, I heard that too. Good for you." It really was too bad about that clean bill of health. It would have made it so much easier, Vallie just dying. But now it was like he was doing the man a favor, wasn't he? Eliminating years of decline, of possible pain and suffering. Really, it was for the best. "I bet you'll beat this thing."

"I intend to."

"That's the spirit, Joe." It was absurd, all this bullshit friendly-enemy banter when Vallie was sticking a shiv into him, holding him up when the bastard was as guilty as he was. A part of him doubted Vallie would blow the whistle because it would send him to jail too, but what did Vallie have to lose? *Nothing.* Still, he couldn't take any chances, a man in his position. "Honest, Joe, if you weren't putting a gun to my head, I'd be crying."

"That's something I'd like to see." Vallie laughed. "You know I got to get out of this dump, and I got that condo ready and waiting. I just have to make the payment."

"You mean *I* have to, which I just did."

"Maybe," said Vallie.

Not maybe, thought Denton. "Sounds real good, Joe, condo in Honolulu, some Hawaiian cutie to bring you a piña colada and suck your dick. Oh, sorry, I guess that part of you isn't quite up to it anymore."

"You're such a fuck, Perry, but you always were."

"Oh, come on, Joe, I was only teasing. We had our good ol' narc times, didn't we?"

"Plenty," said Vallie. "Which is why I think so many other folks would enjoy hearing about them."

Denton's face hardened. He thought about killing his ex-partner right on the spot, save himself some money.

"See you soon," said Vallie. "Real soon."

Denton laughed and cocked his finger at Vallie as if it were a gun. "Not if I see you first, big kahuna."

26

He lifts a Beck's off the tray, eyes tracking the man's wife as she makes her way around the room, lowering the tray for each of them. She disappears and returns with more beer, places it on a low Formica-topped coffee table, and her husband pats her arm the way you would a dog and she smiles.

He wishes his wife were more like this, checks out the matching sofa and club chairs, deep-pile rug, tan wood dinette set seen through an archway, shiny with Lemon Pledge.

A new man to the group, a guy in the military wearing sweats, who calls himself "Ethno," short for "ethnoviolence," says, "To be real masculine men you've got to do violence against the enemy."

He recognizes that Ethno is quoting one of his *über*-heroes, the current leader of the World Church.

"Tell your out-of-work friends and any kids you can to join the army, light infantry the branch of choice because the coming race war will be an infantryman's war, remember that. The army is in desperate need for recruits, and where else can you get the fucking government to train you for free, right?"

This gets everyone's attention, but after a few minutes the talk meanders back to cars and accounting, teaching and trivia, until the host, who calls himself Swift, after the founder of Christian Identity, interrupts. He pushes up his sleeves, exposing small blue-black tattoos, swastikas, as so many of them have. "What we say in public is a lot different than what we do in private."

As he says this he looks right at him and he wonders if Swift knows what he's been doing. He would like to stand up and declare it, but sits there pretending to drink, hand gripping the can so hard it's denting, fragments of pictures flashing in his mind, coming together and breaking apart.

Swift asks for contributions to support legal defenses for two men in prison, Richard Glynn and Duane Holsten, and tells them what Holsten did: "He killed his brother's wife and baby because God told him to." He looks around at each of them, and asks: "Could you make that kind of sacrifice?"

He knows he could.

After that, they take turns reading aloud from Madison Grant's *The Passing of the Great Race* and Ben Klassen's *Nature's Eternal Religion,* and after that Swift leads them in the oath, though he can't concentrate because those pictures of what he is planning next keep vibrating in his head, and after that everyone goes back to stories about their boring day jobs and he's about to leave when Swift takes him aside and leads him into the basement.

Behind a metal door is a small cinder-block room, walls lined with guns and rifles, pistols and flame throwers still in their original boxes, a crate of hand grenades that Swift cracks open for a peek, and he feels a kind of tug in his loins and a wave of reassurance.

Swift says, "For when the time comes," and in that moment he feels so close to the man he wants to tell him what he is doing because he knows he will understand, but decides it's better not to.

27

The NYPD had combined efforts with the bureau, the results of which had produced reams of paper documenting America's leading white supremacist groups. Terri had stayed up most of the night reading and by morning had reached the conclusion that mankind was hopeless.

She had arrived at the meeting with a throbbing headache, washed down two Excedrin with a cup of machine-brewed coffee, and though the headache had abated, her feet were now tapping, nerves jangling from caffeine overdrive.

The G could not dispute the fact that the locals had been supplying some of the best information—thanks to Nate's detection of the logo from *The White Man's Bible*—and Terri was feeling just a little proud for having brought him on the case.

She suspected Denton would have been happier if the PD had been taken off the case, full responsibility falling on the fed's broad shoulders, but that was *his* problem. He was notably absent, some business with the city council, or so he said, though Terri could not imagine what could be more important.

Terri had invited Nate along with her men, anxious for all of them to hear if the Quantico profiler could add anything new to the case.

Collins gave an introductory briefing, basically what the NYPD had provided, then introduced the woman who had already snagged Nate's attention, tall and slender, black suit jacket unbuttoned to expose her fitted white blouse, everything about her flawless except for her auburn hair, twirled into an ad hoc bun that threatened to topple, providing an unexpected louche touch.

"Dr. Schteir comes to us from BSS," said Collins. "She has written extensively about the sociopathic mind, and published several articles on hate crime and its effects on—"

"Thanks," said Schteir, cutting her off. "But I don't think anyone gives a rat's ass about my CV." She flashed a quick smile, and Nate thought he'd fallen in love.

"I don't know if you've had a chance to read the profile I worked up, which is in your folders, so I'll summarize. We'll first do a little Sociopath 101, and after that I'll talk about the hate-crime component." She glanced around the room, and Nate made a point of catching her eye and smiling.

Terri cadged a glance in his direction.

Dr. Schtier counted off on her fingers. "One: The sociopath is unable to give or receive love, though they can fake it quite well when they want to. They are unusually skilled manipulators. Many are the result of abuse and have learned to survive terribly sadistic situations by turning off their feelings. I am not making a case for sympathy, simply stating statistics. Two: They do not feel remorse or guilt like normal human beings. Three: They are egocentric, totally self-centered. These are the general rules—if one can even call them that—which are constantly shifting, and vary from individual to individual. Modern psychology is constantly reassessing them. One must always be prepared for a new manifestation and how the sociopath will exhibit it in a new and novel way." Her eyes were shining; it was obvious that for Dr. Schteir, sociopaths were a sexy topic.

"I'll stop counting," she said. "It doesn't matter. A sense of superiority. Very important. The sociopath feels he is better than you or me, better than anyone. He is above the rules of normal society, just one of the things that aids him in committing his heinous acts. On the other hand, it can be his Achilles heel. Arrogance can lead to mistakes, tempt him to tease the authority he disdains. It is not uncommon for sociopaths to get close to the press and to the police, as I'm sure you know." She unconsciously plucked a comb from her hair, and her auburn locks tumbled to her shoulders.

Nate opened his drawing pad and started sketching.

"In the case of your unknown subject, there is no psycho-sexual release, though he undoubtedly receives pleasure from his acts." She paused. "So, the hate-crime kill-er . . . generally, he regards his victims as lesser human be-ings, or not even human. It's a tactic employed by soldiers, torturers, and sometimes even politicians."

This produced a few laughs.

"But seriously . . ." She pulled her hair back and secured the comb in place. "It's important to remember that he is driven by the belief that he is *right*. Just keep in mind a man flying a plane into a skyscraper, dying for a god and ideol-ogy he believes in, and you will begin to understand the kind of personality you are dealing with." She paused to let that sink in. "There are two profiles in your folder. The sup-position on your unsub, along with a profile I did two years ago on Duane Holsten, who is serving a life sentence at a criminal-psyche facility for killing eight people—four nurses and two patients at an abortion clinic. Holsten main-tains he was doing God's work, and therefore feels no re-morse at all."

Agent Archer raised his hand. "You said eight people. That's only six."

"The other two were his sister-in-law and her unborn child. He slashed her throat before going to the clinic where she was scheduled to have an abortion."

"So he had a motive," said Archer, "other than God."

"Yes, but he does not admit that his sister-in-law's

impending abortion provided any impetus for his crime. He avers that he had been consulting with God for some time, and that God told him to kill these people."

"I don't buy it."

"It is indeed questionable, Agent Archer, an excuse for a hideous crime, and not an uncommon defense for hate-crime killers. But I interviewed Holsten over the course of a year and he never once changed his story. He is absolutely convinced he was right, that he was correcting an affront to God. When I offered the logical argument that *he* might be the one who offended God, since by stabbing his sister he had terminated a pregnancy, he told me I did not understand. He has never once wavered in his belief and continues to insist that God told him to kill, and therefore he did nothing wrong."

"Nut job," said Archer.

"You've got that right." Schteir smiled. "As for your unsub, he may be choosing victims at random, or the acts may have a personal component. You may not discover that until he is caught." She reached for a paper with the symbol Nate had found from *The White Man's Bible.* "Though your man appears to be working solo, he is probably in touch with members of various hate organizations. This sort of personality derives strength from being part of a group. Duane Holsten was a member of both the World Church of the Creator and Christian Identity for at least ten years before his crime. Christian Identity is not an organized group, a shame because it would make our jobs a lot easier. It's a loose-knit network of fanatics that stay in touch via Internet chat rooms. Holsten's computer showed that he spent more than half his day in chat rooms. He had a basement full of neo-Nazi propaganda and three years' worth of journals that documented his personal conversations with God—which is why he's in a psyche ward and not on death row."

"Couldn't he have fabricated the journals after the fact?" Terri asked.

"Absolutely," said Schteir. "And it's possible, though Holsten convinced me he was speaking directly to God, something more than one religious-right sect is pushing these days. It's called divine revelation."

"Direct line to God," said Archer. "Handy."

"Indeed. This sort of man is determined and *righteous*." Schteir looked around the room. "If you believed you were absolutely right—that God told you the world's salvation depended on *you*—would you carry out his bidding? Would you dare *not* to?" She paused. "Holsten, as I said, feels no remorse because he was following orders. Sound familiar?"

Nate raised his hand and spoke simultaneously. "Nazis and neo-Nazis sharing the same excuse, right?"

Dr. Schteir smiled. "Yes. There is something in these men and in your unsub—rather something *missing* from their psyche and emotional core—that allows them to do what they do. They split their personalities, even their lives."

"Are you saying he could be living a normal life?"

"I'd say a *double* life as opposed to a *normal* one, but yes."

After the meeting I stopped to talk with the Quantico shrink.

"Very interesting presentation," I said. "And it sounds like you enjoy your work."

"Oh, I do. I was never interested in having one of those comfortable practices— you know, dealing with everyday neurotics. Interviewing someone like Duane Holsten is a thrill. How many shrinks ever get to work with a true sociopath in their entire lifetime? Me, I get to do it all the time."

"And it's not frightening?"

"Oh, very frightening. Going into maximum security facilities, feeling all of those eyes on you—I can assure you that part is not fun." She shook her head. "I'm sorry, you are . . . ?"

"Nate Rodriguez. Forensic artist."

"Oh, the one who is making the sketches for us."

"That's me." I smiled. "So, what you said about our unsub believing he's right in his actions, I agree; but what about the emotion that drives him?"

"Well, everyone experiences emotions differently, but with your unsub it's obviously anger," said Schteir. "Anger he can't control."

"But he *does* control it. He takes his time making drawings of his vics *before* he kills them, right? After that, there doesn't appear to be much emotion behind the act. It's sort of like he's gotten the anger out in the planning and drawing, and the killing becomes perfunctory, wouldn't you say?"

Dr. Schteir raised an eyebrow and assessed me more fully.

"And anger is usually accompanied by another emotion," I added.

"Such as?"

"Fear, usually. Fear that the object of your anger—the victims, in this case—poses some sort of threat to you."

"I see you've been studying." Schteir smiled. "Who in particular?"

"Paul Ekman, for one."

"Creator of the *Facial Coding System*, of course. I'm familiar with his work."

"Ekman says we often focus anger on people who don't share our beliefs, or offend our basic values." I hoped I didn't sound like I was showing off, though I was, a little. "I've studied anger and fear so I can recognize it on people's faces and be able to draw it."

Terri was suddenly by my side. "Nate can draw a face from memory and create one from the flimsiest description."

"Really? There could be a job for you at Quantico, Nate." Schteir touched my hand.

"He's already been there," said Terri, before I had a chance to speak.

I gave her a look. "It was just a few courses," I said.

"Stop being modest, Nate," said Terri.

"She's right, Nate, don't be modest." Schteir tapped my pad. "Anything in there I can take a peek at?"

I wasn't sure I should, but couldn't help showing off a little more, so I opened the pad.

"Oh," said Schteir. "No one has ever done my portrait."

"They're just doodles," I said.

"No, they're terrific."

I ripped the page out of the pad and handed it to the profiler. "Here. One day I'd like to do something more serious. Maybe you could sit for me."

"You're embarrassing Dr. Schteir," said Terri.

"Not at all," said Schteir. She reached into her bag, came up with her card, and gave it to me. "Call me."

I said I would. I wanted to stay longer and explore the possibility, but Terri tugged me away.

"Sorry to interrupt your little tête-à-tête," she said, "but this is serious."

"Yeah?" I said.

"Yeah," she said. "The *Post* has gotten the story. The connection has been made."

28

NEW YORK POST

PORTRAITS OF MURDER

By Lou Sands

Three vicious murders appear to have a connection. Though the NYPD would not confirm the link, sources close to the investigation suggest that the victims had drawings, portraits which looked like them, attached to their dead bodies. The families of Harrison Stone of Brooklyn, Daniel Rice and Roberto Acosta, both of Manhattan, would not comment, except to voice their frustration that police have not yet apprehended a suspect. Investigators denied the connection, pointing out that the methods of killing has varied: two victims shot, one stabbed. Chief of Department Perry Denton refused comment. But as one unnamed source said, "A serial killer is never something the police department is eager to confirm."

A serial killer?

He shakes his head, thinking he should not be surprised, that it is probably a plant, a conspiracy between the press and the government to make him out to be a monster, a villain in the public's eye.

The fact that the homicides occurred in different locations has brought together several precincts in what appears to be a full-scale, though confidential, manhunt. The recent murder of a young prostitute, whose body was found near Manhattan's Chelsea Piers complex, may also figure into the case, though it has not yet been confirmed. What has been confirmed is that agents from the Manhattan FBI Bureau and Quantico have been brought into the case.

Of course he knew the FBI had joined the case. He'd expected it. And it does not worry him. Many of the people he most admires have been the subject of FBI investigations, and he is proud to join their ranks.

According to an unnamed source, one of the police department's most sought-after forensic artists, Nathan Rodriguez, has been brought into the case. It's been suggested that a witness may have survived an attack and is working with the sketch artist to create a composite image of the killer.

What? His fingers coil and crimp the edges of the newspaper like an insect's teeth about to gnaw at it.
A sketch artist? Making a composite? Of me?
But there is no way he has been seen. He is sure of that. And no one *has* survived, so how is it possible?
He heads down the stairs quickly, unlocks the door, flips on the light, his breathing so loud it's like a growl as he smoothes the newspaper onto his work table and stares until the type blurs.

He paces back and forth, back and forth, trying to get his fury under control, manages to sit, fingers thumping at the keyboard as he signs into a chat room. He finds a few familiar names, proposes a game, and tugs his PlayStation headset over his ears so he can hear the other players, nerve endings tingling as the screen flashes blood-red and one of the players says, "Let's do some damage."

He chooses his favorite over-the-shoulder point of view staring down a rifle's sight line at a surrealistic war zone. Figures dart across the screen, and he fires off virtual ammo at a virtual enemy while the actual men roar racial epithets, their curses and heavy breathing piped through his headset directly into his brain along with the rat-a-tat of gunfire and exploding bombs. The pixilated figures die and spawn, die and spawn, over and over, bouncing back to virtual life seconds after being virtually killed, and it starts to backfire, eroding his confidence rather than building it, and he thinks that he will never accomplish what he needs to do. He tears the headset off and hurls it across the room. It hits the cinder block wall, cracks, and crashes to the floor. He stares at the cyberspace enemy, who refuse to die, skittering across a now mute screen.

He closes his eyes, but the men are still racing across his retina. He takes a deep breath, then another, and when he opens his eyes and sees the posters on his walls and the sketches on his desk, begins to feel stronger. Then he looks at the newspaper article and his paranoia springs back to life like those spawning figures.

He sits forward, shakes out his limbs, lays his fingers back onto his keyboard, and types an e-mail to the man who calls himself Swift.

From: <Nordicman@interstate.com>
Sent: Sunday, March 19, 2006, 2:58 A.M.
  To: <swift@flochart.net>
Subject: Checking in

Do you have time to talk?

He stares at the screen until an e-mail pops up.

From: <swift@flochart.net>
Sent: Sunday, March 19, 2006, 3:03 A.M.
To: <Nordicman@interstate.com>
Subject: Warning

Don't think a call right now is a good idea but what
gives?

He's not exactly sure what to say, why he has e-mailed
Swift in the first place. Perhaps it's because the image of
Swift's basement arsenal made him feel safe. He writes:

Have the feeling someone may be watching me.

Swift responds:

Same feeling here. think something is going down. do
not call. repeat. do not call. better to not be in touch
at all. erase this message.

What does Swift mean? *Something is going down.*

His heart is pounding again.

He closes his eyes, chooses a statement from his readings,
and begins to repeat it:

"To give death and receive it. To give death and receive
it. To give death and receive it To give death and receive it
To give death and receive it to give death and receive it to
give death and receive it togivedeathandreceiveitogive-
deathandreceiveit togivedeathandreceiveitogivedeathand-
receiveit . . .

Light-headed from holding his breath, the anxiety begins
to lift. From behind closed lids, rays of sunlight appear and
the mission statement unfurls like a banner:

And then he hears God's voice, and the plan He offers up is simple.

29

Denton used the new cell phone for the first of two calls he would make before throwing it away.

"How's it going, Joe?"

"I've been waiting for you to call me back is how it's going. I was thinking I might have to call a reporter or something."

"Take it easy, Joe. No need to do anything rash. I was busy. So what's the problem?"

"No problem. I was just thinking I'd like to go to Honolulu earlier, say end of the month."

The cheap phone was breaking up and Denton wasn't sure he'd heard him correctly. "Go where? Honolulu? Now?"

"Yeah. And I could use a little cash to get settled."

"I just gave you the last condo payment." *You little fuck.* But no, he would not lose his temper. There was no need. "Like how little?"

"Just a few thousand. I wouldn't want to squeeze an old friend."

"Real considerate of you, Joe." He thought a moment. "I'll bring it by. How's tonight?"

"How come you're suddenly in such a hurry?"

"Just want to make you happy, Joe. You going to be in?"

"Yeah, where else do I have to go?"

152 JONATHAN SANTLOFER

"It'll be late."

"Like I said, I have nowhere to go."

Denton disconnected and made the other call. "Tonight," he said, gave the particulars again, then tossed the phone into a trash bin. *Aloha, Joe.*

Denton took a deep breath and turned his thoughts to the fact that the media had gotten the story. It was a miracle they hadn't gotten it sooner, but now he'd have to hold a press conference, do some damage control before they got the rest—a serial killer was bad enough, but race killings, the worst. The minute that got out, every bleeding-heart liberal would be clocking in with their opinion.

He opened the *Post* and glanced at the story. How the hell had they gotten wind of Rodriguez? He guessed if someone was sniffing around the story it would not be too difficult.

You read minds, Rodriguez?

Just faces.

So what's my face telling you right now?

That you're a successful and self-satisfied man.

Smug little bastard. So why did it make him uncomfortable? He never should have agreed to let Russo bring him in. No question she was sleeping with the guy. Maybe that's what was pissing him off. But he was going to keep an eye on Rodriguez. On Russo too.

Manhattan FBI Headquarters was streamlined and quiet like a conservative law firm, except the employees were wearing JCPenney instead of Brooks Brothers.

Terri and I were following Agent Richardson. They had a suspect in custody.

We headed down an aisle, cubicles on either side, through a maze of hallways, and finally into a waiting room with a two-way mirror. Through the mirror we could see agents Collins, Archer, and the charismatic Dr. Schteir. Richardson told us to wait, but Terri followed him.

Next thing, there she was, on the other side of the glass with the feds.

I found the switch, flipped it on, and the actors behind the glass started speaking their lines.

"HQ wants Dr. Schteir to do the interrogation," said Collins, the edges of her mouth tugged down with disappointment. "You can watch, Russo, but that's all."

"Sorry," said Terri. "But Denton wants the NYPD represented. He specifically asked me to be in on this." She sucked her lip and rubbed a hand across her eyes, two things people do when they're lying.

Collins sighed so loudly, I could hear it through the speaker. "Okay, but stay out of Dr. Schteir's way. We already have too many people in here."

Schteir turned to Collins. "I'm afraid you'll have to wait outside too."

Collins's mouth opened and stayed open, but no words came out.

"Sorry," said Schteir. "But I don't want the suspect to be distracted, and I think two women are already enough. It would be really helpful to me if you watched the interrogation at a distance, to see if I've missed anything, okay?" She smiled and said, "Thanks," before Collins could get her mouth and brain to work in tandem, the shock of being excluded obviously too much for her to take in.

Then Schteir turned to Archer and asked him to stay.

A second later Collins came out looking like someone who'd just been told her puppy had died.

I moved over to give her some room, but she ignored my gesture and remained standing, staring through the glass and the people behind it like a kid with her nose pressed against a candy counter.

Then the door at the back of the interrogation room opened.

The suspect's hands were cuffed; ankles too. I leaned forward to get a good look at him. His features were bland and indistinct.

The guard pushed him into a seat and Schteir said, "Easy." He gave her a look as the guard attached the ankle shackles to a metal ring in the floor.

"Why all the hardware?" I asked.

"He had a personal arsenal," said Richardson. "According to the agents that brought him, there were more WMD than Saddam ever had. Looked as if he was preparing for World War III, in Queens, of all places."

"Who is he?" I asked.

"Name's Carl Karff. And his arsenal included the same kind of gun that killed the two victims. No matter what, we've got him on illegal weaponry and conspiracy to incite."

"Onetime leader of the World Church of the Creator," said Collins without turning around. "He's not the grand pooh-bah anymore, but still a big cheese in the organization."

"Spent three years up at Fishkill Correctional for assault," said Richardson.

"Was this part of a general roundup of local white supremacists, or what?" I asked.

"Bureau ran a trace of the gun brand," said Richardson. "Lots of names popped up, Karff's among them. The bureau's been watching him—and others like him—for a long time. He spends a lot of time in chat rooms, easy to hack into. And at one time he made his living as a commercial artist. Lots of markers made his name stand out."

I looked through the glass as Archer took a seat opposite Karff. It was obvious why Schteir had chosen him to stay with her and it wasn't because he was big; it was because he was black.

Karff made an attempt to fold his cuffed hands and I caught a glimpse of small blue swastikas tattooed on the inner sides of his wrists.

Terri was pacing, but she never took her eyes off Karff. Her face had hardened in a way I hadn't seen before, lips drawn into a tight line, eyes lidded and squinting. She looked mean as hell.

Schteir was going through her notes, muttering things like, "Wow," and "Oh, brother."

I recalled a visiting lecturer to my Quantico course, a retired FBI agent experienced in the art of interrogation, saying, "Everyone has something to hide, something they are ashamed of—you just have to let your subject think that you know what it is."

I guessed that's what Schteir was doing now.

Archer read Karff his rights, and reminded him he could have a lawyer present.

"God is representing me," he said.

Terri let out a short, disdainful laugh.

"Duane Holsten sends his regards," said Schteir.

Karff turned to look at her, facial muscles neutralized, impossible to read. "I have never met Mr. Holsten."

"But he's a member of your church."

"There are many members of the World Church of the Creator—perhaps you will meet them one day." A smile passed over his lips. "As for Mr. Holsten, I have followed his case with some interest. I understand he recently filed an appeal."

"It was declined," said Schteir. "You wasted your money. We know the World Church has been raising money for his case. The FBI has been charting its activities for some time, and watching you as well, Mr. Karff, your comings and goings." She opened a file and ran her finger down the page. "The name *Swift* ring any bells?"

A micro-expression of anxiety, eyelids and lips ticking, rattled his composed face, but didn't last.

"That's okay, *Swift*. Would you prefer I call you that?"

Karff didn't answer, his facial muscles under control, mask back in place.

"So, your comings and goings," said Schteir. "For starters, we know where you go when you get into your Ford station wagon late at night, after your daughter is tucked into bed and you have kissed your wife good night."

Karff's jaw tightened.

"But let's wait with that. Tell me, Mr. Karff, are you a Christian?"

"Most Christians have abandoned God and their race." He squinted at her name tag. "Schteir? Not a Christian name, is it?"

"It's a Jewish name, Mr. Karff. Does that offend you?"

"Your people have been part of a plot to upgrade the blacks and pull down the white race."

"And no doubt you and your fellow World Church members have a plan to deal with that."

"A very simple one." Karff raised his chin and the hint of more tattoos on either side of his neck poked out of his shirt collar.

"What's that on his neck?" asked Richardson.

"Lightning-bolt tattoos," I said. "Like the ones on Nazi soldiers' uniforms."

"The blacks will be shipped back to Africa where they belong," said Karff. "The Jews driven from power, and as for the Christian traitors, they will be hanged in public squares."

Anthropologists make the case that humanity has evolved, and if you're talking about ape to upright man, I guess that's true, but at the moment I didn't think the species had evolved much at all.

Terri stopped pacing and leaned into Karff's face. "Oh, *someone* will be hanging in those public squares, Carl, you can be sure of that."

Karff pulled back, but Terri trailed him like a magnet.

Schteir let her stay there a minute, then tapped her arm. "Let the man breathe, detective."

"For now," said Terri, backing up.

Archer looked ready to pummel Karff, his hands knotted into fists, and Schteir made sure he noticed. She touched the agent's fists, whispered, "Relax, you'll get your turn."

Without discussing it, they'd all assumed roles: Terri's bad cop to Schteir's good one; Archer the brute enforcer, just barely under control. I was itching to join the act, maybe play my sketch-artist card, do a drawing of the guy to add to his discomfort, and I suggested it to Collins.

"You kidding?" she said, without turning around.

I got the point. If she couldn't be in there, no way she was letting me in.

"And you will enact your plan, how?" asked Schteir. "With the guns and knives you—and others like you—have amassed in basements and attics?"

"We will do what we have to do," said Karff. "Heed my warning. The war is coming." He looked over at Archer and said, "RAHOWA!"

"Ah, yes," said Schteir, affecting ennui. "RaHoWa. Ra for Racial, Ho for Holy, Wa for War. Your group's battle cry. You know . . . it sounds very much like the language used by a tribe in Papua, New Guinea. Fascinating people. I wonder if that's where it comes from."

"You think you're so smart, like all of your kind." Karff's eyes had narrowed. "We'll see how smart you are when the war comes, you Jew bitch—"

Archer grabbed hold of Karff's arm. "Watch your mouth."

Karff eyed Archer's dark hand on his pale white flesh.

Schteir allowed the agent to do a little damage—Karff would be bruised by morning—then she laid her hand gently over Archer's, and said, "I think that's enough—for now."

Archer gave the man's arm another good squeeze before he let go.

"So, Mr. Karff, let's get back to the present war, the small, sad little war you and your fellow World Church members are fighting, the one where you kill off one person at a time." She slid crime scene pictures of the victims onto the table.

"Who are these mud people and race traitors supposed to be?"

"Come now, Mr. Karff, you can do better than that," said Schteir.

"I have no idea what you want me to say."

"Say whatever you want to say, Mr. Karff. After all, this

is a free country, a country that allows you to espouse your religious and racial views without threat of punishment. So speak your mind. Go on. Tell me what you think of me, of Agent Archer here, of the people you refer to as the mud people and race traitors." She slapped her hand down hard onto the photos and Karff flinched.

Terri snatched the photos up and one by one raised them to his face.

"These are *people*," she said. "Do you even get that concept? I realize it might be difficult for an emotional cripple like you, but *try*."

Karff stared straight ahead, freezing his expression.

Was this the face I had been trying to see? I wasn't sure. There was something generic about it, the kind of man you might pass in the street without noticing.

Terri dropped the photos and planted her face into Karff's, nostrils flared, eyes narrowed. "Your weapons have been confiscated, Carl. So what are you now, huh? Just a sad little man with Nazi tattoos that make you feel tough." She laid her fingers onto one of his blue-inked swastikas. "You're being watched, Carl, like the song says: '. . . every move you make.'"

Karff continued to stare, but his lids were flickering; she was getting to him.

"We're seeing it. All of it, Carl. My friends here at the Federal Bureau of Investigation, hell, they're just itching to publicize your anti-American activities. Not a popular subject these days, and getting less popular by the minute. We're going to take you down, Carl. Way fucking down."

I'd never seen Terri like this, and believed she could take him down.

The veins in Karff's neck were standing out in high relief as he strained his head back like a turtle's.

Schteir put her hand on Terri's shoulder. I wasn't sure it was the right move, but maybe she just wanted to run the show.

"What?" Terri barked.

"I think it's time we showed Mr. Karff the photos we have of his late-night drives." She maneuvered herself in front of Terri, who backed up and took a few deep breaths to regain her composure.

Schteir spread a new set of photos across the table. I couldn't see them, but Karff could, his eyes twitching, frontalis muscles wrinkling his forehead, mentalis muscles quivering his chin. "Here we have you leaving your Queens home and getting into your station wagon at eleven-fourteen P.M.," said Schteir. "You can see how the digital camera notes the time and date in the lower corner. Terrific invention, the digital camera, don't you think? Not to mention the zoom lens."

"I see the date," said Karff. "And I also see these are six months old."

"We have similar ones from one week earlier, and then a week or so before that. I suppose the photographer got bored taking the same pictures over and over." She laid another photo in front of him. "Let's see where your car ends up, shall we? Ah, here it is, on the other side of the river, in Manhattan, at eleven forty-seven P.M., on West Fourteenth and Greenwich Street. I wonder what you were doing there at close to midnight?"

She slid another picture out of the stack. "Here you are, on the corner, and there's a really tall woman leaning into your driver's-side window. A black woman. I've misjudged you, Mr. Karff, thinking you were a racist. It just goes to show you how wrong snap judgments can be." Schteir peered at the photo. "No, wait a minute—that's no woman!" She handed the picture to Terri.

"Oh, Carl, what a bad boy you are." She snickered. "Would you look at that, Agent Archer." Terri waved the photo. "Carl here gets off on she-males."

Karff had turned pale.

"And what is happening here at eleven fifty-two P.M.?" Schteir had already turned to another photo. "It appears as if that same tall woman—excuse me, that tall black *man* dressed as a *woman*—has gotten into your car, and the two of you are . . . oh, my, look at this." She raised the photo for Archer and Terri to see.

"I've got an idea," said Terri. "Let's put these pictures on Carl's personal website—or even better, the World Church's website. What do you think?"

"Great idea," said Schteir, smiling.

"Those pictures are a fake," said Karff.

"Well . . . Let's just see what others make of them, shall we?" said Schteir.

"For starters," said Terri. "How about . . . Carl's wife?"

"You can't do that."

"Mr. Karff," said Schteir. "I am the FBI. And I can do whatever I want."

Karff's lower lip was trembling. "I told you I don't know those people."

"Well, maybe you do and maybe you don't," said Schteir. "As we speak, our lab technicians are checking your weapons and we will soon know for sure whether or not they have been fired recently. If the bullets match, we will know if you knew these people. In the meantime, I'll tell you what I want. I want *names*. Names and addresses of everyone who is connected to your church in this geographic section of the world. I want to know who you talk to and who talks to you. I want to know who has come to you for guidance, orders, repentance, or whatever the hell else you people talk about. You understand, Mr. Karff? I hope so, because I am one tough Jewish bitch who would like nothing better than to put your pathetic white ass in an Attica cell with murderers and rapists and let them know that you refer to them as *mud people*."

Karff's face hardened again, features pulled toward the center and tensed. "My Aryan brothers will protect me."

I knew he was referring to the Aryan Brotherhood, The Brand, as they liked to call themselves, which had started back in the sixties in San Quentin, a way for the whites prisoners to protect themselves against the blacks and Latinos.

"Oh, I think we can find a place where the Aryan Brotherhood is outnumbered," said Terri.

Schteir nodded. "So, what do think, Mr. Karff? It's either you or someone you know who is responsible for these killings. And even if it isn't you, we're going to hold you—which we can do for a very long time—if even one of the *forty-six* guns recovered from your home is not licensed. And that's just for starters. So, any of this getting through to you?" She turned to Archer. "I'd like a set of close-ups of this African American gentleman in the wig and hot pants and his statement as well. It's in the large file on Mr. Karff. I believe the gentleman goes by the name of Veronique, who, by the way, Mr. Karff, will testify that you are the man in the Ford station wagon that she, excuse me—*he*—has been servicing for quite some time now."

Karff raised his head, ice-blue eyes gazing at the ceiling. "Any day now the angels will sing and the trumpets will herald the end of days, and chains like these"—he yanked at his handcuffs and rattled the shackles at his ankles—"will fall from my body, and we will take up arms and all will be restored with the world."

"Yeah," said Terri, hissing the word. "While you rot in a prison cell."

Schteir slid the victims' photos back in front of Karff, but it was no good. He was gone, hiding behind rhetoric.

Terri took a step toward Karff, ready to go at him again, but Schteir stopped her.

Karff had neutralized his face, but his fingers were twitching.

It gave me an idea.

"Get him to draw," I said.

"What?" said Collins.

"Have Karff draw something. Anything. So we can compare it to the sketches left at the scenes."

"He's not going to do it just because we ask him to."

She had a point, but I could see she was considering it. She wanted to be in there, to contribute something. I just had to convince her.

"Look, just take his cuffs off, leave a pencil and paper on the table, and let him sit there for a while, alone. He was a commercial artist, right? People who draw, just do. They doodle all the time. It's like a reflex."

Collins didn't say anything, but the next thing I knew she was on the other side of the glass, whispering to Dr. Schteir. A moment later they took the cuffs off Karff. Archer disappeared and came back with a big cup of coffee. Schteir gathered up the photographs and files, but made it look accidental when she left a few blank sheets of paper behind. She also left a black pen.

"Nice idea," said Schteir when she came out. "But he's probably too smart to fall for it."

"Well, he's not going to do some full-out drawing for us, but maybe a doodle." I turned to Terri. "You did good in there."

"Not good enough," she said, directing her comment to Schteir. "You see how he reacted when Archer touched him or when I was in his face? He didn't like it one bit—a black man and a woman invading his space. We could have done more with that if—"

"Detective." Schteir spoke quietly but clearly. "You were a participant by our permission. Lest you forget this is a bureau interrogation. We do things a bit differently. You did . . . just fine. But we'll take it from here."

Terri pressed her lips together, hard, containing her rage.

"At least the coffee is going make him want to pee," said Archer. "And I'm not letting him out of there for . . . a long time."

"I think you showed great restraint," I said to Archer.

"So far," said Archer.

Then we all stared at Karff like a bug behind glass.

After a few minutes he picked up the pen and we leaned forward. He put it down and we sat back.

We watched for a few minutes and I filled the time chatting with Dr. Schteir, which seemed to annoy Terri, who had gone unusually quiet.

Fifteen, twenty minutes passed, then Schteir had to leave, and a moment later Collins did too. She took Archer with her.

"Lest," Terri whispered to me. "Does anyone actually use the word *lest*?"

"Apparently," I said.

When Karff didn't do anything for another fifteen minutes, I started to think I'd miscalculated. Richardson starting talking about the Mets, how they were already off to a bad start. He asked me what it was like to be a sketch artist and I asked him what it was like to be a G man. We were filling the time. It was better than watching Karff pick his nose or yawn.

Then Karff picked up the pen and while looking at the ceiling he started doodling away on the paper.

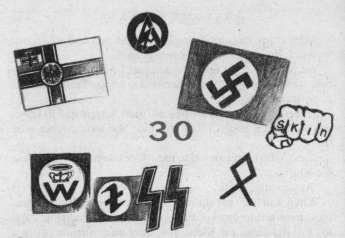

Carl Karff had really gotten into it, a half hour of serious doodling. But he had a limited repertoire. He was also left-handed, and I didn't have to explain what that meant to the bureau or the NYPD.

I was back at the station with Terri, both of us keyed up but tired.

"Could he be faking it?" she asked.

"Only if he's totally ambidextrous, and I never saw him use his right hand except to pick his nose."

Terri's phone kept ringing, but she ignored it.

A suspect's arrest was big news. Though Karff's name was being temporarily withheld, CNN had already broadcast a segment called "Behind the Scenes with America's Hate Groups." By tomorrow, newspapers would be running stories and Op Ed pieces, and from what I'd heard, the surveillance pictures of Karff and "Veronique" were on their way to the tabloids. Karff would be crucified in the press, though Ballistics had already proved it had not been one of his guns that had fired either of the fatal shots.

"He's already out on bail," said Terri. "Some slick World Church lawyer came to his defense. Don't you just love it when these guys start crying that their civil liberties are being stepped on?"

"Yeah, they want to overthrow the government, but try to touch them and they invoke the constitution," I said. "Tell you the truth, I would have enjoyed seeing Archer pummel him."

"I would have lent a hand if Schteir hadn't stopped me." Terri sighed. "At least Karff supplied a list of names before his lawyer showed up. I'm guessing he gave up names the G already had, but maybe something will come of it." She glanced over at her ringing phone.

"Not going to get that?" I asked.

"I don't need to hear J. Q. Public and every one of his crazy neighbors give their opinion."

When the ringing stopped she picked it up, asked for the desk sergeant and told him to stop putting calls through to her office. "That's why we have a tip line," she said. "Yes, I realize the calls are coming in faster than they can be logged, but I don't want them coming to my personal line, is that clear?" She slammed down the phone and turned to me. "If I don't get out of here I'm going to explode."

It was dark outside. I had lost track of the time, and so had Terri. We were still keyed up, so I suggested a drink and was surprised when she said yes.

It was a nice night and we decided to walk west. We ended up at Market, a local place over on Ninth, and sat at the bar. I ordered a beer and Terri ordered a vodka martini.

"I would never have taken you for a martini girl," I said.

"You're thinking strictly a Bud girl, that it? Well, I am, but I'm teaching myself to drink this paint thinner. It's part of my Terri Russo Improvement Plan."

"Terri Russo seems fine to me as she is."

She smiled and patted her hair, which was down and framing her face in a way that made her look softer. She clinked her glass against my bottle. "Here's to the white supremacists going straight to hell."

"I'll drink to that."

Terri took a sip and made a face. "You were impressed with Schteir, weren't you?"

I had a feeling it was a trick question, so I shrugged.

"Oh, come on, Rodriguez. You drew her *portrait,* for Christ's sake."

"It was a . . . reflex."

"Yeah, I can think of another reflex. Give me a break." She tried another sip of her martini and made the same face.

"Maybe you should stick to beer."

"And maybe you should stick to regular girls."

"What's that supposed to mean?"

"Nothing."

I aimed my beer bottle at her. "Out with it, Russo."

"It's just that women like Schteir piss me off. Okay, I'll admit it. I'm jealous. She pushes my buttons, and I can't help it. Did you read her bio?"

"How would I do that?"

"Easy. Look her up online. I did. So sue me. She went to Smith College for undergrad, Columbia for a master's, and Harvard for a Ph.D. I mean, give me a fucking break."

"Hey, you can't hate the woman for going to pedigree schools."

"Who says? And she's a profiler, not a cop. She shouldn't have been doing the interrogation."

"She wasn't bad."

"She didn't nail him, did she?" She sighed. "So where did you go to school? Never mind. I know. Hunter College. A city school."

"You looked me up too?"

"Didn't have to. It's in your file." She grinned.

"Detective Russo does her homework."

"Naturally. I'm a cop." She arched her eyebrows for emphasis. "It's bad enough Schteir has all the fancy degrees, but does she have to be good-looking too? I mean, shit, that's just not fair. And I can tell you that outfit she was wearing was not from Target."

"And when was the last time you shopped there?"

"Yesterday. I was visiting the homestead on Staten Island. Believe me, Target was like an escape to paradise." She snared a piece of her jersey between thumb and forefinger. "Eight bucks. I bought three."

"So you're a good shopper."

"No, I'm a schlepper. But what the hell." She tried her martini and it seemed to go down easier.

"Going back home is difficult?"

"No, it's a fucking nightmare. My dad sits in front of the TV and orders my mom around like she's his slave. Mom is clinically depressed and will never do anything about it. She married a mean, withholding son of a bitch who will never give her anything, but it's too late for her to get out. I'm sure the guy was a shit from day one. He used to beat the crap out of us, me and my brother, but . . . oh, God, why am I unloading this on you? Forget it."

"No, it's okay. I'm just sorry to hear it."

"Don't be. I'm used to it. I mean, it's the past, right? Over."

"Yeah," I said, trying to feel the way she did, that the past was over. I didn't think it ever would be for me.

"You okay?"

"Yeah, great." I started chewing on a cuticle, realized it, and replaced the finger with my beer bottle.

"Sure you are," she said. "Me, I try to avoid going home as much as possible. What about you?" She finished her drink and ordered another.

I checked my beer. "No, I'm fine."

"Not your beer. I meant your home life."

"Oh. I grew up here, in Manhattan, and it was fine. Well, except, you know, the part . . . about my father." I finished my beer and tapped the bar for another. Just talking about my father had that effect on me. "My mother lives in Virginia Beach. She's a therapist. There's a naval base there. She says it produces more peacetime casualties than war, though the wounds are not so easy to see with the naked eye."

"You see her much?"

"Not really. Once or twice a year." I didn't want to talk about my mother either.

"No sisters or brothers?"

"You read my file, didn't you?"

"Right. Forgot." She smiled. "You don't seem like one of those spoiled only children types."

"Thanks. I think." I smiled and Russo smiled back.

"It must have been hard after your dad died."

"It was." My muscles tensed. "Is it okay if we don't talk about this? It's not my favorite topic.

"Sorry," she said. "I didn't mean to overstep my bounds." She laid her hand on mine and said she was sorry again.

"It's okay," I said, aware of her hand, the heat it was producing.

She smiled up at me, lifted her hand, but kept smiling.

"You're quite something, you know that, Russo?"

"How do you mean?" She tilted her head back and waited for my answer.

"For one, the way you handled Karff in that interrogation; you were good, a little scary too."

"Oh. That."

"What's the matter? You expected me to say something else?"

"Yes," she said, looking into my eyes.

A moment passed, the two of us sharing a look, then she took a big slug of her martini, stood up, and peered down at me.

"What?" I said.

"I was just wondering . . . You feel like taking me home?"

31

Terri's apartment was a one-bedroom on East Thirty-seventh in the Murray Hill section. She'd fixed it up nicely, walls painted in shades of gray, a big brown leather couch with lots of pillows. She said most of her salary went to pay for the place, but it was worth it because she loved the city.

After five minutes in her apartment I didn't know what to say. We were both pretty uncomfortable. I could see Terri was having second thoughts, her facial muscles ticking off a whole slew of nervous expressions.

She offered me another drink, and I said yes though I didn't want one. She got a beer out of her fridge, handed it to me, and said, "You'd better kiss me before I totally chicken out on this."

I did.

It was going pretty well until I got my pants stuck on my shoe and practically fell off her bed. Terri helped me yank my shoe off and we laughed, which helped ease the tension until we were both naked and stopped laughing. I backed up to look at her and she tried to hide under the blanket, but I held it away and told her she was beautiful. Then we kissed and our bodies took over, and for a first time I thought it went pretty well. Afterward, she curled against me.

"Was that like a huge mistake? You don't think I'm like some big slut now, do you?"

I laughed.

Terri slapped my chest. "I'm serious. I need some reassurance here, Rodriguez."

"Well, for starters, how about calling me Nate?"

"Nah, I like the way 'Rodriguez' rolls off my tongue. *Rod-riii-guezzz,* see? Nate doesn't have any rhythm."

"How'd you get this?" I touched a scar on her shoulder.

"Bullet. Pretty cool, huh?"

"Oh, sure, Wonder Woman. That's you, I'm sure."

"No question," she said. She outlined the angel tattoo on the inside of my arm. "What about this? When did you get it?"

"When I was too young."

She rolled over and displayed her ass, which was very nice, her left cheek sporting a small rose. "Night of my high school prom. I was totally stoned. Lucky I didn't end up with an anchor."

I ran my fingers over the rose tattoo, and Terri leaned back against me. "I'm glad we did this."

"Me too," I said. "Even if you are a *big* slut."

She slapped my chest again, harder, and we both laughed.

"Well, it wasn't so bad, was it?" she asked.

I could see she needed the truth. "Bad? No. I think it falls under the heading of 'really good.' " I pulled her closer. "But hey, I come from a long line of Latin lovers, so how could it be bad?"

"Pretty sure of yourself, aren't you, Rodriguez?"

"Oh, yeah, that's me."

"Well, you did okay," she said, and curled into my side. "So, Latin lovers . . ." She stopped and her mood turned serious. "Earlier, when I asked about your father—"

I felt my muscles tense again.

"Talking about it can help, you know. Didn't anyone ever tell you that?"

"A shrink or two."

Terri ran her fingers along my arm. "I don't want to push, but I swear I'm a good listener."

I shrugged.

"Don't you trust me?"

"Sure, but . . ." I took a deep breath, thought about the picture I'd been carrying around of myself for a very long time. It was a cartoon of a guilty little boy looking for his dad.

Terri touched my cheek. "You okay?"

"Sure," I said, but the movie had already started to play, with all the attendant feelings I could never sort out: sorrow, guilt, grief, anger. The shrinks hadn't helped, but maybe I hadn't given them a chance because I didn't want to admit all the things I'd worked so hard to bury.

"Hey, Rodriguez, talk to me, okay?"

I looked into Terri's face, compassion in her eyes, a bit of sadness in the furrowed brow and slightly down-turned mouth, and that, coupled with our lovemaking, was enough to loosen me up, so I told her.

I didn't go into details, but enough so she would understand.

After I finished she questioned my guilt, but I thought she was trying to make me feel better and said so.

"No," she said. "I'm just being a detective. I like to know all the facts. How can you really know?"

"I know it in here," I said, and tapped my heart. I swallowed a few times and blinked because my eyes were burning, and turned the subject around. "So, what about you?"

"What about me?"

"What happened with you and the feds, before this case, I mean?"

"Oh, that." She sighed, and hesitated. "I ignored a tip line they'd set up. The NYPD was logging calls for them, which was my job. I'd logged in like a thousand, but how was I supposed to know which call out of that thousand was on the level? I didn't assign anyone to check it out, so it became my fuck-up. And maybe it was, but we didn't have the manpower." She sighed again, and I wrapped my arm around her. "I got six months suspension along with six months of mandatory therapy. Like neglecting a tip line means I should be on a couch with Dr. Freud?"

"So how was he?"

"Who?"

"Freud."

"Better than *you*." Terri laughed and hit me.

"Do you always hit?"

"Only when necessary," she said. "According to the NYPD shrink, everything I've been doing in my life, from becoming a cop to ignoring the tip line, is all due to my selfish son-of-a-bitch father. Apparently I was trying to get his attention." She gave me a look. "Guess we both have father issues."

Then she told me what it was like growing up on Staten Island, the daughter of Old World Italian Americans who thought she should marry and live next door with her Italian husband, three and a half kids, aluminum sided house, and aboveground pool.

"I figured since I didn't like aluminum siding I'd skip the whole thing." She laid her head on my chest. "I can feel your heart beating, Rodriguez. Good to know you have one."

"It's a loaner," I said.

"So you consider yourself Catholic or Jewish?"

"Both. Neither. My mother's parents were Polish Jews who decided the Lower East Side was a lot better than Eastern Europe's pogroms. My father's parents exchanged Puerto Rico's Mayaguez for Manhattan's El Barrio. I tried Judaism on for about a minute, went to temple a couple of times, put the yarmulke on and all, but it wasn't for me. Same thing with the church, all those smells and bells. I guess my religion is New York."

"You like being back in action?"

I stroked her leg. "You mean in the sack?"

"No, asshole. I meant as a cop."

"I knew exactly what you meant, and yeah, I like it. I like it a lot."

"And you're good, a natural."

"Thanks." I was flattered. "But I like being a sketch artist too."

"And a great one, no argument there."

I shrugged with false modesty. "So tell me about you and Denton."

"Why?"

"I don't know. I'm interested?"

"I don't remember asking you about your past with other women."

"There weren't any. You were my first." I smiled, but she had already rolled away from me and wrapped the blanket around her.

"So what do you want to know—how many times we did it, or what sort of lover he was?"

"Forget it. I'm sorry. I didn't realize it was a sore spot."

"You think I fucked Denton to get ahead, is that it?"

"I never said that."

"But you're thinking it."

"I'm thinking that you're overreacting."

"I am *not* overreacting. And by the way, one fuck does not entitle you to my entire sexual history."

"I didn't ask about your sexual history. I asked about Denton. And I said I was sorry."

"This was a mistake," she said. "You should go."

"Oh, come on. Get over it."

"Why?" Terri's features screwed up with anger. "Because *you* say I should?"

"Just forget it."

"Forget what—that you're telling me how to feel or interrogating me about my sex life?"

"Forget it *all*." I stood up and tugged on my pants. "Forget I ever came here."

"Were you ever here?"

"I thought I was, but I guess not." I reached for my shirt and continued to get dressed, the whole time waiting for Terri to stop me, but she didn't.

* * *

Why the hell did I do that?

Terri Russo flopped onto her bed and tried to answer the question.

Do what? Invite him home, or throw him out?

She couldn't come up with an answer, but it didn't matter because clearly it had been one more mistake in a long line of mistakes, always with men. But damn it, she'd thought Rodriguez was different.

She traipsed into the bathroom, wound her hair into a ponytail, washed her face, and stared into the mirror thinking when it came to men she just never got it right. Maybe what that cop psychiatrist had said was true, maybe her father had screwed her up for life—and love.

"What a jerk," she said to her reflection. She didn't need anyone to point out that she had just broken one of the cardinal rules—Do not sleep with someone you work with—for the second time.

And now what? For starters, how was she going to deal with Rodriguez on the job? Like it never happened? Too late for that. And damn it, she liked the guy. She slammed her towel into the hamper so hard the wicker basket toppled and fell.

Had she slept with Denton to get ahead?

No. She'd been telling the truth when she said she didn't know Denton was on his way up. Or did she?

And what about Rodriguez, the sketch-artist cop with a special talent? Was she using him too?

Terri got back into bed and dropped her head onto the pillow though she knew it was going to be a rough night. Rodriguez had stirred up too many questions that she couldn't answer.

I walked home to burn off my anger. I had asked about Denton because I was curious to know why she'd slept with him.

Yeah, it was the wrong thing to ask, but I still thought she'd overreacted. It made me realize I didn't know anything about Terri Russo, except now I knew what she looked like naked and how she smelled, and I liked both of those things.

But the fight had set off a little paranoia and I started to wonder if she really liked me or had an ulterior motive for taking me home. *But what?* Clearly I wasn't powerful, like Denton. I couldn't help her career. *Or could I?*

I didn't know what to think except now I wished I hadn't told her about my father. There had been a moment, obviously a weak one, when I wanted to tell her, a way to get some of the grief and guilt off my soul and share it with someone I was starting to like. Now it felt like a mistake, all the feelings about my father I had worked hard to suppress bubbling to the surface.

Shit.

Plus, it was going to be really weird to see her at the precinct. Didn't everyone know that sleeping with a colleague was a huge mistake? Obviously, not me.

I headed crosstown, stores and offices closed up for the night; streets that overflowed with people during the day, now desolate. An icy drizzle had started and my old leather jacket, already worn and edging on shabby, was going to get soaked and go over the edge, but nothing I could do about that. I turned the collar up and as I did, the man in the long coat and ski mask slid into my mind. I rounded Thirty-ninth Street with the feeling that someone was behind me, but when I turned to look, there was no one there.

I shivered and blamed it on the cold. I'd never been scared in the city. It had been my home for too long. I told myself I was being ridiculous, that it was the result of working a triple homicide, having my father on my mind, and my emotions stirred up by Terri Russo. I passed a few delis that serviced the fabric-and-button industry, all closed, and quickened my pace.

There were people on Eighth Avenue—late-night commuters on their way to Port Authority, winos and junkies going nowhere, a few businessmen skulking out of porn shops—and I was happy to see them all, even the Hispanic transvestites stumbling out of Club Escuelita on my corner. Three of them huddled together under the street lamp, passing a joint, adjusting their minis and tank tops.

"Hey there, *guapo*," said one, and the rest joined in, whistling and hooting, offering sex and a good time—though black stubble pricking its way through smudged pancake makeup was never my idea of a good time.

I told them I was tired and they called me a *mentiroso* but left it at that, and I was relieved. Despite the makeup and heels, the Escuelita crowd were not sissy boys. Most of them sported prison-made tattoos and packed shivs. The week I'd moved into the neighborhood, there had been a stabbing in front of the club, and someone had created a makeshift altar—plastic flowers, pictures of saints, candles, writing on the wall, *"In Memory of Angel"*—to mark the spot, along with bloodstains that permeated the porous concrete and survived for a week before heavy rains washed them away. Now it felt like an omen, a prediction of murder. I shook it off and told myself to get a grip.

After Escuelita there was nothing—a couple of empty parking lots and deserted office buildings, including mine. For the first time since I'd moved in I wished I were not the only resident in my building.

I had just made it to the entrance when I had the feeling of being watched for the second time. I cast a look over my shoulder and could have sworn I saw something, a figure or a shadow, but wasn't sure if I was confusing reality for all the images I'd stored in my brain over the years.

Inside, one of the two entry lights had burned out, the back half of the lobby in shadow. I unlocked the elevator and rode up to my floor.

I was too hyped to sleep, got a beer out of the fridge and considered giving Terri a call, but was in no mood to apologize. I sat down at my drawing table, flipped on my high-intensity lamp, opened my drawing pad, and started over.

This time with no coat or ski mask. Just a face. But where was this new information coming from? I had no way to judge it. Was this the man we were hunting, or was I inventing him?

I'd have to show it to Terri and the witnesses, but there still wasn't enough of a face to identify. Even if there was, none of the witnesses had seen the guy close up, some not at all.

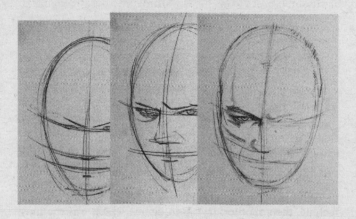

The lamp above my table hurt my eyes, but I waited a few minutes to see if anything else came to me. When it didn't I turned off the light and sat in the darkness thinking about Terri Russo, my father, and the face I'd just drawn that was shimmering as strongly in my mind as it had on paper.

From across the street he watches the light die in the window. An afterimage of yellow orbs dance in front of his eyes, then fade to black as he makes his way toward the Times Square subway station thinking about the images he has collected and recorded in his brain and what he is going to do with them.

32

Harvey Tutsel's desk reminded Terri of a teenager's bedroom: brown-ringed coffee cups with varying amounts of sludge at the bottom, a Dannon yogurt container well on its way to becoming a biology experiment, crumpled napkins, and an opened gym bag with a pair of rumpled socks sticking out.

"What brings you to Deadwood?" he said, lifting one coffee cup, then another, trying to decide which was the most recent. He sniffed at a third, made a face and put it back down.

"That's about three days old." His partner, Mary Perkowski, came into their shared office with two Starbucks and a couple of fresh bagels, swiped the mess off Tutsel's desk into the trash, and dropped his gym bag onto the floor before placing the new coffee and bagel down in front of him.

"How's it going, Mary?" asked Terri.

"Busy, but sharing an office with this slob makes it all worth it."

Tutsel gave his partner a look. "Guess this isn't a social call, is it?"

Terri handed him the murder book on Rodriguez. She'd spent some time in a dusty room looking for it, had read it through and come up empty, same as the cops who had worked the case back in '86.

"Juan Enrique Rodriguez," said Tutsel. "This have anything to do with what you're working on?"

Terri just shrugged. She had her reasons, but didn't want to share them.

"We got a lot on our plate right now, Russo." He laid his hand onto a stack of folders. "See these? They go back over ten, fifteen years. And this is just a fraction."

"I realize you guys are busy," said Terri. "But Rodriguez was a cop—one of us—and they never found the shooter. It could have been a case he was working on or . . . I don't know. According to the file, there was blood on the gun and it didn't all belong to the vic."

"In 1986 . . ." Perkowski cocked her head. "That would have been before DNA, no, just on the cusp, so it wouldn't have been tested back then. But if there was blood or tissue, it's possible the DOJ have it on ice."

"Can you check?"

"Hey, we'd like to help you, Russo, but we're real short on staff."

Terri could see the murder book on Juan Rodriguez was going to end up under yogurt containers and coffee cups. "I'd rather not wait another twenty years," she said. "Oh, and by the way, Toots, that nephew of yours who wants to intern in Homicide this summer—"

"My sister's boy, yeah, really bright kid, needs two credits to graduate John Jay."

"Right," said Terri. "I know. His letter landed on *my* desk, of all places."

Tutsel gave Terri a knowing smile and reached for the book on Rodriguez. "You know, I think one of our guys might have a little time." He turned to his partner. "Horton's free, isn't he, Perkowski?"

"Not anymore," she said. "I hear he's working on Juan Rodriguez."

* * *

The hallway was dimly lit and the stairs creaked despite his rubber-soled shoes, though it did not worry him. He was a professional and he knew what he was doing. He had been watching the apartment for the past two hours. He had seen the man hobble in with a bag of groceries and had not seen him come out. The job had to be taken care of tonight, something about the guy wanting to take off for the Caribbean or someplace, which he had not paid attention to because the less he knew about a contract, the better.

At the top of the stairwell he checked to make sure he had everything ready, then rapped on the door and mumbled the name he was told to say.

A voice from inside called out, "It's open."

He walked into the apartment and followed the flickering TV light down a narrow hallway until he saw the man sitting in a chair eating ice cream out of a container. The man had just put a spoonful of Cherry Garcia in his mouth.

He put two shots into the man's heart. The chair tipped backward and fell over, and the body hit the ground with a dull thud.

The shooter waited a minute, distracted by an old black-and-white movie on the TV screen, Richard Widmark pushing a wheelchair-bound old lady down a flight of stairs, and cackling. He laughed along with the actor, then leaned over to check the man's pulse and noticed the Rolex. It surprised him, a good watch like that on a man who lived in such a fleabag, but he didn't give it much more thought. Even if he were not being paid for the job he would not steal it; stealing went against his principles. He pulled his leg back, kicked the man in the mouth, and checked to make sure he'd shattered his teeth. Then he removed a small tin of lighter fluid from his inside jacket pocket, emptied it on the man, and struck a match.

33

The briefing room was full, standing room only.

Archer and Richardson were in the front row with a few unfamiliar gray suits. New recruits, I suspected, and not a good sign for the NYPD. Terri and her men were just behind them, the pecking order clear.

She glanced up when I came in. Our eyes met, and she looked away.

I moved toward the back of the room and leaned against the wall as a few more precinct chiefs filed in, finally Chief of Department Perry Denton and Special Agent Monica Collins. Denton was whispering something in her ear, hand on her shoulder in a way both conspiratorial and flirtatious. From the look on Agent Collins's face she was enjoying it. The man had an effect on women that was lost on me.

Denton asked for everyone's attention, though he already had it—the room had gone quiet the moment he'd entered with Collins. He went on to discuss the various news stories, Carl Karff, and the ensuing investigation into the names he had supplied. He stressed it was now a "federal case," and that the FBI would be running the show from here on in. He asked for all NYPD files and information gathered in the course of the investigations to be handed over to Collins and her crew, then turned the meeting over to Collins, who introduced the new BSS and CIU agents and said that everything would now be processed through the National Center for the Analysis of Violent Crime.

"All existing evidence will be reexamined, the victims' bodies transferred to a Washington lab for further testing." She looked over the room without making eye contact with anyone. "Naturally the bureau will expect full cooperation."

I couldn't see Terri from where I was standing but expected any minute to see a cloud of steam rising and be able to find her.

I wasn't sure if this meant the PD was in or out. If the feds wanted the local police to cooperate, they were in, right? It was hard to figure. But I realized something: I wanted to stay in.

"We will confer with the NYPD on a routine basis," Collins finally said. "And naturally, if anything should turn up in regard to this investigation, we expect to be notified immediately."

"Agent Collins." It was Terri. "We are receiving hundreds of calls a day, as are the other precincts. Detectives have been checking out all credible calls and—"

"The Manhattan bureau has tapped into all of the PD's tip lines, Detective Russo, so *you* needn't worry about that going awry. We will follow up as we deem necessary."

The tip line was a sensitive issue with Terri and it appeared Collins knew it.

Denton interrupted to address the crowd. "Please have all files pertaining to this case burned onto discs and turned over to Agents Richardson or Archer. For the computer-impaired among you, get one of the recent academy grads to teach you how to burn a CD." He smiled again, a wolfish grin exposing sharp little teeth. "Don't look so unhappy, folks. The bureau has just given you back your time. And I'm certain you can all put it to good use."

After the meeting broke up I wanted to slip out without being noticed, but Terri and her detectives were conferring with the FBI agents and Denton just inside the door. I tried my best to evade them, but Denton caught my arm.

"Guess it's back to the drawing board, huh, Rodriguez? Drawing board, get it?"

"Good one," I said. "But I wish I could have done more."

"Probably better to stick to your crayons," said Denton. "A lot less dangerous, right?" He grinned at Terri, and it pissed me off.

I turned to Collins. "If you don't mind me asking, what more can the bodies tell us? I mean, why ship them to Quantico now?"

Denton's eyes narrowed in my direction. "You have a problem with that, Rodriguez?"

"No. I was just wondering what Agent Collins hoped the lab would find."

"Well, why don't you tell us, Rodriguez. You're the one who reads minds."

I had clearly entered a big-dick contest. "I don't read minds, sir." I couldn't believe we were going back over the same territory, but Denton appeared to be enjoying himself, a genuine smile stretching his lips and compressing his eyes. He turned to Terri. "Your boy here says he doesn't read minds, Russo. That's not what *you* told me."

I could see Terri wanted to say something, maybe *Cut the crap, Perry,* or *Rodriguez is so far from being my boy you wouldn't believe it,* but she couldn't with a crowd around them. "Rodriguez has a talent," she finally said.

I appreciated the effort. Maybe she didn't hate me. Or maybe she just hated Denton more.

"So come on, Rodriguez, it's been a long meeting and we could all use a little entertainment. Read a few minds."

"I left my crystal ball at home," I said.

Denton laughed and so did everyone else. I thought it was over, but then I looked at Denton and the weirdest thing happened—a picture flashed across my brain.

It didn't last long, maybe five seconds, but it was perfectly clear, the afterimage still clinging to my optic nerve. I could

feel my eyes blinking, and knew I must have looked startled, because I was.

"You okay, Rodriguez?" Denton asked. "You're not getting a message from the great beyond or anything, are you?"

The room was in focus again, and so was Denton's grinning face. "I'm fine."

"Really? You look like you've just seen a ghost."

"Woo-woo," said Perez, and everyone laughed while the image of the burning man flickered in my brain.

"You'd better take Rodriguez for a drink, Russo. He looks like he can use one." Denton turned to me, still grinning. "So, was it a ghost, Rodriguez?"

"No, it was a man on fire."

Denton's facial muscles ticked. Then he laughed hard and loud. The others laughed too, all but Terri, who looked straight at me.

When Denton stopped laughing, he said, "I know. You can be our in-house psychic." He turned to his audience. "Hey, you all read about that case last week over on Staten Island, the one where the psychic was trying to help the PD find that missing woman? Drags half the local PD to a site where he says the woman is buried. They dig for hours, and what do you know, they find a skeleton. Problem was, the skeleton turned out to be a *dog!*" Denton laughed even harder this time.

"My father tells the story of the psychic who helped them back in the seventies, also on Staten Island," said Terri. "It was with this kid who'd been kidnapped on the way to school. Five, six weeks go by and they give him up. Then some psychic calls the station, says she's seen the kid in a dream tied up in a room with a sign that says something about hot dogs. A day later they find the kid in an abandoned building in Coney Island right beside the famous Nathan's hot dog stand. You believe that?"

"No," said Denton. "My guess is the psychic was in on it from the get-go."

"Actually, no, Chief Denton," said Collins. "I know that case. We studied it at Quantico. The psychic was totally unaffiliated with either the victim or the perpetrators."

"Is that so?" Denton was trying to control a sneer but losing. "Don't tell me you believe that sort of stuff, Monica."

"There are some things that just can't be explained," said Collins. "And if you're hearing *that* from an FBI agent, well . . ." She laughed.

But Perez wouldn't let it die. He nudged me with his elbow. "So, Rodriguez, can you tell me what's going on in my head?"

"Yeah, sure, Perez. I'm looking in there right now. But all I see is *dust.*"

Denton really guffawed over that one. He gave me a slap on the back, but that was it. He'd spent enough time with the commoners. He took Agent Collins by the arm and led her into the hall.

34

It was just the two of us, alone now, in the briefing room.

I waited for Terri to say something, but she didn't, so I said I was sorry.

"I don't need your apologies."

"And I don't need to give them. But I want to."

"Fine," she said.

I touched her hand and said I was sorry again, but she shook me off. "The only reason I came to your defense back there was because Perry Denton is an asshole—and because you're my responsibility."

"Your *what*?"

"You heard me."

"Is that so? Because I thought I was carrying my weight around here just fine. Fact is, I think I'm carrying it better than fine. A whole lot better."

"You going to turn this into another drama, Rodriguez?"

"*Me?*" I started to laugh.

"Don't you dare laugh at me."

"I'm not laughing at you. I'm laughing at the absurdity of the situation." I wanted to say it was not me being a drama queen, but I knew that would go over like the proverbial lead balloon. Plus, I wanted to make nice because I needed to know where the case was going now that the feds were taking over and, if I admitted it, I wanted to know where I stood with Russo, but no way I was going to say that. "Look, this is stupid. We have a job to do."

"Oh, so that's what this is about, the job. I thought you were apologizing."

"I thought you didn't want apologies." I sighed. "Look, what do you want me to do, fucking bleed?"

"I don't want you to do anything, Rodriguez. *Nothing,* get it?"

"Fine."

We stood there another minute not speaking, Terri sucking her lip and pushing imaginary hairs out of her face the way people do when they want to hide their expression. Every few seconds our eyes would meet and one of us would turn away. Terri looked really upset, so I finally asked, "Are you okay?"

"No, but it has nothing to do with you. I'm just upset about the case."

I didn't think she was being entirely honest, but didn't think it was a good idea to say it. "So what do we do?"

"We?"

"I'd like to stay connected to whatever goes on—and I think you could use my help."

I expected another fight, but she directed her anger at the case.

"What do they expect me to do, sit on my hands while the G brings in more BSS and CIU and the rest of the fucking alphabet? I'm not going to roll over and play dead." She stopped. "Forget it. I don't know why I'm telling you this."

"Because I'm your *responsibility,* remember?" I added a smile, and after a moment something let go in Terri's face and her muscles relaxed and she smiled too. Then she got serious.

"So, tell me, did you really see a man on fire?"

"Yeah, and it was totally fucking weird. My grandmother would say it was a spirit sending a message."

"This happen to you a lot, Rodriguez?"

"No. The pictures I've seen in my head have always been connected to a drawing I was making with a witness. But this came out of nowhere. I've never seen anything like it." It was true I had a tendency to see things in line and tone, more like drawings than real life, which I chalked up to extensive art training, but this was a whole other dimension. "Maybe I'm starting to see things."

Terri looked at me like I was a freak.

"Hey, it's your fault."

"Oh? How's that?"

"Trying to create the unsub's portrait for you must have triggered a chemical in my brain that just won't quit."

"So you're doing that sketch entirely for *me,* that it?"

She was right, of course; I was doing it for me as much as for her.

Terri still had that look on her face and I told her to stop, and she told me to stop biting my nails, but in the process we'd gotten past the fight, though we were both a little wary.

I needed to get out of the station to clear my head, and asked if she'd take a break with me.

"Now?"

"Why not? Your big case just went to the G."

"Thanks so much for reminding me, but I've got a deskful of other cases waiting."

"So let them wait."

His eyes track them like prey in a rifle's sight line, and he sees it in his mind's eye: bullet propelled in slow motion until it reaches its target, then, *wham!* a direct hit, aorta bursting, blood spurting out of the woman's heart, white blouse soaked a deep wine red, body thrown back, the look of shock on her face. Then the man, turning to the woman, eyes darting in every direction trying to locate the bullet's trajectory, and just when he figures it out, just when they make eye contact, it happens: *Kaboom!* another round fired right into his head!

He blinks and the pictures fade and there they are, the

man, sketchbook tucked under his arm, and the woman, crossing the street, getting into a car, no idea they have just been killed.

He waves down a cab. "Follow that car," he says as he gets in, and forces a laugh. "Sounds like we're in a movie, huh?"

The driver, head wrapped in a turban, asks, "Where to, sir?"

"I said, follow that car."

"Whatever you like, sir."

He stares at loose strands of shiny black hair that have escaped the turban, imagines wrapping a wire around the man's neck while thinking up the excuse he will give for leaving his desk so suddenly.

With its colonnaded court and Central Park just across the street, El Museo Del Barrio belied any connection to the real barrio only a few blocks east.

"I used to come here when I was a kid," I said.

"Really? This place has been around *that* long?" Terri grinned.

"It was started by some Puerto Rican educators and activists around 1969, I think, which happens to be before my time."

I hadn't been here in a while, but inside it looked the same—large room, lots of tile trim, nothing fancy. It brought me back.

Julio and I used to come here when we were teenagers and had nowhere else to go and didn't feel like getting into trouble. It was the only museum where Julio said he felt comfortable. A couple of times we'd gone to the Met, but he said the guards would watch him like he was going to steal something. I said they were probably right.

"This place was a sort of haven for me and my best friend, Julio." I remembered the time we were looking at a show of art from the Caribbean Islands. The tour guide was speaking to a class, in Spanish, about the pots and artifacts that had been made hundreds of years ago, and what Julio had said.

Yo, mira, *you hear what she said: hundreds of years ago? I can't get my head around that. The teachers at Julia de Burgos, they always saying there weren't no history, no nothing, so like I figured all the Puerto Ricans were like me,* un mamao, *y'know, worthless.*

That day had made a difference to Julio. And when he got out of Spofford we'd come up here to see the exhibitions. Later, after he got the job with the law firm, he became a member and started donating money.

Terri crossed the room to check out the brightly colored portraits that covered a wall of doors, *Soul Rebels,* painted by the artist Yasmin Hernandez.

I started pointing them out. "That's Julia de Burgos, a famous Puerto Rican poet; and Piri Thomas, who wrote *Down These Mean Streets;* and I think that's Eddie Palmieri."

"What'd you do, Rodriguez, study up before you brought me here so you could show off?"

I hadn't, but she was right that I was showing off.

Terri pointed to another portrait. "Bob Marley," she said, and started to sing, " 'No Woman No Cry.' You're not the only one who can show off."

We headed into the main gallery, an exhibition of works by Felix Gonzalez-Torres, spare and austere.

Terri pointed at a stack of papers on the floor maybe two-by-three-feet and six inches thick, an image of sand or waves or clouds on top, it was hard to tell. "What's this?"

"Pick one up."

"You want me to set off the alarms and get arrested, that it?"

"No, I'm serious."

She gave me a look, but did it. "Oh. I hadn't realized it was a stack of the same picture."

"Gonzalez-Torres wanted his art to be disposable—democratic, you know, just a stack of photocopies."

Terri rolled up the print. "Maybe I'll frame it. Free art, why not?" She moved to a wall of small framed statements, and read one: "Center for disease control 1981 streakers 1974 go-go boots 1965 Barbie doll 1960 hula hoop 1958 Disneyland 1955 3–D movies 1952." She turned to me. "What's this about?"

"I'd say it's about juxtaposing fads and cultural phenomena to create unexpected associations."

"Wow. You're either too smart for me, Rodriguez, or really full of shit. Forgive me, but art intimidates me."

"It intimidates lots of people, but you just have to know the language."

"You mean like the G, with their BSS and CIU bullshit."

"Exactly," I said. "For me, art always came naturally, but put an algebra problem in front of me and I go brain-dead. Gonzalez-Torres is a conceptual artist. He works with ideas as opposed to, say, paint and canvas."

"Sounds a lot cheaper."

I laughed, and ushered her into another room, walls covered with papier-mâché masks made in the seventeenth century for the carnivals in Ponce, Puerto Rico.

"Jesus!" Terri gasped.

I looked back and forth between a hideous horned fanged devil mask and Terri's pretty face.

"Can't tell us apart, huh?"

"If it weren't for the horns, no." I laughed, then squinted at Terri.

"What?"

"It's gone, but a second ago when you looked at that mask, your anatomy—your *facial* anatomy, that is—rearranged itself into a classic fear face."

"How so?"

"Your eyes opened and tensed. Your brows raised, and your forehead wrinkled."

"Not my forehead, Rodriguez. I'm way too young. Go on."

"Your lips drew back, then opened, and for a second, just a second, your jaw dropped open and quivered."

"It did not."

" 'fraid so. Dropped wide open—and it wasn't pretty."

Terri whacked my arm.

"Sorry, but the classic elements of fear were written all over your face."

"You know, I see people lying dead in the street and I barely flinch. But I walk into a room with a papier-mâché mask and I freak out."

"Facial muscles have a mind of their own. It's totally involuntary."

"You really know this stuff, don't you, Rodriguez?"

"It's my biz, but I'm still learning. And I spared you the anatomical muscle names because I didn't want to show off."

"I think you did a pretty good job—of showing off, I mean." She looked up at me. "So what's my face telling you now?"

I cocked my head and studied her. "Aside from your raised lip and the one cocked eyebrow—sure signs of disgust and arrogance—there's a telltale sign of sadness in the downward slant of your outer eyelids, but I think what your face is saying is, 'Hey, I'm gorgeous and I don't always know it because I'm insecure, but I think this guy I'm looking at is *way* cool.' "

"Asshole." She laughed, and raised a hand to hide her face.

"Right on the money, huh?"

"All but that last part about you being cool." She kept the hand over her face. "Just don't look at me, okay, Rodriguez? I can't have you reading my face all the time."

"Afraid of what I'll see?"

"Believe it," she said and slapped my arm.

"You're hitting me again."

"Take it as a good sign."

We ended up in the museum shop where Terri bought a box of Frida Kahlo stationery and I bought some postcards of tacky Spanish-language movies from the fifties.

Outside, a slate-gray sky was framing the naked winter trees of Central Park.

I looked at Terri, pulled her to me, and kissed her.

"Whoa," she said, her hand pushing against my chest, but not before our tongues had done a little tango. "You could have asked."

"I couldn't take the chance of being turned down."

She shook her head, but she was smiling.

He feels the bile rising into his throat; the picture of them kissing, vibrating on his optic nerve, sickening.

But what did he expect from her? Maybe she is half Spanish too, like Rodriguez. It was possible, some of them passed.

A school group is heading into the museum and he uses them like a shield to get closer. They are only a few yards apart. He sees them talking and laughing, completely unaware of him. Then the guy raises his arm and the sleeve of his jacket slides back.

He takes a deep breath and ticks off a few more pictures, then pulls the cap lower on his forehead and follows them.

We didn't make it back to the precinct. We went to my apartment instead. Terri said it was her first day off in a year, but she still felt guilty.

After we fooled around, I pulled myself out of bed and got my pants back on. I wanted to show her my latest drawing.

"It's still not enough for an identification," said Terri, "but there's something familiar about it. When did you add to it?"

"The other night. I just had a feeling about it."

She gave me a look, like she was trying to see inside my head.

"Don't look at me like that. It makes me feel like a crackpot, the way Denton was looking at me."

"Oh, Denton just likes to have someone around to torture, and he thinks I'm sleeping with you, so you've been elected."

"How would he know that?"

"He doesn't. He's just guessing," she said, still gazing at the drawing. "What if we got one of the computer nerds to play with this, see what they could come up with?"

"You mean *another* sketch artist?"

"Oh, don't look so wounded, Rodriguez, it was just a thought."

"Well, it's a sore spot with me. Most of the sketch artists who work on computers have no art training at all. They take a course in moving noses around on a computer screen and they think—"

"Okay, relax. It was just a thought. But do you think you're going to get more of this face?"

"Maybe," I said, but had a feeling I would. I thought I might show it to my grandmother too. It didn't seem so far-fetched these days, particularly with her weird connection to the case.

"And you'll show it to me if you do." It was not a question.

It brought up my suspicion or paranoia or whatever you

want to call it, that Terri just wanted me around to do my drawings. I don't know why that annoyed me. I wanted to complete the drawing too.

"What?" Terri asked, looking up at me.

"Nothing."

"Bullshit. I'm no face-reading expert, Rodriguez, but I can recognize annoyance when I see it."

"I'm not annoyed."

"Suit yourself," she said.

I walked her out and we didn't say anything until Terri slid into a cab.

"You know, Rodriguez, if something's bothering you, it's okay to say it."

I tried to think of what I wanted to say, but I'd been tamping down my feelings since I was a kid and all I could come up with was "I'm going to Boston tomorrow."

Terri sighed, pulled the door closed, and I watched the taxi drive away.

*F*inally.

He has watched them come out of the building, the woman get into a cab, the man stand in the street until the cab turned the corner. The whole time his lids opening and closing like a camera's shutter, one fragmented picture after another sent to his brain, again . . . and again . . . and again.

35

I pulled myself out of bed around eight. I was feeling edgy and sad but didn't want to analyze it. I got my art supplies together and headed down Seventh Avenue, the morning sky over Manhattan silver, the tops of skyscrapers dissolving, a talc-like snow turning everything into sculpture.

Penn Station was crowded, people rushing for trains balancing briefcases and Starbucks. I bought a ticket for the ten-twenty Acela Express, which shaved the trip down to just under four hours. I got a seat to myself, and opened the latest issue of *Rolling Stone* but couldn't concentrate on the music reviews or a story about Al Gore and his fight to save the environment, my mind going from Terri to the case to the sketch I was trying to make.

I closed my eyes and tried to picture something else: Terri, nude, the first thing that came to me, distracting but hardly relaxing. I exchanged it for a memory: sandy beach, blue sky, my first and only trip to Puerto Rico when I was nine years old, my father beside me, the enormous sand castle that had taken us half the day to build and five minutes for a wave to wash away. I could still picture the soft mounds of the castle's remains and hear my father's soothing voice: *We can always build another.* But I don't think we ever did.

* * *

He watches the man leave, art supplies tucked under his arm, follows him on foot to Penn Station, where he stands on a ticket line, cap tugged low over his features, only three people between them, once again thrilled to be so close yet anonymous. When he hears the man ask for a ticket to Boston, he cuts out of the line, walks back to his building, slips inside behind a couple of workers who are not paying attention, takes the elevator and waits until the hallway is empty, then sets to work on the apartment's shitty hardware-store lock, which is easy to pop.

The place reminds him of a big cage, no America the Beautiful accoutrements that make life worth living: no Ethan Allen sofa, matching chair, and ottoman; no acrylic nonstain rug. Nothing about the place makes any sense to him—no actual rooms, a beat-up sofa in the center of the space, lamp on a wooden crate that's been painted blue, bed behind a half-wall, unmade, blankets tossed about, enough to set him itching. He can't imagine that anyone would want to live like this. Clearly the man doesn't know any better, more proof that some human beings have evolved and others have not.

He moves away from the bed, afraid it will contaminate him, and crosses the space to a long table covered with dozens and dozens of sketches, pencils, erasers, drawing stumps, sharpeners, graphite and wood shavings, a mess, even worse than the bed.

He switches on the high-intensity lamp and begins to sort through the sketches, studies the man's style, the way he must hold his pencil to make such marks. It's not difficult, the line and tone uncomplicated. He hates to admit it, but the man has some talent.

He taps the iPod resting in the docking station, and salsa music blasts into the room, shrill and ugly. He tries to stop it and knocks it to the floor. When he goes to retrieve it, he sees the drawing pad propped under the table, opens it, and freezes.

It's true, what that reporter wrote! He can hardly believe it. *How is it possible?* A mud man with such a gift. Of course this is why he has been following him; he just didn't expect to find it.

He grips the pad, gloved hands shaking as he stares at the incomplete portrait. He is about to rip it from the pad, tear it to pieces, but no, he can't. The man must never know he was here. He has to think this through, figure out what to do. He closes his eyes and waits. He knows God will tell him.

The train was delayed in New Haven and again in Hartford and I arrived in Boston almost two hours late. I caught a cab, which dropped me in front of the impressive granite-and-glass building that housed the PD and their state-of-the-art DNA and Ballistics labs, as well as a couple of in-house forensic artists I'd met the last time I was here, computer variety, who had obviously failed to deliver, which gave me a slight jolt of schadenfreude.

A uniform led me to Detective Nevins's office, which was bigger and better than the cubicle she'd had three years ago. The lettering on the door indicated she was now heading up Robbery.

She glanced up and pushed the blond hair out of her eyes. She looked good.

"Congrats on the promotion," I said.

"You're late," she said. "The witness has already left."

"Hey, not my fault. The train was delayed. Can you get him back?"

"Not till morning. Any chance you can stay overnight?"

I didn't see any reason why not. "Sure," I said, giving Detective Nevins a smile.

She didn't return it. She raised her left hand and wiggled her ring finger to show off the gold band.

"Wow," I said. "Congrats again. When did that happen?"

"Year ago. You didn't think I was going to wait around for you, did you?"

The last time I'd come to Boston she'd been so happy with my sketch she'd taken me out for a drink and one thing led to another.

"When you didn't call, I wrote you off as just another jerk."

"That's me," I said.

"There's a hotel in Crosstown Center, walking distance. We'll reimburse you," she said.

It has not taken long for God to provide an answer. Though He is busy, He is always there for him. God reminded him that nothing is more important than the mission, the role he is playing pivotal, that he will be remembered, written about, his name passed down by generations of men and women as a martyr to the cause.

He closes the pad that contains his half-finished portrait

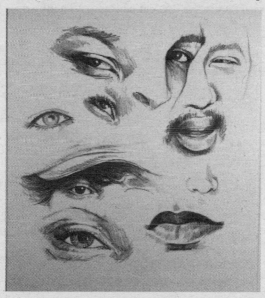

and slides it back under the table. The cracked iPod he arranges to look like an accident: book plucked from a shelf above the table and placed onto the docking station as if it had fallen, iPod on the floor just below it. He feels pleased to have broken the sketch artist's toy.

He peruses the man's drawings, page after page of sketches, and stops at one in particular to study the partially drawn faces, details of features—eyes, noses, lips, a slightly open mouth—and carefully notes again the man's technique, the way he uses his pencil to create line, tone, and shadow.

He does not think this one will be missed.

He folds the page into his pocket along with a pencil.

At the door he takes his time refitting the lock, getting all the screws back in place.

Outside on the street, he feels calm. Though the man is creating his portrait, it no longer worries him. He will go home, do the work, come back, and finish up.

He peers up at the sky and whispers, "Thank you."

36

The hotel was better than expected, a modern ten-story businessman's hotel, sleek and superclean. I checked into my room: double bed, ER-sterile bathroom, TV the size of a mini drive-in theater. I asked the bellhop where I could buy a toothbrush and get a bite to eat and he directed me to a CVS and a local café, where I had a glass of Shiraz and a decent dinner spoiled by a young couple at the next table who were practically making out. I was going to tell them to get a room, but thought it would make me sound bitter, and maybe I was.

Back in the hotel, I watched the end of *CSI,* which did a good job of combining glamour and gore, but couldn't concentrate. I was feeling antsy and frustrated, wondering why I'd come here when I should have been home chasing a phantom, which, according to the feds, I was no longer supposed to be doing.

I stared out the window, snow coming down, flickering like glitter in a snow globe.

The snowflakes turn to icicles, steam hissing as they hit the pavement. Somewhere salsa music is playing—the next room?—men and women laughing and dancing as the snow changes to water spurting from an open fire hydrant, spraying the night air with a million tiny diamonds. One of the dancers holds the sketch of my grandmother's vision. It bursts into flames and burns. My eyes burn too, hot and tired. A woman dressed in white, candles all around her, whispers: *Cuidado, cuidado.*

The killer's sketches are suddenly around me, flapping like injured birds. I grab one and it springs to life. But it isn't one of the victims. It's a different body, though one I know.

I turn and see a man with a gun aimed at the body. I try to stop him, but it's too late.

The gunshots startled me awake.

I blinked, trying to gauge my whereabouts.

I was in the Boston hotel, steam hissing; voices and music coming from the television. I pulled myself up, shut off the TV, stood in the dark watching flakes of white snow flutter past a black window and looking at my reflection, ghostly and unformed. It gave me a chill, it was so much like the man I'd been trying to draw, there and not there, features blurred or missing.

37

Dickie Marwell turned the simple act of entering the small Boston conference room into a three-act play: cape off with Zorro-like panache, Act I; gloves plucked daintily from each finger, Act II; trying out the two identical chairs, sagging into one, jiggling his bottom around in the other, Act III; a deep histrionic sigh as coda.

He smiled, or tried to. Nothing moved, his face a Botoxed mask. There were pale surgical scars around his ears. Still, I took him to be close to eighty.

"Can't we do this in a cocktail lounge?" he asked.

I was about to point out that it was not quite 10:00 A.M. when he launched into his résumé, starting with, "I used to make movies."

"Wait a minute, you're *that* Dickie Marwell? I've seen all of your films on video and DVD—*The House That Dripped Blood, Die, Die Dracula*, and my all-time favorite, *Killing the Undead*."

I thought the skin on Marwell's tight-as-a-drum face might split as he attempted to smile, though the simple act had been rendered close to impossible by the botulism injected into his facial muscles. "The one and only," he said. "Retired. Beverly Hills paled and my hometown Beacon Hill beckoned."

I wanted to ask him everything about making cheapo horror films in the fifties, but I was getting paid to ask other, more important, questions, so I opened my drawing pad to get started.

Marwell gripped my hand. "What have you done to your cuticles? Good-looking boy like you. My God, it's a sin."

I tugged my hand free.

"With your looks and name—*Rodriguez*—I can see it on a marquee faster than you can say *'Qué pasa,* baby.' No offense, darling, but today it's all Latin Latin Latin. Am I right, or am I right? I may no longer be in the film biz, but I keep up." He framed my face. "If I were still making films I'd sign you up in a minute."

"Another horror film, huh?"

Marwell's hands continued to form rectangles around my mug. "I know a face when I see a face, and *you* have a face."

"Yeah, I always knew that. I see it like two or three times a day."

"But clearly *not* this morning. When was the last time you shaved? No matter. It's a *look,* I know. And the camera will love you just the way you are. But promise me you will stop picking at your fingers."

I promised. "So, tell me about the perpetrator."

"The *perpetrator.* I *love* that." He took a deep, dramatic breath. "Well, I had a party and showed a movie in my screening room, *Brokeback Mountain,* to make my old-fogy Boston amigos sit up and take notice, and—"

"Can we cut to the robbery, Mr. Marwell?"

"I'm the director, sweetie, I'll say when we cut. And call me Dickie."

"Okay, Dickie. The robbery?"

"Well, after my friends left I was exhausted from all of the party chitchat, you know how it is."

I did not.

"Anyway, I went directly to sleep. Next thing I know, I'm awake, it's the middle of the night, and *oh my God,* there's a man in a black jumpsuit—awful, by the way, so seventies, and he was way too big for spandex—stealing my things! Here, in Beacon Hill, of all places. I mean, really, in Beverly Hills it's to be expected, but—"

"Mr. Marwell—"

He raised a finger. "Dickie."

"Right. Dickie. The man? In spandex? Can you describe him?"

"He had a big sack, like Santa, and he was putting my gold candlesticks in it—a gift from Vincent Price, by the way. I pretended to be asleep. I'm lucky to be alive!"

"But you saw him?"

"Indeed I did. A big man. Real rough trade. If I wasn't so tired . . ." He laughed.

I took a deep breath and went through my usual questions—race, shape of the face—and Marwell was good.

I was doing fine for a while; Marwell had an excellent visual memory, but then something went wrong. When I looked down I was shocked.

I hadn't been listening to Marwell at all. That other face in my mind was all I could see—and draw.

 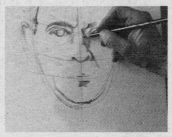

I didn't want to show Marwell, but he turned it around. "Oh, my, what's this? You need a Xanax, m'boy—or maybe just a good colonic?"

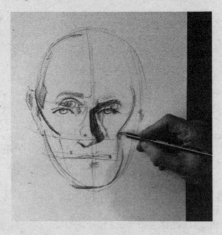

I said I was sorry. I didn't know what had happened.

We took a coffee break and I asked Marwell a few questions about his life in Hollywood, which he was more than happy to answer. Afterward I tried again and did better. Marwell deemed my sketch brilliant and said if he ever made another movie he was going to call me.

"You'll be the new Andy Garcia," he said. "Only taller."

"Oh, sure," I said.

I gave the sketch to Nevins, who barely looked up from her desk when she said, "Thanks. Make sure you leave your social security number with the desk so you can get paid and reimbursed for the train and hotel."

38

Denton plucked a paper clip off the file and began to bend it.

Had Rodriguez actually seen into his head?

No, that was impossible. But who knew what sort of voo-doo shit went through these people's minds?

Psychics. ESP. All bullshit.

But what if it wasn't bullshit?

Denton skimmed through the files, father and the son, Juan and Nathan. The father had been a narc. Before his time. Had worked with his current chief of operations, Mickey Rauder.

Could Rauder know anything?

He had to know Vallie too. Were they still in contact? Had Vallie said something to Rauder?

The paper clip snapped.

No, he was getting carried away. If Vallie had so much as hinted at anything to straight-arrow Rauder he'd have heard about it by now. And so would everyone else. He had taken care of everything. There was nothing to worry about. He was just being paranoid.

It was Rodriguez's fault for looking into his head.

And Russo's. For bringing him into the case.

Oh, yes. I understand all about protecting your reputation.

Russo's words echoed in his mind, her thinly veiled threat. She wouldn't dare say anything. It was her career on the line too.

Russo. Rodriguez.

Denton picked up another paper clip and started to twist it.

Of course if Rodriguez fucked up, it was Russo's fuck-up too. She'd go down, he'd see to that. One less cop around who could do him damage.

Terri wasn't sure why she was looking at the crime scene photos again. Maybe she wanted to feel as if she still owned them, these dead bodies she had come to think of as under her care even if they were now federal property, the bodies flown to Quantico for more slicing and dicing. And Rodriguez was right: What more could the bodies possibly reveal? If the G found anything she and her team had missed, she'd be surprised.

Rodriguez.

She had not expected anything like this to happen; she'd been down this road one too many times to be a wide-eyed romantic, and she didn't need it. But hell, he'd apologized. *Apologized.* Now that was a first. Maybe she'd been right, that he *was* different. Not that she was looking for a relationship. Right now, all she was looking for was a solution to this case. *Her* case. No matter what the G said.

Maybe she should be happy the G were taking over, let it be their headache, the way Denton thought, right?

Denton.

She pictured him, chest puffed out, needling Rodriguez. It would not have surprised her if he'd whipped his dick out. A contest he would have lost. The thought brought a smile to her lips, but it didn't last. She couldn't figure it out, what Rodriguez meant to her: Was he the talented cop who she'd thought could win her the case, or the guy she was falling for, or both?

She cracked open a new jacket: a cabdriver murdered, something that might knock the Sketch Artist off the front page, the press always hungry for a fresh kill. She tried to read the report, but the words blurred.

Was it too soon to check back with Perkowski and Tutsel, see if they had looked into that old murder book yet?

Terri closed the file on the taxi driver and stood up. As she had told Rodriguez, she liked to have all the facts—and wouldn't he?

By the time I got back to the city it was dark.

I knew there was nothing in my fridge but a six-pack and a block of cheddar past its prime, so I stopped at the Cupcake Café and bought a wedge of quiche and two cupcakes. Whoever said real men don't eat quiche didn't know it was okay if you washed it down with real beer and finished it off with real cupcakes.

The daytime workers had cleared out of my building, the lobby empty.

The elevator was a mess, small anthills of dust in the corners, scraps of crumpled paper on the floor. Likewise, my rusty apartment door covered with peeling alarm warnings that had been there since I'd moved in, all bogus.

I balanced my drawing pad and art supplies along with the quiche and cupcakes in one hand and put the key in the lock. It got stuck and took ten minutes to get out. In the process I dropped the cupcakes. By the time I got inside I was in a really bad mood.

My apartment looked worse than usual—walls dingy, wooden floors scuffed, my clothes draped over my Goodwill furniture. Maybe it was my overnight stay in a sterile hotel that made everything look worse.

I asked myself: Is this the home of a man or a teenage slacker?

I set the food down, plucked my clothes off the furniture and stuffed them into the laundry bag. My bed was unmade and Terri's smell was still on the sheets. It made me miss her. I flipped open my cell to call, then closed it, went back to the kitchen, glanced across the room, and noticed my iPod was on the floor. I picked it up, saw the crack, and stared at it trying to will it back to life. I felt like a little kid whose favorite toy had been busted.

One of my big anatomy books had fallen off the shelf and landed on the iPod docking station. But when I checked the shelf it looked secure, and no other books were out of place. It seemed odd.

I glanced at the drawings on my work table and started sorting through them. I didn't know what I was looking for, but something seemed wrong. I tugged my drawing pad out from under the table and opened it. I had a really weird feeling and needed to see if my drawings were all there. They were. I looked at the most recent one of the face I'd been trying to draw.

That's when I felt it, a presence accompanied by a chill so palpable I was afraid to turn around. But when I did, there was nothing.

I made a beeline for the closet. My Smith & Wesson was still there, and for the first time in seven years I put in a new clip. I went around the apartment, checking closets, the bathroom, even under my bed, holding my breath, heart pounding. But nothing was out of place. So why did I feel as if someone had been here?

Santerian gods were in my head, Akadere, who protected the home, Abaile, messenger in charge of moving things from one place to another. I went over to the window and gazed out at Thirty-ninth Street, the face I could not complete shimmering in my mind. The candle my *abuela* had given me for protection was sitting on the sill.

There is a man in that room with you, Nato.

I found a match and lit the candle.

Dolores Rodriguez had slept fitfully, her mind replaying the vision, her *nieto* in a burning room with someone evil.

She had already consulted her shells, and lit candles, made appeals to Santa Barbara, and bought quail eggs as an offering to the powerful Babalu-Aye. But the bad feeling, the *algo malo,* had persisted. It was the strongest feeling she had experienced since her son was killed.

She knew her grandson was not a believer, but it made no difference. She spread a clean white cloth over the *bóveda,* filled seven glasses with water, added a crucifix and a string of rosary beads, glanced up at the photograph of her son, Juan, and asked that he keep a watchful eye over Nato. She believed this was the moment Juan's *ori* had been waiting for, that it was being called upon to fulfill his destiny on earth; after that, he would stand before Olodumare and Orunla, and they would finally allow his soul to rest.

39

He has had no sleep, but is not tired. He has been here and home and back again, a new drawing tucked into his pocket. He has talked with God. An hour ago he saw the man come home, go into the building, turn on the lights. Now he sees the man in his window.

Two factory workers, dark-skinned women, come out of the building. He lowers his cap, darts across the street, and gets a gloved hand on the door just before it shuts. The women are nattering away in Spanish and barely notice him. He thinks another time he might just as easily have killed them.

Inside, the lobby is quiet. He heads to the back stairwell, removes the small piece of wood he wedged into it earlier, and opens the door.

My *abuela*'s candle had burned down, leaving a trace of ginger scent in the air. In the last two hours I'd eaten the quiche, washed all the dishes that had piled up in the sink, swept the floor, scrubbed the bathroom sink and shower stall, but had been unable to wash away the bad feeling that someone had been in my apartment. I was overtired but too antsy to sleep. I turned on the television, watched a few minutes of a *Seinfeld* rerun, but couldn't sit still. Plus, I was cold. The heat was off and there were ice crystals forming on my windows. I decided to call the super, a mean-spirited drunk who lived in the basement and was quick to turn down the heat the minute the businesses closed for the evening regardless of the temperature. We had argued about this for years, but being the sole resident in the building I always lost. But this was ridiculous; the radiators were stone-cold.

I called his number but he didn't answer. I pictured him crapped out in front of his Panasonic, warmed by the booze in his system. The guy was a Dominican and he seemed to hate me, maybe because I was Puerto Rican, and because, according to him, I was a *bohemio* and a *hippi*.

I pulled on a sweater, left the TV on for company, and went over to my work table unsure of why I was going. I blew on my hands to warm them, then sharpened a new Ebony pencil, and got to work.

The whole time I was drawing it was as if someone were guiding my hand. I'd never really believed in anything that could not be explained, a cynic if you got right down to it, but lately things seemed to be taking on a spiritual significance that was unexplainable.

When I saw what I'd done I was surprised. I hadn't realized I'd been stuck in one spot. The detail in the eye gave the face a sense of reality that hadn't been there before. One of my Quantico instructors always said you had to find the anatomy under the facial expression, and I thought I was starting to do that. There was something recognizable in the face, but I didn't know what. Had I seen him before? In real life? In a dream?

My *abuela* used to say that I was *intuitivo,* but the only time I ever felt intuitive was when I was doing a police sketch. Now it seemed to be true at unexpected moments, like seeing into Denton's head, for one. I couldn't quite believe it, but something had definitely happened in that moment.

A man in flames.

It seemed strangely connected to my grandmother's vision.

Could Chief Denton be the man in the room, the one my grandmother had warned me about? I glanced back at the eye I had just drawn. It didn't look anything like Denton's.

I picked up my pencil, but whatever force had been guiding my hand was gone. I laid the pencil down and tuned into the ambient noise: television playing; car alarm going off somewhere not far away; and something that sounded like scraping, maybe rats in the walls, which I did not want to think about.

I got up and tapped my hand against a heat pipe. It was still cold. I plugged in an old space heater, but it sparked and died.

That did it.

It has taken nearly two hours for the heat to die down after he switched it off.

Now, as he tiptoes down the dimly lit hallway, he mutters his favorite new word, *Rassenhygiene,* German for race hygiene.

He finds the rusting metal door and stops to unsheathe his new mail-order hunting knife. He leans an ear to the door and hears a TV sitcom laugh track, and is thankful for the distraction it will provide. It takes him less than a minute to pop the lock.

40

Crime Scene shuffled around the room, cotton bootees swishing along dusty floors as they collected evidence, difficult to ascertain what was new and what was old, the place a mess. They'd chalked an outline around the body and beyond that an eight-by-eight-foot square, off-limits to everyone other than the medical examiner until they completed their search.

Terri had received the call around 4:00 A.M., tearing her from a dream of Rodriguez on top of her. She was smiling when she'd raised the phone to her ear. This was Midtown North's jurisdiction, but the drawing had been noted and the bureau had been called, and they were officiating, Terri and her men assigned to supporting roles.

It was now almost 6:00 A.M.

Terri watched the scene, holding her breath, a sourness growing in her stomach. She had not eaten and worried she might be sick.

Across the room, Agent Richardson was asking questions and making notes in a pad.

The ME was leaning over the body and Terri saw him pluck a thermometer out of a wound. Then he rolled the body over and noted the way the blood had pooled under the skin. "Lividity suggests approximately six to eight hours."

Terri did the math. He'd been killed sometime between ten and midnight.

Another technician was scraping under the nails and bagging the hands.

The ME opened the victim's shirt. "Four, maybe five stab wounds here. Difficult to tell till we wash him down."

"A bit more brutal than the others," said Perez. "Could be he's getting angrier."

"Maybe he'll get sloppier too," said Dugan, trying to stifle a yawn.

A photographer tiptoed around the body as if he were practicing ballet, snapping pictures, a flash blinding Terri every few seconds.

"Press is going to love this," said Perez. "But hey, it's the G's headache, not ours, right?"

"Shut up," said Terri.

"Sor-ry," said Perez, hands up.

Terri took a deep breath and made her way over to Agent Collins. This imbalance of power had gone on long enough. "I need to see that drawing," she said.

"Go home, detective. We've got it under control."

Terri made a show of looking at the body, then back at the agent, the message clear: *Sure as shit doesn't look like you have it under control.* "I need to compare it to the other drawings."

"Our lab will run the tests," said Collins. "Type the paper, the pencil, see if it's a match with the others. I imagine it is, but with all the press there could be a copycat out there who wants to get his name in the funny papers."

"I understand that, but—"

Agent Archer interrupted. "He's Spanish, which fits the profile."

Collins's cell phone rang. "Yes, sir. No, sir. There's no press on the scene. Yes, sir. I think we can contain it, keep it under control."

Terri glared at the agent. Why was the bureau always so concerned about control, the press, keeping everything such a goddamn secret? Didn't they know it was hopeless? Didn't they know about Watergate and Travelgate and Monica Lewinsky and Abu Ghraib? Didn't they know the press eventually got it all?

"Hopefully this one will give us the information we need, sir." Collins had the cell phone pressed against her ear with one hand, the sketch in the other.

Terri tried to sneak a peek.

Agent Richardson was still across the room asking questions. She should get over there, she thought, but wanted a good look at the drawing first.

She glanced up at Collins. The woman looked exhausted. Terri could see she was under a lot of pressure, her job probably at stake—and she knew the feeling. She recalled the look of disappointment on Col-

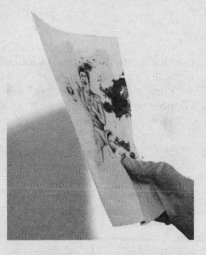

lins's face when Schteir had gotten to play the starring role in Karff's interrogation. Maybe she had more in common with this woman than she had originally thought, and if not, she could play it.

She laid her hand on the agent's arm. "How are you holding up?"

Collins's eyes narrowed. "I'm doing just fine, Detective."

"I know the kind of pressure you're under and have no intention of adding to it or getting in your way."

"Well, that's just great to hear." Collins let out a deep sigh. "Listen, I know we can look like the bad guys to the locals, but we've got a job to do, just like you."

"I hear you." Terri offered Collins a sympathetic look. "To be honest, it's a relief not to have all the responsibility, everyone just waiting for you to screw up." She paused to see if Collins was taking it the right way. "But I've been on the case from the outset and I'm happy to help you out any way I can." Terri paused. "I understand the drawing has to go to Quantico for analysis, but if I could just see it . . ."

Collins let out another deep sigh. "Here," she said, and handed her the drawing. "Knock yourself out."

Terri crossed the room, sketch in her gloved hand.

"You mind if I have a word with him?" she asked Richardson, meaning Nate.

Terri waited till Richardson moved away.

"You okay?"

"I have no idea."

Terri turned the drawing toward him. "I need you to look at this."

"I've seen it," said Nate.

"I realize that, but I need you to tell me about it, if it's the same or . . . I don't know, but it looks different. He's added a little sketch on the side, maybe a close-up of the vic's mouth? Or maybe it's something left over from when he started the sketch. I'm not sure. What do you think?"

Nate's hands were trembling. He'd seen the detail too, and it had sent a shiver down his spine, though he didn't know why. He'd been up all night, too tired to focus. "It looks . . . more developed, less sketchy. And that separate mouth on the side . . ." He felt the chill again, glanced around the room, the windowless basement apartment, rent receipts and papers stacked up on an old fax machine, dirty dishes piled in the sink, and the super dead on the floor. He still couldn't believe it.

"You think it was made by the same guy?"

"Who else could it be?"

"Well, the drawings, the MO, have made it into the media. So it could be a copycat. I just want to be sure."

Nate squinted at it with tired eyes. "There is something different, it's a little softer, and I don't see the pronounced crosshatching, but . . . maybe he's just using another kind of pencil—" Another chill shook his body. "Can I take it out of the plastic?"

Terri cadged a glance over her shoulder. Collins was huddled with her men.

She handed Nate a pair of gloves. "Make it fast. And put these on."

Nate tugged on the gloves and removed the drawing. "Yes, it's a softer pencil than he ordinarily uses. He's blending and modeling more too."

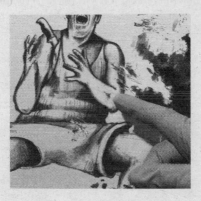

"And what's this?"

"I can't tell," said Nate, but the chill intensified. "Maybe it's another one of those white supremacist symbols."

"I need to get it magnified, but there's no way Collins is going to let me hold on to this." She glanced over at the fax machine, then back at Collins, who was half turned away, her cell phone at her ear.

Terri didn't waste any time. She slid the papers and bills off the fax machine and fed the sketch into it. Thirty seconds later she was folding a halfway decent copy into her pocket. She handed the original back to Collins.

"Thanks," she said. "I appreciate it."

"It tell you anything new?"

Terri shook her head. "Not really."

Collins turned to Nate. "You've got to come with me to give a statement."

"I thought I already did that," said Nate.

"Yes," said Collins. "But it has to be official."

41

He could stop now and no one would ever know.

But is that what he wants? To never be known? With his most important project still ahead of him?

He spreads a few sketches he has made for inspiration across his work table.

Yes, this is it, but he wants to see it all again, to consider the where and when.

He stops a moment to think about the drawing he's taken, what he has done, and how to take it a step further.

Yes, he is seeing it, the place and the idea fixing in his mind.

Now he has to get the timing right. This one has to be big. This one has to be perfect.

42

This was the second time in a week I was walking down the corridors of FBI Manhattan, this time less comfortably between Agents Collins and Richardson. My adrenaline had kicked in for the third or fourth time of the day. I felt edgy and itchy, the way I did when I was fourteen and had pulled an all-nighter high on drugs. Richardson kept up a steady stream of chat—baseball, politics, the weather—but Collins was quiet.

They ushered me into a windowless room with two chairs and a desk, and asked me to wait. They said they'd be back in a minute. Ten minutes passed. Then another ten. I paced, measuring the room with my steps, twelve one way, nine the other. I kept seeing Cordero lying on the floor, blood pooled under him. I checked my watch every other minute, and chewed my cuticles. Another twenty minutes passed before Collins came back.

She took a seat, carefully tucking her skirt under her, ladylike, but there was nothing ladylike in her face, which was frozen, intentionally immobilized. She flipped open a notepad and angled her head toward a video camera wedged into a corner where the wall met the ceiling. "We're recording this," she said. "It's procedure."

"Guess the FBI videotapes everything, huh?" I forced a laugh.

She didn't, just looked up at the camera, stated the date and time, her name and mine, then asked what time I'd come home from Boston, which I'd already told them more than once, and asked about my relationship to Manuel Cordero.

"We didn't have a *relationship*. He was the superintendent of my building."

"Did you get along?"

"What the hell sort of question is that?"

"Take it easy," she said.

I couldn't. There was something in her tone and even more in her frozen face that was setting me on edge.

Collins cadged a look at the video camera, then at a mirrored wall. I knew there was someone on the other side, watching.

She referred to her notepad. "So you found Manuel Cordero's body around eleven-thirty."

"Yes, I said that earlier, to Richardson."

"But now you're saying it to me." Her eyes narrowed, lids compressing the way they do with the onset of anger.

"I'm really tired," I said, losing patience, adrenaline seeping out of my veins like I was donating blood.

"We're all tired. But you've got to say it for the camera."

"Yeah, it was sometime around eleven-thirty."

"And you know that because . . . ?"

"Because I looked at my watch."

"Before or after you found the body?"

"Before. When I was upstairs. I had been debating whether or not it was too late to go downstairs."

"And you decided it wasn't?"

"Obviously."

Collins glared at me. "I don't think that response was called for."

Maybe it wasn't, but I didn't feel like apologizing.

"So it was eleven-thirty," she said, flipping pages in the coroner's report.

"Give or take a few minutes."

She made a note in her pad. "And Cordero was lying face-down when you found him?"

"Yes. I've already said that. About ten times tonight."

"Did you touch him? Roll him over or anything?"

"Why would I do that?"

"I'm just asking."

"No. I didn't touch him. I could see he was dead."

"And you could see that *how*?"

"He was lying facedown in a pool of blood—a lot of blood—and he wasn't moving. That spelled dead to me."

"Really?" Collins noted something in her pad, then looked up at me, face neutralized though there was some leakage in the way the triangularis muscle had tightened around her mouth. "Because some people might have thought the man was just hurt, injured, you know, but somehow you *knew* he was dead."

"Yes, I—"

"And his door was open?"

"Yes—"

"So you could see in?"

"Yes. Well, no—"

"Which is it?"

"It was only open a couple of inches, so no, I couldn't really see in. I explained that to Richardson, and—"

"Could you please stop referring to Agent Richardson's report?"

"No, I don't think I can." My heart was pounding and the muscles in the back of my neck had tightened. "I'm getting tired of saying the same thing over and ov—"

"I explained that." Collins nodded at the camera. "I don't know why you're making this so difficult." Her icy tone matched her frozen mask. "It really doesn't look good."

"What's that supposed to mean?" I could feel things unhinging, as if screws were being loosened to allow easy entry to my brain and psyche.

"So you went in."

"What?"

"To the apartment. You went in."

"Yes. You know that. I knocked, but he didn't answer. I waited a minute and knocked again. I could hear the television and I could see the kind of bluish light that comes off a TV screen. It was reflecting into the hallway. You know how that is."

"No. Tell me."

"I just did."

"All you told me was that the door was ajar and you went in. You didn't explain *why* you went in."

"Well, I . . ." *Why had I gone in?* "I had a feeling—"

"A *feeling*?" Collins's mask was cracked by a raised eyebrow.

"Like I said, the door was partially open. I knocked and—"

"Went in. Yes, you already said that." Collins scratched her head with the back of her pencil. "You mean to tell me the man's door was unlocked and open in a basement apartment in a fairly crappy neighborhood in New York City? I don't mean to insult your neighborhood, Rodriguez, but come on."

"Hey, I know it's not Park Avenue. But what's your point?"

"My point is, it's weird. The door just being open like that, wouldn't you agree?"

"Yeah, I fucking *would* agree. It was unlocked because it had obviously been left open by the perp, the unsub, by whoever killed Cordero." I could feel my pressure rising, blood pulsing in my ears.

"And how do you know that?"

"I don't know it for a fact, but like you, I was there when Crime Scene said the lock had been popped, and since *I* didn't do it, I'm presuming it was done by whoever killed Cordero, right?"

"If you say so."

"*I* don't say so. *Crime Scene* said so."

"Fine," she said.

"What are you suggesting? That I . . . killed Cordero?"

My palms were sweating. I had that feeling you get when a store security guard is watching you: that you're guilty though you haven't done anything.

"I'm not suggesting—"

"I've had enough. I'm leaving." I stood up.

"Sit down," said Collins. She glanced first at the mirror, then at the video camera, and I remembered people were watching me, that I was being filmed acting guilty when I had nothing to be guilty about.

"Just take it easy, Rodriguez; relax."

I took a deep breath, but I did not relax.

"Just a few more questions. Nothing to get so upset about." She offered up a clipped fake smile, and I sat down.

"Let's get back to what you did when you came in and saw Cordero on the floor."

"Like I said, I called 911."

"Right away?"

"No. Not immediately. I was frozen for a minute, stunned, I guess. Then I noticed the drawing beside the body and it hit me that it wasn't just some ordinary break-in."

"So you waited to make the call?"

"I didn't think about it right away, no. And . . . I wanted to see the drawing."

"So you went over to look at it."

"Yes."

"Which is why the soles of your shoes had Cordero's blood on them and why you tracked your footprints across the room."

It sounded awful when she said it. "I didn't realize what I was doing at the time or I never would have done it." Jesus, what the hell had I been thinking? I knew all about contaminating a crime scene. "I wasn't thinking straight."

"But you were thinking straight enough to go over and see the drawing."

"I've been working this case—" My annoyance ratcheted up a notch toward anger. "So, yeah, I wanted to see if it was like the others."

"And then?" I could see she was assessing me, head tilted back, eyes narrowed.

"I looked at the drawing and made the call."

"Could you look at the camera and repeat that? And say *who* you called?"

"Who the hell do you think I called, my broker?"

"There's no need for sarcasm. This is simply procedure."

"Really? Because it doesn't seem like it." I blew a breath out of the corner of my mouth. "Look, I'm tired. I've been up all night and—"

"I know that," she said. "But you're the one who found the body."

Homicide 101: He who finds the body is always the first suspect.

"Wait. I found the body, so you think *I* killed him? Give me a fucking break. I've been working the case, you know that. You can't possibly think I had anything to do with the guy being killed."

Collins just sat there.

"Look, I found the guy, yeah, and was stupid enough to track his blood across the floor on my shoes, really stupid, but like I said, I wasn't thinking. But I didn't do anything to Cordero."

"Okay," said Collins.

"Okay what?"

"Okay, you weren't thinking."

"And I didn't kill him either."

"Okay," she said again, in the same noncommittal tone.

Did she believe me? I searched her face for evidence, but she'd frozen her features.

I was beginning to feel like a character in a Kafka story. "I had nothing to do with Cordero getting killed. You know that, right?"

She didn't say anything, not even okay, and then I saw it, the tic of suspicion, her eyes narrowing ever so slightly.

"How many times do I have to say it? I've been working this case. That's why I wanted—*needed*—to see the drawing!" I could hear the shrillness in my voice. I wanted to stay calm, but couldn't.

"I heard you."

I didn't want to utter the classic line, but had to. "Should I be calling a lawyer?"

"If you want to call a lawyer, fine, but I'm just asking questions for the record—and the camera." She sat back and laced her fingers together. "You're an awfully paranoid guy, Rodriguez.."

Was I? God knows I'd walked around feeling guilty for twenty years. Maybe it was finally starting to show. I kept telling myself to relax, but my mind was spinning. Should I call a lawyer, or would that confirm I had something to hide? I could call Julio. He was a real estate lawyer, but he'd know a good criminal lawyer. *A criminal lawyer. Did I actually need one? Was this really happening?*

Collins unlaced her fingers and sat forward. "It's just a few more questions. After that, you can go home." Her voice was calm. She sounded perfectly reasonable. But I knew what I'd seen in her face. Words lie. Faces do not.

But I nodded, hoping she was telling the truth. Maybe I was being paranoid. I was so tired I couldn't reason it out.

"So why do you think Cordero turned the heat off?"

"I don't know. I suppose because the owners tell him to save on heat when he can."

"And he's done this before?"

"Yes. You should be asking the building owners why Cordero turned the heat off, not me."

"We will," she said. "Okay, just a few more things. We've got to make sure we don't miss anything. You don't want to go through this again, do you?"

I didn't bother to say the obvious. And we did go through it again. And again.

The air outside felt colder and brittle, but maybe it was just me. I made it halfway down the street and had to stop. I could barely breathe, my head aching and light, my body like sludge.

Could they possibly suspect me? It was absurd. I was being paranoid, like Collins said. If they really suspected me of anything they'd have arrested me, right? And here I was, on the street, a free man.

But I couldn't shake it. I had seen it in her face: doubt.

I'd seen something else too, something I had not yet processed, but was too tired to figure out what it was.

I headed toward the subway but hailed a cab instead. I couldn't take another step.

I sagged into the seat and tried to relax. I told myself everything would be okay, that I was getting carried away. I was first on the scene and they had to question me. It was their job. It was my bad luck, a coincidence that I'd found Cordero's body.

What was it they'd taught us at the academy about coincidence? That there's no such thing.

I shivered though the taxi was hot.

There was something else in that rule that was nagging at me, some other coincidence that wasn't a coincidence, but I couldn't see it, not with my head pounding and exhaustion so bad my muscles were twitching.

I got out my cell to call Terri and found two messages from her. She needed me to come to the station right away. It was urgent.

43

Terri's mouth was set tight, lips compressed.

"They cleaned up the Cordero sketch. That thing drawn on his arm that you suggested might be another white supremacist symbol—I had it enlarged." She laid the paper down in front of me. "Look familiar?"

I stared at the image, trying to make sense of it, my hand involuntarily sliding up my shirt-sleeve, covering my tattoo, which he'd copied and added to his drawing. "Jesus. He must be stalking me!"

"Why would he do that?" Terri's face had the blank stare of someone who was trying hard to look neutral.

"Well, he must have read about me in the newspaper. Stalking is his stock-in-trade, right? What he's done with all his victims." The idea of him close to me, watching me, sent a chill up my back. "It makes sense, doesn't it?" *It did, didn't it?*

Micro-expressions slid across Terri's face like fast-moving clouds, but I was too tired to read them.

"Okay," she finally said. "So he reads about you and stalks you. I guess I can see that."

"You *guess*?"

"Hey, I blow up the unsub's drawing and find your tattoo in it. It's taking me a minute to digest this, all right?"

I saw her point.

"So why put your tattoo in the drawing?"

I tried to think it through, but I was exhausted, going on empty from no sleep. "To let me know how close he's been? To . . . unnerve me? I don't know, but it's working."

Terri just looked at me when all I wanted was to have her put her arms around me and tell me everything was okay. I guessed she liked her men tough and heroic and right now I felt anything but.

"When I got home from Boston I had a feeling someone had been in my place. I can't explain it. My iPod was broken and—"

"Your iPod?"

"That's not important. Well, it is, but— Look, you've trusted my feelings before, right? Well, I'm telling you now that I had a feeling he broke into my place, our unsub, the Sketch Artist. He was there. Before he killed Cordero." It was as if I was listening to myself from a distance, judging my own words—and they didn't exactly add up or make sense. How could I really know he'd been in my place? I couldn't. But I knew what I felt.

"I'll get Crime Scene to dust for prints, see if they can find anything." Terri flipped open her cell.

"Oh—shit—wait. I cleaned up."

"You what?"

"I cleaned up. The place was a mess. I wasn't thinking."

There it was, that same expression of doubt I'd seen on Collins's face, orbicularis oris muscle puckering the lips, depressor glabellae lowering the brows.

"Don't look at me like that, like you suspect me of something."

"No one suspects you of anything."

"No? I just spent a couple of hours with Agent Collins, who sure acted like I was a suspect."

"It's procedure."

"That's what she said."

"And I'm sure she meant it. You're not a suspect, not—" She stopped.

"Not *yet*? Is that what you were about to say?"

"Don't put words in my mouth." She laid her hand onto my shirtsleeve, slid it up to expose my tattoo. She glanced back at the sketch, my tattoo drawn onto the superintendent's arm, her brows drawn together even more tightly. "The G is going to find this in the drawing—if they haven't already."

"But they don't know it's *my* tattoo."

"No, but the minute they realize it's not on the victim's body, they'll know it means something else. They'll be sending the image out to every tattoo parlor in the country."

"I got this tattoo twenty years ago and can't see how—"

"And no one in the precinct, in the NYPD, has ever seen it?"

"Shit. I don't know."

Terri started pacing.

"Maybe he's showing off for me, showing me how good he is, you know, one artist to another."

"Maybe," said Terri. "And if he was that close—he'll be back."

"The FBI should be putting a guard on me rather than suspecting me of something, grilling me."

"They had to ask you those questions. So would I. It's standard operating procedure."

"Yeah, I know that. But if it's standard, why do you look so worried?"

"I'm not." She tried to smile, and failed. "Look, the vic, Cordero, was in your building and you found him. They have to look at you first. It's proximity. It doesn't mean anything. It'll be okay, Nate."

"Oh, shit, now I'm really worried. You're calling me Nate."

I thought that would make her laugh, but it didn't. I glanced down at my tattoo. It had been a mistake twenty years ago, and here it was a mistake all over again. "Why would I put my own tattoo in the drawing? Why would I want to implicate myself?"

"Right," she said, but her face said something different.

"What?"

"Well, you just said it when you were describing the unsub, that he was showing off. I mean . . . well, the G could apply that reasoning to you—that *you* were showing off, taunting the cops. They could say it was the next logical step, that you're pushing the envelope. It's not uncommon for psychos to play with the cops."

"Could you stop making it sound so plausible?"

"It's just the way it could look to them. But it won't. Don't worry. And I know you had nothing to do with this." That same micro-expression flashed across her face: the shadow of a doubt.

If Terri didn't believe me, who would? I tried to swallow, my throat dry. I could see the look of doubt on her face spreading like a virus to her men and to the feds. And what defense did I have? A feeling? A lousy feeling.

"It'll be okay."

"You're just saying that."

"No, I . . ." She tried to smile. "It'll be okay."

"Stop saying that."

"What do you want me to say, Rodriguez?"

"Tell me that you're on my side, that you believe me."

"Of course I'm on your side." Her face softened, and

she touched my cheek. "They have nothing more than proximity."

"So what do I do now?"

"Go home and get some sleep."

44

I fell into bed, body aching, mind in overdrive. If only I hadn't gone down to complain about the heat I would never have found the body.

If only . . . if only . . . if only . . .

I played it over and over like a song stuck on repeat. I tossed and turned, fluffed the pillow up, punched it down. I kept hearing Collins's questions and my answers, which now sounded lame. But they were the only answers I had. I took a deep breath, closed my eyes, tried to picture clouds, sky, seascapes, but kept seeing my tattoo drawn into the sketch.

He had been following me. And he'd been in my apartment. I'd felt it. But that wasn't enough. I needed proof. And there was none.

I thought Terri believed me, but if it came down to protecting her job or protecting me, which would she do?

I kicked off the blankets, went to the window, and stared down at Thirty-ninth Street. Could he be out there now? Watching? Waiting?

I flopped back into bed, but my eyes wouldn't close. It was the middle of the day and I'd never been good at naps no matter how tired I was. I stared at the ceiling and asked myself why I had not called the station the instant I'd seen Cordero lying in a pool of blood.

Because I wanted to see the drawing.

But why had I needed to see it close up? And why had I been stupid enough to slog through Cordero's blood to get at it? I knew better. I was a trained cop. What was it about the drawing that made me lose my reason? What was it I had said to Terri when I described it?

Softer pencil. Less crosshatching.

And what about that little drawing on the side of the paper? That little detail.

That was it.

Jesus Christ! It looked like one of my drawings!

I sat up in bed and thought it through. He'd stalked me, broken into my apartment, seen my drawings, made his sketch of Cordero, added the detail from one of my drawings, then my tattoo as a sort of signature. After that, he killed Cordero, left the drawing on the scene, and led me to it.

A setup. Brilliant. Perverse. And no way I could verify it. I hardly believed it myself, and yet . . . I knew it.

I got out of bed. I had to do something. Collins was already suspicious and she didn't yet know about the tattoo or the similarity to my drawing. But she would. Soon.

My brain was spinning. I pictured FBI lab techs laying the Cordero crime scene drawing next to one of mine. Would they see the similarity? Maybe they wouldn't even know I drew fragmentary faces to keep my hand and eye in shape.

Who was I kidding?

I went over to my work table, glanced down at my sketches, so many of them like the one he'd chosen to replicate.

For a moment I considered destroying them all.

But this was nuts. No one was going to start comparing my drawing style to the unsub's, and even if they did, any artist who could draw could imitate another's style, right? And he hadn't really done that.

Except for that detail of the mouth.

I closed my eyes, pictured myself on the subway, could see the young black man, mouth open, talking to his friend, the look he gave me when he caught me staring; how I'd turned the pad around, pointed to the little drawing I'd made of his mouth, and how he'd smiled.

I started pushing my sketches around. There were dozens of half-finished faces, but not the one I was looking for. I was making a mess, scattering drawings across the table, knocking them to the floor, frantically searching, all the time knowing I would not find it.

But I never threw a sketch away. Never. Not even the bad ones. It was a habit I couldn't kick.

He'd taken it. It was the only thing that made sense. To me.

I pictured Cordero dead in his apartment, the TV behind him, Jay Leno doing his monologue, the pool of blood, and the drawing that looked like mine on the floor.

I locked my hands together to stop them from shaking. I had to calm down. I'd explain it to them and they'd see it, that I was being set up. What was I worried about? Collins was right: I was a paranoid guy.

I went to the bathroom and splashed cold water on my face, caught a glimpse of that damn tattoo on my arm, and broke into a sweat.

I went back and opened the pad with my sketches of the unsub's incomplete face. I had to see more of it. That was the answer. The only thing I could do.

I sharpened a pencil, dropped it, my hands trembling. I took some deep breaths and told myself to relax, got a grip on the pencil and waited for something to guide my hand, but nothing happened. I closed the pad, but couldn't sit still. I needed to get out. I needed to *do* something. But what?

There is a man in that room with you, Nato.

I called my grandmother and told her I was coming over.

I put on jeans and a clean white shirt so I wouldn't worry her. I went into the bathroom and ran my hands through my hair. My eyes were red-rimmed. I looked awful. I thought about shaving because it would make my grandmother happy, but didn't think it was the best time to hold a razor to my throat. I splashed on some lime-scented aftershave and decided that would have to do.

I tucked my drawing pad under my arm and left.

"*¿Qué pasa,* Nato?" My grandmother's first words when I walked in the door.

"*Nada, uela.*"

"You don't look good." She got a hold of my face with both hands.

"*Estoy cansado.* That's all. I was in Boston, working, and I didn't sleep well."

She narrowed her eyes.

I tried to think of something to say. "I met an old movie director."

"You going to be in the movies?"

"Oh, sure, *uela.*" I had to smile. "I'm going to be a star."

"*Te estás burlando de mi?*" She pointed a finger at me.

"*Nunca, uela.* I swear." I looked down and saw the bowl with shells and beads and stones beside the front door, an Eleggua, used to protect the home. "Since when do you need protection?"

She waved off my question. "It is like, what do they call them, what your mother's people have at the doors, with the prayers inside?"

"You mean a mezuzah?"

"*Sí,* like that."

In the living room, the *bóveda* was all set up with glasses of water and shells. "What's going on?"

"You want a *cerveza*?" she asked, avoiding my question.

I didn't press. I was too tired. And I knew my *abuela.* When she was ready to tell me what was worrying her, she would. And then I might tell her what was worrying me too. We were both stalling. She asked if I was hungry and I realized I hadn't eaten since the night before.

I followed her into the kitchen and she started ladling food onto my plate: *arroz, habichuelas, tostones y chuletas fritas.* I didn't think I could eat, but I did, everything, all of it great, which I told her and she smiled. She didn't take much for herself, just picked at *arroz* for a while. Something was definitely bothering her.

"¿Qué pasa, uela?"

"Come," she said. *Eat.* She forced a smile.

My *abuela* took eating very seriously and did not want to disturb the process. She changed the subject, mentioned that she'd spoken to my mother, and I felt guilty because I hadn't. We usually spoke once a week, but I hadn't called her since I'd started the case. I knew it would worry her.

"Llama tu mami." She aimed a slightly crooked finger at me.

I promised I'd call.

When I finished, my grandmother stood up and beckoned me to follow. I knew it had to be serious if she was ignoring the dishes. She never let them sit around, afraid of roaches or mice.

She led me down the hallway. We passed the living room, the TV on, a Spanish soap opera she was addicted to. She ignored it and continued down the hall toward the last room in the apartment, at one time the master bedroom. She'd given it up years ago, moving her bed into the tiny room off the living room.

"We will speak in the *Ile*," she said.

It was the first time I'd heard her refer to the room where she saw her clients as a *house church*.

"Why *Ile* and not *cuarto de los santos*?"

"My friends encouraged me. *Y así paso.* I do not mean to say that it takes the place of church."

I knew what she meant: that she was still a churchgoing Christian. She prayed to Olofi—who served as humanity's personal God on earth—but she prayed to God's son Jesus as well. For her, there was no conflict.

"When someone comes to me to consult the *orishas,* I tell

them, ask your church and your congregation to pray for you too."

"So you have become a godmother, a *madrina*?"

"I am . . . just me. There are others with much greater knowledge." She told me about some kid named Carlos, twelve years old, a child of Obatala, she said, with great powers, but I'd stopped listening. We had stepped into the *cuarto de los santos,* which I hadn't been in since she had given it up as her bedroom, and I was stunned.

There were makeshift shrines everywhere. One with a dish and rock like the one by the door, this one much more elaborate, adorned with red and white beads, a jewel-encrusted crucifix, a dollhouse draped with a wilting vine. A few feet away another with pictures of saints wrapped in colored cellophane and a small cheap-looking plastic skeleton covered with rosary beads. And there were more: dolls with peacock feathers and fake flowers, stacks of fruit, toys, candles, pictures of saints and *orishas,* even a Buddha. I didn't see a Star of David, but there probably was one.

My grandmother had always had a few modest shrines made from candles and pictures of saints, but nothing had prepared me for this.

"It looks like you've spent way too much money at the local *botánica, uela.*"

She told me not to make fun, that it was a *pecado,* a sin, that almost everything had been created by people who came to her for consultations.

In the center of the room were three benches like pews, plain wood, pockmarked and weathered as if they had been left outside during some church demolition, which was entirely possible. I asked her where she'd gotten them and she said that a local *padrino* had found them for her.

She told me to sit down in one of the pews, and I did. She touched the sleeve of my white shirt. "This was a good one to wear, *una señal.*"

"It was my only clean shirt," I said.

"And you think that is not a sign?"

Then she told me she had seen another room, but not to draw, just to listen. She had felt something in this room, a presence of something evil. Then she described what sounded a lot like my apartment, an apartment she had never seen.

I was about to show her my sketches of the man I was trying to draw, but she had more to say, and another vision she wanted me to draw.

45

"**I** realize this is delicate," said Collins, "which is why I came to you, Chief Denton."

"*Perry,* please. And I appreciate that, Monica." Denton tried to imagine the FBI agent nude, but could not.

"There's just a bit too much coincidence. Nothing concrete, not enough for an arrest, but I have to say we're watching him."

"Of course. I understand," Denton tried not to smile. This was the best news he'd had all day. "I can see where you're coming from. I'll keep an eye on Rodriguez too."

Agent Collins tried to concentrate but was getting lost in the chief's blue eyes. She didn't think a man like Denton would be interested in her, but there had been his arm on hers at the meeting, a conspiratorially wink or two, and now the way he was leaning in to whisper.

"Personally, I was against the idea from the beginning. It was Russo who encouraged it. Could be Rodriguez convinced her he'd be able to help." Denton shrugged to make his comment seem offhand, but he wanted to be sure he seeded the possibility there was something going on between Rodriguez and Russo. "Don't get me wrong. Russo's a good cop. Sure, she's made a few bad decisions in the past, but what cop hasn't?" If Collins had not remembered Russo's past, now she would.

"Right now it's mainly a question of proximity," said Collins. "And Rodriguez left prints all over the vic's apartment, though there's no way to date them. For argument's sake, let's say they're new, that Rodriguez made them when he discovered the body."

"That's very generous of you, Monica." Denton smiled.

Collins sat back and crossed her legs. "What I don't like is that he traipsed across the apartment. I mean, why would a cop intentionally contaminate a crime scene?"

"I see your point."

"I understand he was curious to see the drawing, but still . . ."

"If you'd like, I can put one of my own men on him."

Collins looked surprised, and Denton worried he might have pushed it too far, supporting her suspicions over one of his own men. He laid his hand on her knee to distract her. "Can I be honest with you, Monica?"

"Oh." Collins flinched a bit. "Please do."

"I suggested my own surveillance because . . . well . . . if it turns out Rodriguez had anything to do with this, I'd like to know first."

"I understand completely," she said, feeling the heat from Denton's hand. "And you needn't worry. Whatever we find on Rodriguez, I'll make sure you know about it."

I had been drawing for a few minutes, my grandmother beside me, but I wasn't getting anywhere.

"It is . . . an *explosion*," she said, her eyes closed. "But I cannot tell you more. I cannot see more than that."

"And do you know where this explosion is happening?"

"No sé. Es un . . . presentimiento."

We were both into feelings these days.

I tried to get more information, but it was all she could

come up with, so I put it aside and told her that I thought the unsub had been in my apartment.

She crossed herself, but did not seem surprised. She said she had been worried for days, that she had consulted the *orishas* and set up the *bóveda* all for me. She said she wished I was part of the faith and she could make me a saint.

"Me? A saint?" I laughed.

"*Pórtate bien,*" she said, *behave,* then asked what else had happened.

I didn't want to tell her about Cordero and my fears that I'd become a suspect.

She looked into my eyes and laid her hand on my heart. "There is a problem, *aquí adentro.* Sometimes we anger the *orishas* and we do not know it. Sometimes it is not our fault and still the gods are angry with us."

I knew exactly what I had done to piss off the gods, but couldn't say it.

"There are things we can do, Nato, to scare away the *espiritus malévolos.*" She explained about receiving Eleggua and the warriors. Then she draped one of the beaded necklaces around my neck and I didn't fight her. It felt strangely comforting.

She smiled, but it faded fast. "I do not have the power. It

should be a *babalao*." A male priest of the highest order with power over the future, she explained. A part of me wished he were here. My whole life I had resisted, but now I wanted to believe. I was like the dying man who has never been to church who suddenly wants the sacrament.

My *abuela* plucked a double-headed ax covered with red and white beads out of a shrine. She explained it was a symbol for Chango, god of thunder and lightning, and very powerful. It looked as if a kid had made it, half the beads fallen off. My cynic's mind flipped back on: How could this hokey piece of fetish folk art possibly have any power?

My grandmother seemed to know instinctively what I was thinking. "The *orishas* will forgive you."

She gave me new candles for my apartment and told me to create an Eleggua by the door. "*Haslo, chacho. Esto es importante.*" She gave me beads and shells. "For the Eleggua's face, for his *ojos y boca.*"

Then she told me to tear off a little piece of the drawing I had been making and put it under the Eleggua.

"Why?"

"Because he is an enemy and if you place him under the Eleggua he will lose his power. And it would be good if . . . you sprinkled some blood on the Eleggua."

"*Like what?* Kill a chicken or something? Perform some sort of voodoo rite?"

The muscles in my grandmother's face tightened with anger, and I was immediately sorry. "*Perdón, uela.*"

"It is not voodoo. You know that. I never do *el sacrificio*, but now you must make *el ofrecimiento*, maybe some coconut and candy."

I was tempted to make a joke, ask whether the Eleggua preferred Snickers to red licorice, but I didn't dare.

"*Algo rojo*," my grandmother said, which sort of spooked me as I'd just been thinking about licorice, *red* licorice.

She lit more candles, took my hand, asked me to pray along with her, and I did.

It's a funny thing when one chooses to believe. I knew

people, serious business types, who believed in feng shui, who rearranged their furniture so that they faced the door to invite money in, who placed tiny Buddha statues in corners to bring them luck. I'd always scoffed at them and here I was thinking that as soon as I left my grandmother's apartment I was going to stop in Central Park to collect rocks for a god to ward off evil, and buy him some red licorice in case he got hungry.

When I got back to my apartment I found a big bowl, put the rocks into it, and wound the beads around them. I felt a little foolish but couldn't ignore that one of my *abuela*'s visions had already proved prescient, and another—her description of my apartment and an evil presence—rang too true. I tried laying the shells onto the rocks to create the face, but they kept falling off, so I resorted to a glue stick. It was like a sixth-grade arts and crafts project, but I got into it, gluing down the shells to create the eyes and mouth. I didn't know what to do with the licorice and ended up sticking it in around the edges of the bowl. They looked like headless, flowerless stems.

I spent a minute staring at my creation, wondering if I'd finally lost my mind, then figured what the hell, and pricked my finger with a pin. Three droplets of blood landed on the stone and were instantly absorbed into its porous surface. It was as if the Eleggua had eaten it. Then I tore a corner off one of my sketches, slid it under the rock, placed the whole thing beside my front door, stood back, and shook my head.

Rodriguez, you are definitely losing it.

But I didn't stop. I took the glass-encased candles with pictures of Chango and Babalu-Aye that my *abuela* had given me and put one in my living room, the other in my kitchen window. I had no idea if that was right. Maybe Babalu-Aye didn't like the cold and shouldn't be in the window; maybe Chango needed sunlight? I switched the candles. I had no idea why, it just felt right. Then I stripped off my clothes, lay down on my bed, and for the first time in twenty-four hours fell into a deep sleep.

46

Terri spread the first set of the Cordero crime scene photos
across her desk. They showed the superintendent lying face-
down in a pool of blood from every conceivable angle; the
second set, details of the body; the third, pictures of evidence collected by the CS team—the unsub's drawing, a
pizza box, a matchbook, a half-smoked cigarette, a pencil.
At first none of it registered. But the next group of photos,
these taken after the body had been removed, stopped her.

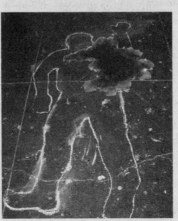

Terri shuffled through the evidence photos again. She had to be sure of what she was looking at.

Her hand was shaking as she called the G. She needed to know if they had this too.

Terri had called, rousing me from a deep sleep to say she was coming right over.

I was still a little groggy, but when she slid a crime scene photograph onto my kitchen counter, I was wide awake.

"Please tell me this isn't *your* pencil."

I tried to think. Did I have a pencil with me when I went down to see Cordero? I didn't think so, but my thoughts were bouncing around like a ball in a pinball machine. "Maybe it fell out of my pocket when I leaned over to see the drawing."

She placed a second photo in front of me, an outline of where Cordero's body had been, the pencil inside it. "The pencil was *under* Cordero's body."

She didn't have to spell it out.

"Maybe . . . it was Cordero's," I said, though I knew it sounded lame. "The unsub must have stolen it. He stalked me, right? We know that because he saw my tattoo. Then he breaks into my place, steals a pencil, and, Jesus, Terri, he's setting me up!" My head was pounding again. I got some aspirin, Terri watching me the whole time, that look of doubt registering in the narrowing of her eyes and tightened mouth.

"I thought you believed me."

"I do, but—" She shook her head. "This isn't going to look good."

She didn't have to tell me that. I took a deep breath. "And there's more."

"What?"

"The new drawing, the one of Cordero . . . You thought it looked different and . . . it does." I took a deep breath. "He's copying my style. The softer pencil—" I tapped the crime scene photo of the Ebony pencil. "I'll bet he made the drawing with this pencil—with *my* pencil. And that little detail you noticed—the one of the mouth drawn on the side? It's a direct copy of a sketch I made—which I no longer have. He's been in my apartment, Terri. How else could he have my sketch—and my pencil?"

"Oh, Jesus, Rodriguez. The G is running DNA on that pencil. A chewed pencil equals saliva. Saliva equals DNA."

"How do you know that?"

"I called. I pretended I already knew. As soon as I saw the picture of the pencil I knew they'd be testing it, so I asked when the DNA results would be ready. Some techie told me he didn't know, that they were backed up, which, thank God, is the only good news." She sighed. "I'd say we're looking at a matter of days."

I eased myself into a chair, trying to comprehend the extent of the nightmare. "I'll go to them, tell them before they find out."

"Tell them *what*? That it's *your* pencil they found under Cordero's body? That a phantom you cleaned up after took it from your apartment to plant at the murder scene, along with a sketch that you say looks like *you* drew it?" She stopped me before I could say anything. "Your DNA isn't on file, is it?"

"No, of course not."

"Okay. So let's say they get the DNA results from the pencil in two days. Then it's another two days before they think to test yours."

"So what are you saying?"

"That we've got about three or four days."

Dolores Rodriguez had first consulted Eleggua because that was the way it was always done. Eleggua, messenger of the gods, who had cured Olodumare was always the first to be honored in any ceremony. Now she lifted the shrine from the floor, poured rum over the rocks, and sprinkled the surface with shredded coconut, though she knew the *orisha* favored the blood of roosters and turtles. She promised herself if things did not improve—if the feeling something bad was going to happen to her beloved Nato continued—she would find someone who would help. She would do anything to protect her grandson.

She stood over the Eleggua and recited the prayer she had memorized in English.

"Divine Messenger, do not confuse me. Divine Messenger, do not confuse me. Let someone else be confused. Turn my suffering around. Give me the blessing of the *calabash*. Owner of all four corners, head of the paths, my Father, remove evil so Nato can walk without death."

Then she made her way from shrine to shrine, offering cornmeal to Chango, sunflower seeds to Osain, toasted corn to Ochosi, and finally dripped almond oil over Inle. She sat on a pew and asked all of the Santerian gods to watch over her grandson and protect him from those who would harm him. Then she tied a scarf over her hair, wrapped a shawl around her shoulders, and headed over to Santa Cecilia to ask the same of Jesus.

47

The Cordero crime scene photos and drawing were pinned to the corkboard wall behind Monica Collins's desk.

"We should be getting DNA results soon," she said.

She and her men, Archer and Richardson, along with profiler Roberta Schteir, had just reviewed the bureau's file on Nathan Rodriguez and watched the taped interview he'd done with Collins.

"He looks nervous, doesn't he?" said Collins.

"You would be nervous too, Agent Collins," said Schteir. "Everyone is nervous in that sort of situation. It's a normal human response. Of course having a guilty conscience compounds it."

"I say we search his place," said Richardson. "Take away his crayons and pencils."

"It's a little more complicated than that," said Collins, thinking of her conversation with Perry Denton. "If Rodriguez allows the search, that's one thing, we would not have to get a warrant. But any search, if we come up empty, will be an embarrassment for both the NYPD and the bureau. This is a serious allegation. We can't search a cop's premises without hard evidence."

"The timing is perfect," said Richardson. "ME says the vic was killed between ten and midnight. Rodriguez was back from Boston by seven, home all night, and admits to being in Cordero's apartment around eleven-thirty. Damn close."

"Too close," said Archer.

"It's not enough," said Collins.

"What if he runs?" asked Richardson.

"I don't see that happening," said Collins. "He doesn't know we're really looking at him."

Richardson glanced back at the computer screen. The interview with Rodriguez was playing again. "He sure does look nervous."

"Rodriguez is carrying a lot of pain," said Schteir. "His father, a cop, shot and killed when he was a teenager. And if this latest wrinkle is true"—she tapped the report from Cold Case—"we might be looking at something much more serious."

"It isn't conclusive," said Collins.

"I said *might,* Agent Collins. But there is certainly some ambiguity according to what these detectives have turned up."

"How come the PD was already investigating this?" asked Richardson. "They have some suspicion about Rodriguez?"

"The Cold Case detectives said Detective Russo came to them to reopen the Juan Rodriguez shooting, but asked them to keep it quiet," said Collins.

"Do we know why she did that?" asked Schteir.

"No," said Collins. "But I'll find out."

Agent Archer was skimming the Cold Case report. "So they now have DNA that was not available twenty years ago."

"Yes, and it's being fed through the Department of Justice DNA data bank to see if they can find a match."

"Is Rodriguez in the bank?"

"He hasn't turned up, no."

"So that will fall to us?" asked Archer.

Collins was thinking again about her conversation with Perry Denton and the surprise follow-up call, the invitation to dinner. "It's better if the PD takes care of that in-house.

Once they get all the data-bank updates, they will undoubtedly collect DNA from Rodriguez for comparison. That would be standard operating procedure. And once they get his DNA they will turn it over to us." Denton had promised her that. "That way we get it without having to step on their toes or embarrass them." Collins looked at her men, and managed a smile for Roberta Schteir. She suspected that anything she said would be reported and was careful in her choice of words. "There's a solid team sorting through everything at Quantico. This case will not get away from us."

"But it seems odd," said Archer. "I mean, Rodriguez *wanting* to be on the PD case."

"He was asked on by Russo," said Collins.

"It's not uncommon to find that a killer has been close to a case," said Schteir. "How many times has an unsub been found in the crime scene photographs of bystanders to a crime?"

"Yeah," said Archer, "but there's still some distance there. This is up close and personal. I mean, committing a murder while you're actually on the case?"

"Well, here's one for you," said Schteir. "Martin Smithson, Seattle PD, investigating officer in the deaths of six young women raped and murdered between 1998 and 2000. Smithson *volunteered* to head up the investigation and . . . *he* was the one who had killed them. Being literally on the case could be viewed as a brilliant move. Rodriguez would know everything the PD was doing and be one step ahead of them. Think about it. You're a killer, a cool, manipulative, narcissistic personality who thinks you are not only above the law, but above society's rules. How would it feel to push the envelope that much further, to commit a heinous act right under the nose of authority?" Schteir thought a moment. "I found Rodriguez to be an amiable, charming guy. But I don't have to tell you that fits a whole category of sociopaths."

"Bundy, for one," said Collins.

Schteir nodded. "You ever read the transcripts of Albert DeSalvo, the Boston Strangler? In it, DeSalvo describes a family gathering where his sister says, 'I'm taking judo lessons to protect myself,' and DeSalvo says, 'So you think you can handle the Strangler?' and she says 'Yes,' so he gets her in a stranglehold and says, 'Try and get out of this!' and practically kills her while everyone is sitting around laughing—at least that's the way DeSalvo describes it. You see what I'm saying?"

"Yes," said Collins, happy to find some commonality with the Quantico profiler. "David Berkowitz would join in conversations with his fellow postal workers about the Son of Sam, about whether or not the guy was crazy, and say things like, 'I hope they catch that son of a bitch!' "

"And he'd *sing* after each killing."

"And DeSalvo would go home, have dinner, and play with his kids right after committing rape and murder."

Archer looked from Collins to Schteir. He had a feeling the two women could go on like this for hours. "Okay, I get the point. But then Rodriguez screwed up, right? I mean, if we're looking at him for this, he's not so smart after all."

"Could be that he's gotten tired," said Schteir. "Ready to get caught." She scanned the bureau stats on Rodriguez. "He's a loner, never married, and certainly has the talent to make the drawings. And there's the father issue."

"Okay," said Archer, thinking it through. "But our unsub is targeting minorities. He's a hate killer. And Rodriguez is Puerto Rican. Does that make any sense?"

"I'm sure you know that serial killers hunt in their own pack," said Schteir.

"He's the product of *two* minorities," said Collins.

"And he probably took a lot of grief for that growing up," Richardson added.

"We could be looking at self-hatred turned outward," said Schteir. "Eradicating people like himself, symbolically wiping himself out, killing the part of himself he despises."

"I don't know. Plenty of people take crap for being Puerto Rican or Jewish or black," said Archer, thinking about his own life experiences. "And they don't become serial killers."

"Absolutely correct," said Schteir. "There is always the unknown component. What makes one person, say, merely sensitive, and another, a killer. Science is investigating that, and one day we may have the answer. Look, I'm not saying Rodriguez is your man. I'm just saying it's a *possibility*."

"So we wait for the DNA," said Richardson.

"Yes," said Collins.

Schteir glanced up at the Cordero crime scene pictures, then at the recent sketch. She plucked it off the wall. "You must have copies of earlier drawings left at the scenes, yes?"

"Of course," said Collins. "Why?"

"I'm not sure," said Schteir. "But there's something about this one that's a little different, isn't there?"

48

I had become a suspect. It seemed inconceivable, but true.

Terri promised she'd help, but didn't say how. She told me to be patient, but didn't tell me how to do that either.

I couldn't sit still. My head was throbbing, muscles in my neck and jaw at a level of tightness I did not think humanly possible. Was I going to have a heart attack? A stroke? It felt like it. I took two aspirin. I chewed my cuticles. I called Julio.

The law offices of Russell, Bradley and Roach looked like the fanciest funeral parlor in the world, everything muted and gray, including Julio's office. Even Julio was in gray pinstripes.

"*Pana,* take it easy. No way they think this is you."

I had told him about Cordero's murder, my tattoo in the sketch along with the detail that was exactly like one of my drawings, my pencil at the scene; that it was only a matter of time before they connected it all to me.

"Circumstantial," he said, trying hard not to frown. "All of it."

I reminded him he was a real estate lawyer, not criminal, and he kidded me and tried to make me laugh but his face betrayed him, the worry impossible to hide.

Then his phone rang. He was late for a meeting. *Mi pana a broqui,* my bodyguard, had to go. I painted on a smile and told him I'd be fine. He said I should go to his apartment and hang out till he got off work, that he'd think of what to do. But I did not want to be a child who needed babysitting.

I just went home.

I checked the Eleggua. It looked ridiculous, wilted licorice sticks lying over the rocks. I thought about taking the candy out before it attracted roaches, but didn't, because I was afraid to offend the gods.

I'd never felt like this in my life. But this was like no other time in my life. I tried to think of what I could do, and there was only one thing: I had to finish the sketch.

I went to get my pad and it wasn't there. I had a moment of panic. *Had he been here again?*

Then I remembered I'd left it at my grandmother's.

My *abuela* was happy to see me, but worried too. I told her I just needed my drawing pad. I could see she wanted to ask me a million questions, but controlled herself, and left me alone. I went into the living room and opened my pad to review the sketches I'd made of the unsub's face so far.

I sharpened a pencil and waited for inspiration, something to guide me, but nothing happened. I closed my eyes and tried to relax, but I couldn't clear my mind enough to let anything in.

My grandmother came into the room with a beer—an excuse to interrupt me. She saw the look on my face, sat down beside me, and touched my cheek. It was all it took to reduce me to her little *nene.* I told her what was going on, how I feared I was already a suspect.

"This is *loco.*" She shook her head and muttered, *"Coño carajo,"* words I had never heard come out of her mouth.

"This man—*este demonio desgraciado*—he has put a curse on you."

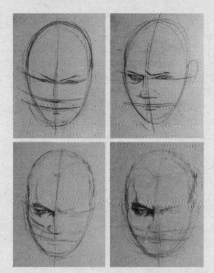

"No," I said, trying hard to look confident for my grandmother. "It's just a . . . mistake."

"No hay errores, chacho. Everything happens for a reason." She stood up and told me to wait. I could hear her on the phone in the other room. A minute later she was back.

"Entra."

"Where?"

My grandmother stood over me, all five feet two inches, hands on hips, eyes narrowed. "You are coming with me, *chacho,* and you will not say no."

I could see she was serious, but I was no longer feeling like little *nene*; not quite grown up, but old enough to ask where she was planning to take me.

"To the *botánica.*"

"What for? A radish root? A frog? This is serious, *uela,* and you can't make it go away with herbs and incantations."

"And *you* have fixed it? You, who are here now in my

house with your pad and pencils and looking like hell?" Her face was screwed up tight. I'd never seen her like this. "I have done what I could, Nato, prayed to Chango, Osain, and Ochosi, but it is not working. I do not know why, but the forces have turned against you. It is time to try something more powerful."

"More powerful than *what*?" I asked.

"Than me, or you. *Ven*."

49

We walked six blocks, my grandmother nervously playing with a strand of rosary beads. We turned onto 118th Street and I saw it, the *bótanica*. It looked like a junk shop, signs in English for party favors and gifts mixed in with hand-painted lettering in Spanish.

"It looks closed," I said, with a sense of relief. A part of me wanted to run.

"No *para nosotros*." My grandmother rapped on the window. "I know the *consejos espirituales*. She is expecting us, and she will help."

A moment later a big dark-skinned woman opened the door.

"Nato," said my grandmother. "This is María Guerrero."

Guerrero, the Spanish word for warrior. She looked it.

"*Entra, mi hijo.*" She put her hand on my arm to steer me in.

Inside, the place was small, crowded with herbal remedies, statuary, glass-encased candles, fake flowers and real ones, a large plastic Madonna beside one painted black. There were rows of multicolored beaded necklaces hanging from hooks above mundane religious articles one could find in a Christian gift shop. On the floor near the door, a shrine with cowrie shells not unlike the one I'd created at home. A few weeks ago I would have been shaking my head and sighing, but I had just made my own Eleggua, so how could I?

"You know Quincy Jones?" asked Maria Guerrero. "A very nice man. He comes whenever he is in Nueva York." She smiled, showing two front teeth plated with gold. "My customers are black and white, Catholics and Jews. Only two days ago, a rabbi. I am a Catholic, but I welcome all people. But I am also a *santera,* and before that an *espiritista.* I was born an *espiritista.*" She looked me over and said she was glad I was wearing a white shirt or she would have made me change. I remembered what my *abuela* had said the last time about my white shirt, and I knew white was an important color for Santeria, the *bóveda* referred to as the *Mesa Blanca,* the white table, a color of purity, empowerment, associated with Obatala, the sculptor of human form, all the lessons my *abuela* had taught me coming back to me.

Maria Guerrero laid her hand on my chest and told me there was much pain in my heart. At first I flinched, but she kept it there for several minutes and I began to relax, the warmth from her hand spreading through me. Then she touched my forehead and asked how long I had suffered from *dolor de cabeza.*

"Headache," my grandmother translated.

How did she know?

She recommended tea made from rosemary, plucked a statue off the *Mesa Blanca,* Saint Jude, patron of the hopeless, waved him over my head, and said, "For the *dolor de cabeza.*" It seemed ridiculous, but seconds later my headache disappeared. I touched my head, trying to locate the pain that had been there a moment ago.

"Muy bien," she said, and was right. I was much better.

But how was it possible?

She closed her eyes and said, *"Dios está en la atmósfera."*

"God is in the air," said my grandmother.

I looked around the shop, at the beads and candles, dusty shelves crowded with herbal remedies and statuary, my rational brain still protesting. *There isn't room for God among this mess.*

Maria Guerrero said, "This is no *bilongo*."

"Witchcraft," said my grandmother and frowned at me.

Then the *espiritista* said it was time, and my grandmother handed her a wad of bills. I didn't know how much, but the bill on the outside was a twenty and the wad was thick; it could have been a couple of hundred. I was appalled, but my grandmother gave me a look and I didn't say anything.

Maria Guerrero led us into the back room. It was stark and simple, in contrast to the packed storefront—white walls dotted with a few pictures of saints and a *Mesa Blanca,* the focal point, with plastic saints, glasses of water, a wooden crucifix wrapped with beads, angel figurines, books, and candles waiting to be lit.

I was trying hard to be open-minded—*was it really any different from a church, a synagogue, a Buddhist temple?*— but a part of me was still resisting, having trouble giving myself over, believing.

"Is *importante* to believe." Maria Guerrera touched my head, then my heart.

It was as if she'd just read my mind. She smiled, then excused herself.

When she was out of the room I turned to my grandmother. "You gave her money."

"*Por supuesto*. She is working. It is the *derecho,* and expected."

"This is crazy, *ulea*."

My grandmother put a finger to my lips and told me to be *"tranquilo,"* that Maria Guerrero would hear me. Then she took my hand and held it firmly. "There are things we do not understand, Nato. Things that are not easy to explain because they come from another place, *el más alto,* from the *espiritus.*

But when we see them we start to believe. You must believe." She looked into my eyes. "Sometimes it is necessary to believe in something to get out of something else, *entiendes*?"

I didn't know if I understood or not. I had spent a lifetime of not believing. Could I start believing now? I took a couple of deep breaths and tried to relax. My grandmother squeezed my hand, sending support and love while trying to telegraph her entire belief system into my being. I could see it in her face, every muscle constricted with concentration.

Maria Guerrero returned wearing a white smock. In her right hand she was holding a knife.

I took a step backward.

"The *cuchilla*," she said softly. "Used to cut through problems." She laid it on the *Mesa Blanca* and picked up one of the books. *"Colección de Oraciones escogidas,"* she said, and my *abuela* translated, "Prayer book."

She crushed some powdered incense into a small iron pot and lit it, whisked the smoke into the air, handed me a box of wooden matches, and asked me to light two white candles on the table.

My hands were shaking, but I did.

She recited a prayer from the book, turned off the lights, and the room took on a warm glow. She touched my hands and they stopped shaking; tapped my forehead and my thoughts stopped racing; drew her fingers across my chest and my breathing and heartbeat slowed. Then she said she was going to perform a *limpia,* a ritual cleansing. She sent my grandmother into the front of the *bótanica*. She came back with an aerosol dispenser decorated with a bird and a Native American in full feather headdress, the words CAST OFF EVIL printed on the label. She gave it to Maria Guerrero, who sprayed it toward the ceiling, the altar, and finally on me. It didn't have any detectable scent and it seemed like nothing but bottled air with a fancy label.

But I felt something, a sense of being physically lighter,

as if I'd lost weight or someone had lifted something off my chest.

Then she started lighting the other candles, and explained they were for "*protección*," brown to ward off ill will, the black to help me against my enemies. I tried hard to believe her. I wanted it to be true.

She closed her eyes. "I see a man and he means to do you harm. And I see a *corona*."

"He's wearing a crown?" I asked.

"No." She shook her head, eyes still closed. "Not on the man. The *corona* is . . . *está dentro del circulo*."

The crown symbol in *The White Man's Bible* that had appeared in my grandmother's vision and in the crime scene drawing.

There were things to be done, she said, and sprinkled me with powders and pungent herbs and spoke of Eleggua, who would either open or close the roads for me, and I thought: *Please open them.* She told me to stop eating red meat and potato chips—and how she knew I lived on burgers and chips I didn't know, but she was making a believer out of me. She said I had to change my life patterns, start eating well and exercising, stop drinking beer and engaging in pre-marital sex. That last one got to me, but I nodded. She slipped a beaded necklace around my neck. "*Un collar*," she said. As she did, the muscles in my neck eased in a way they had not in weeks.

She asked me to take off my shirt, and when I hesitated my grandmother started tugging it out of my waistband like I was a kid, so I took it off and stood before the two women feeling vulnerable and naked.

Maria Guerrero broke an egg into a pitcher of water and poured it over my neck. It oozed down my back and chest. I shivered, a kind of electric energy coursing through my body. Maybe it was nerves, but I didn't think so. It was unlike anything I'd ever felt before, anything I had ever experienced.

Then she snapped blossoms off gladiolas, crushed them

in her hands and rubbed them onto my chest. There was a slight burning sensation, not unpleasant, but it sent more shivers rippling through my body, and my gut churned.

"Somos parte de la naturaleza," said Maria Guerrero, talking about plants versus people, and how human beings were consumed with vanity and how I had to give up my ego or I would be in trouble.

My desire to believe was battling with my doubt and cynicism, and standing there covered in slimy water, crushed flowers over my heart, the room began to spin, pictures of saints coming in and out of focus, and I thought I might faint. The women took hold of my arms. My grandmother hummed an old lullaby she'd sing to me when I was a boy and Maria Guerrero mumbled some Spanish incantation, and I started to feel better, the dizziness abating, my mind clearing, stomach settling.

Maria Guerrero cleaned the egg off my chest with my white shirt. She rolled it into a ball and told me I had to dump it into a trash bin as soon as I left the store, that the shirt had absorbed the evil spirits, and I must now cast them off. Then she prepared a jar of water with crushed herbs and colored it with a blue dye and told me that over the next week I was to pour portions of it over my hands and it would keep me safe and pure.

When she was quiet I asked a question. "This man who you saw, the one who wants to do me harm, how do I find him?"

Maria Guerrero opened my sketch pad and looked at my drawings.

"Tienes un talento," she said. "You can see things other people tell you and you can see this man." She reached out with her fingertips and gently closed my eyes.

When she did, he was there. But just for a second. Like the burning man I'd seen with Denton, but much faster.

"He was there," I said. "But he's vanished."

Maria Guerrero took one of my pencils and swirled it over the votive candles. Then she handed it to me and I started to draw.

Time became elastic, impossible to gauge. I just kept working, the image coming to me.

When I looked at my drawings, I had done it. He was there. On the page.

I was amazed, speechless, staring at this face I had drawn: the tightly knit brows, the taut scowling mouth, all the facial anatomy conspiring to create a classic face of anger to the point of fury and hatred.

"You have seen this man," said Maria Guerrero. It wasn't a question and she was right—I had seen him.

"But where?" I *had* no idea.

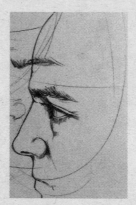

"Eleggua will open the road," she said. *"Es tuyo. Tú lo tienes."*

He is yours now. You have him.

What I always said to victims but never fully believed until this moment.

"You will no longer see him in your mind," she said.

"But how will I find him?" I asked.

"In your own way," she said.

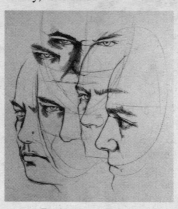

* * *

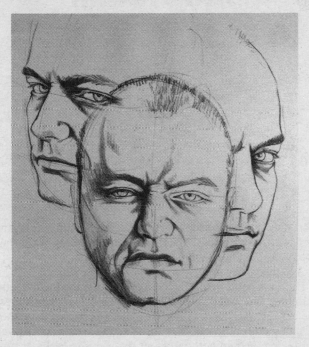

Outside, I tossed my stained white shirt into a garbage can and felt another wave of unexpected relief. I walked my grandmother home, jacket buttoned up against the cold and to hide the fact that I was shirtless. I kept trying to remember where I had seen the man I had just drawn.

"*Para empezar,*" my grandmother said. "You are trying too hard. *Deja que suceda.*"

I knew she was right, but I couldn't stop.

At the entrance to her apartment building she told me she was proud of me and loved me, that she would pray to Jesus for me. She was going to change clothes now and go to church. Then she kissed my cheek and made the sign of the cross.

50

He stands in the shadow of an abandoned building slath-ered with city notices, watches a kid balancing a blaring boom box pass by, bobbing to the salsa music.

And there they are.

His optic nerve snaps pictures of the man and the old lady with him. He watches them hug and kiss. The man leaves, the old lady begins to climb the stairs. As he takes another mental picture, the old lady turns and sees him, dark eyes narrowing, and something about the way she looks at him causes him to shudder.

He slinks back into the shadows and waits for the door to close behind her. Then he takes another picture. This is just what he needed.

He thanks God for the idea that has just come to him.

51

When I got home I was flying, adrenaline pumping. I had completed the drawing. It was astonishing. A miracle.

But now what?

I had to show the sketch to Terri, have her run it through every possible mug shot on file and computer. But I did not want to go to the station. I called her cell, got voice mail, and told her to call me.

I closed my eyes and tried to picture the face I had drawn, but could not. What Maria Guerrero had said was true: Now that I'd put him on paper I could no longer see him in my mind. I had the drawing; now all I had to do was figure out who he was and where I had seen him. But how?

I heard Maria Guerrero's voice. *In your own way.*

Of course.

I sat down at my work table, flipped to a clean page in my pad, and started drawing.

What was it? I couldn't place it

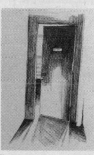

and it didn't tell me anything. But there was something about it on the edge of my psyche.

I stared at it, but was trying too hard.

I called Terri's cell, left another message, then tried her office.

A man answered, O'Connell, I was pretty sure. I hesitated, didn't know if I could trust him, but took a chance.

"O'Connell?"

"Rocky?"

"Yeah."

"Listen, there's trouble here," he said. "But I can't talk."

"Trouble with what?"

"The G has something."

"DNA?"

"I don't know. Just that they want to see you," he whispered.

I froze a moment, not sure what to say, then, "Where's Russo?"

"With Denton. I can't talk."

I hung up, my hand shaking. They must have gotten the DNA results from the pencil. And now they'd come looking for mine. But this was too fast, wasn't it? Maybe I was wrong. But what else could it be? And what was going on with Terri and Denton? Whatever it was, I'd know soon enough.

I looked back at the sketches I'd made and it happened. One of those brain flashes. I saw it, the lettering on the door, though I couldn't make sense of it till I got it down on paper.

Of course. This had to be where I had seen him.

I called the precinct and asked for Detective Schmid in Special Victims.

She answered on the third ring.

I tried to sound casual. "Hi, it's Nate Rodriguez. Remember me?"

"Sure, the sketch artist. You did a good job for me. And you know we caught that guy, the rapist."

"Yeah, I heard that." Two good signs; she was not acting like anything was wrong, and she remembered she owed me.

"So what can I do for you?"

"Public Information is down the hall from you, right?"

"Yes, what about it?"

"That day I did the sketch for you I was there—"

"Why were you in DPI?"

"I wasn't. Not exactly. It was when I was dropping off the sketch." I wasn't sure what to say or how to say it. "I need to find someone in that office."

"Who?"

I described him.

"Has to be Tim Wright. He's the only man in that office. But you won't be asking him any questions."

"Why not?"

"He's been canned."

"When?"

"Just. I don't know the details," said Schmid. "From what I hear he'd been missing lots of days, just not showing up, so they fired him. Why'd you want to talk to him?"

"No longer matters," I said.

I called Public Information.

A receptionist answered.

"I'm calling from . . . Personnel. We're going to need Tim Wright's address and phone number to process his dismissal."

I listened while she tapped on a keyboard. A moment later she gave it to me.

Tim Wright lived in Queens.

I had to reach Terri. We had to go there. But Terri was with Denton. And if I was wrong about Tim Wright, her job would be on the line.

I had to find out if Wright was the man in my sketch. I didn't know for sure. But it was the guy I had seen in the hallway coming out of Public Information. I'd logged his face into my brain. We had exchanged the briefest greeting and he'd smiled. I could see it now, a big smile, all lips, no eye muscles, totally fake.

But I needed proof and had to get it now. While I still had a chance. Once they had my DNA, that was it.

There was no rational way to explain Maria Guerrero or crushed gladiolas or an egg dripped over my neck as the method by which I had completed the sketch. Hell, it sounded crazy to me, how was it going to sound to the cops and the feds?

I called Julio and asked to borrow his car. He asked why, and I said, "Because I need it."

"What's wrong?"

"Nothing."

"You're lying."

"No. I just need your car."

"Hey, *pana,* whatever it is, you can tell me."

"I will. Later."

"You want me to come with you—wherever it is that you won't tell me you're going?"

I wanted to say yes. I wanted my best buddy along with me, but no way. It was bad enough I was going without authorization or back up. I couldn't get him involved.

"I hope you know what you're doing," he said.

I hoped I did too.

I thought about the way I had finished the drawing, and how Maria Guerrero had said I would find the man in my own way. I needed to keep going, have faith, and trust my instincts. I had to believe.

"You have to trust me, Julio."

"I always trust you," said Julio. "You know that."

"Then let me have your damn car and stop asking questions."

"**Q**ué pasa, man?" The parking attendant, who knew me, tried to make conversation, but I just nodded. I slid into Julio's dark blue Mercedes SLK350 Roadster, drove it out of the lot, and pulled to the curb, my hands shaking too badly to drive.

This was crazy, a mistake. I needed backup. A witness. A partner.

There was only one person for the job and I didn't know if she would do it, or if I could ask. I'd pretty much lived my life without asking anything of anyone and now, when I needed to, I didn't know how to do it.

A couple, arm in arm, passed in front of my windshield like a framed video, a picture of happiness, smiling faces, actually looking at each other.

Maybe I was afraid of asking because then I'd have to give something and I didn't know if I had it in me.

The couple disappeared and the glass became a monitor, images flashing across it every time I blinked: *Cordero dead, my pencil at the scene, the drawing with my tattoo.*

Terri answered her cell on the second ring.

"It's me."

"Where are you?"

"Did you get my messages?"

"Yes. But—" I heard her take a breath. "They've got DNA from the pencil," she whispered. "They want to test you."

I could see it all happening—my DNA matching, the arrest, trial, my mother and grandmother sitting behind me in court.

"Are you there?"

"Yes." I tried to ignore the nightmare in my head. "I finished the sketch. The portrait of the unsub."

"How?"

I didn't know what to say, how to explain it. "I need to show it to you and I need you to . . ."

"What?"

"I need you to help me."

A moment passed. I pictured Terri, cell phone to her ear, considering my plea, weighing consequences. "Where are you?"

I gave her the address.

"Stay there."

I sat in Julio's car wondering what was going to happen next. Would Terri turn me in? Would I suddenly be surrounded by cop cars? I didn't know if I trusted her, didn't know what I meant to her, or what she meant to me. I couldn't stop the pictures in my head—a by-product of a life spent inventing them—and right now I saw myself being led into a patrol car, cuffs on my wrists.

The sketch pad was on the seat beside me, open to the finished drawing. I touched the edge of the paper to make sure it was real. Was this man simply a phantom who had been in my head for so long, or was he real? I had to know.

When I looked up I saw Terri's Crown Victoria slowing to a stop. Her window rolled down just beside mine.

"So what you'd do, Rodriguez, steal a car?" She shook her pretty head and smiled.

It opened up something unexpected in me, a flood of emotion, and I laughed to cover it. "Yeah," I said. "Get in before the cops get here." I closed the pad and tried to move the jar of Maria Guerrero's blue water, but too late.

"What the hell is this?" she asked as she slid in.

"If I told you, you wouldn't believe me." I hardly believed it myself.

Then I showed her the sketch.

"I know him," she said. "I mean . . . I've seen him. I'm sure of it."

"His name's Tim Wright. Works out of Public Info, at the station house."

"Jesus Christ. That's it! Where I've seen him."

"He was fired a day or two ago."

"How the hell did you get this, Rodriguez?"

I wasn't sure how to begin, but I realized something: My drawing had been confirmed. It *was* Tim Wright. Terri recognized him. It wasn't total lunacy. "I just did what you've been asking me to do, to draw, and do that transference thing I do, remember?"

Terri's eyes narrowed. There it was again, the look of skepticism.

"You don't believe me?"

"I believe you, Rodriguez, I just don't know how the fuck you do it and . . . it's a little scary, you know?"

I did know.

"You've got to come in," she said.

"Aren't you the person who told me I couldn't, that they had too much that couldn't be explained away—the tattoo, the drawing, my pencil?"

Terri sighed. "I don't see an alternative."

"We go find Wright."

"No. You come in and I'll send out an APB on Wright."

"How? There's no way they can search his premises. Where's your probable cause? What are you going to say to the judge—*Rodriguez concocted a forensic sketch out of thin air, your honor?* Come on, Terri. There's not a judge in New York who will grant you a search warrant, and you know it."

Terri sat there a minute. I could see the doubt shifting to worry or maybe even the onset of fear, eyebrows raised and knit together.

"This is my job, Rodriguez. I do this and it turns out it's not Tim Wright, I'm fucked, you understand what I'm saying? My career, over."

"I know that." I touched her hand. "But I need you to believe in me for all the reasons you wanted me on the case to begin with."

"Stop touching me." She tugged her hand away. "I can't

think if you're touching me." She took a deep breath and let it out in a slow sigh.

I didn't say anything. I just sat back and watched her.

Terri looked back at Nate and tried to make sense of what she was seeing and thinking. Was she actually going to do this, take a chance on this guy? Her luck with men had always been bad and she didn't see why it was suddenly going to change. And this was bigger. Much bigger. Screwing up a relationship was one thing, but screwing up her job—*for a guy*? No, she didn't think so.

"Look, Rodriguez, I just—"

"It's okay," said Nate. "I knew it was a crazy thing to ask you to do. I understand."

"Oh, fuck that," said Terri. She sighed again and touched his hand. "You know how to fucking drive this boat, or what?"

I gripped the steering wheel as I headed over the 59th Street Bridge, Terri right beside me. We hadn't said much after I started driving. I'd told her Wright lived in Queens. She told me again that I was crazy, that *she* was crazy, then she just stared straight ahead. Every few minutes I looked over at her, worry and fear etched on her face, lips tight, lines around her mouth and on her forehead. She didn't have to tell me how she felt.

Crossing the 59th Street Bridge brought me back to when Julio and I were kids and we'd boost a car and drive over to Long Island City, park in some abandoned lot, get stoned, and gaze back at the city floating over the East River like Xanadu, bridges strung like Christmas lights, majestic sky-scrapers lit up winking against a night sky. It was thrilling. Now it was the same bridge, but the thrill was infused with fear. I could have used a little of the dope Julio and I used to smoke.

"So what's with this?" Terri held the jar of blue water up to the light. "You into watercolors?"

I thought about saying yes, but didn't want to lie to her. "It's something . . . from my grandmother. Well, from her friend, actually. It's hard to explain."

"Try me."

I did. I told her about the *bótanica* and the *limpia,* and the way Maria Guerrero had released something that allowed me to finish the drawing.

When I stopped talking Terri was staring at me, mouth open, so I decided not to tell her the part about the egg and the gladiolas. Sometimes less is more.

"And this blue water, I'm figuring it's not Tidy Bowl?"

"It's supposed to keep me safe and pure."

"Probably a little late for purity, but I'll settle for the safe part." She looked down and I followed her glance. The Smith & Wesson was sticking out of my pocket.

"You were planning to do this alone, weren't you?"

"Me? No. Never."

"Bullshit," she said, a wry smile twisting back into worry as the city slid behind us like a memory and Queens came into view.

52

It makes perfect sense to him now, what he's been doing and what he's been working toward for so long. The plan is set. God has told him what to do and he will not fail.

He takes a moment to admire his craft, but no longer needs any props, everything set sharply in his mind. He crumples the drawing in his hand and drops it into the wastebasket.

He stares up at the ceiling as if he can see into his perfect living room—the matching sofa and armchairs, wide-screen

TV, everything he had at one time worked for and thought important. He knows better now. None of it matters, not the sofa, nor the armchairs, not the TV, not even the home itself; not the wife who has left him, nor the child whom she has taken with her.

How long ago was that? A few days, months, a year?

For a moment he wonders if they ever existed. Perhaps he has invented them. Perhaps they were a fiction. He tries to reconstruct their faces, but there is no room in his brain for anything other than the picture of what he is about to do, so big, so extravagant it blots out everything else.

He checks over his supplies. Everything is ready. This is what he has prepared for. This is his moment.

53

"Jesus, is it Twenty-third Street or Twenty-third Avenue?"

"I don't know. I just wrote what the receptionist told me, 202 Twenty-third. How was I to know the numbered streets crossed the same numbered avenues? Whoever devised this system was a fucking sadist!"

"Well, we've been up and down Twenty-third Street and there's no number 202," said Terri. "So it must be Avenue."

I found my way onto Twenty-third Avenue and Terri called out the numbers until we reached number 202, a small one-family brick house on a tiny plot of land. It didn't look like much. But what was I expecting, flames whipping through the roof like the drawing I'd made of my *abuela*'s vision?

"Keep going," she said.

I cruised past, then doubled back and cruised by it again, trying to determine if anyone was home. There was no car in the driveway, but that didn't really tell us anything. I parked across the street and rolled down my window.

"Can you see in?" she asked.

"What, you mean through the walls, like Superman?"

"I meant into any of the windows, but if you can see through the walls, go for it."

The windows were obscured by blinds or drapes.

"This is so fucked," said Terri. "You realize that, don't you?"

"Yeah. I do. But if Wright is the Sketch Artist, he's gone to a lot of trouble to set me up." The irony did not escape me: *Would the real Sketch Artist please stand up?* "He could disappear now and leave me to pay the price. I just need to get some proof . . . to clear my good name." I added that last part to get a smile out of Terri, her face a map of worry. "I'm sorry I dragged you into this."

"Forget it," she said. "I was the one who dragged you into the case."

A good point and I appreciated her saying so.

I glanced down at my drawing, noticed what I'd scribbled in a corner, and pointed it out. "I totally forgot—Wright's telephone number, the receptionist gave it to me."

Terri punched it into her cell.

"Anything?"

"It hasn't even rung yet. Relax." She chewed her lip, cell pressed to her ear. "It's ringing. One . . . two . . . three times."

"What are you going to say?"

Terri clamped her hand over the mouthpiece. "I don't know. Five . . . six . . . seven. No one is picking up. Eight . . . nine . . . ten rings. No machine picking up either." She shut the cell.

"If he's in there, would he answer?"

"Not if he's spotted us sitting here staking out his house."

We sat for another fifteen minutes, waiting for something to happen. When nothing did, Terri said, "Come on."

She reached for the door handle, but I stopped her.

"What? You drag me out here and now you're going to wuss out on me?"

"No. Give me your hand."

"We don't have time for a Hallmark moment, Rodriguez."

"Just give me your hand."

I opened the jar of colored water and let some trickle onto

her hands, then mine. It didn't feel foolish. It felt right, like part of a ritual, as if I were preparing us for battle.

"Oh, Jesus. Is this like *The Exorcist* or what?"

"It can't hurt," I said.

She gave me a look as she dried her hands on my sleeve, then checked the service revolver she had holstered beneath her jacket. "You ready?"

"Yes," I said. I'd been getting ready since I started the Sketch Artist's portrait, from the minute I drew the first pencil stroke on paper, but hadn't known it until that moment.

I got out of the car, heart beating fast, hand gripping the revolver in my pocket. I stared at the house as we got closer, trying to feel if there was a presence inside, but obviously my gift for feeling things did not include houses.

Terri pressed the bell and we heard it chime somewhere inside. "What are you going to say?"

Terri thought a moment. "That I'm from NYPD Personnel and need to discuss a few things about his dismissal, how's that?"

"If Wright is the unsub he probably knows who you are."

"Right. Okay. I'll give him a version of the truth. That I'm investigating a case, that's all. Maybe he'll play along, try and act normal."

"Or try to make a break for it, or—"

"Well, it's too late to turn around and change our minds. You wanted to do this, Rodriguez, remember?" She tried the bell again. There was no answer.

"I'll check the back," I said.

"Okay," she said. "But wait for me."

Terri watched Rodriguez round the corner of the house and disappear. She had to stop herself from calling out "Be careful." Then she sidled over to a window and peered through a gap in the drapes. She could make out a couch and a big flat-screen TV. There were no lights on. Maybe he wasn't home.

Or maybe he was waiting for them.

She knew he was patient, good at planning, taking his time. He could be watching her right now.

The backyard was small, a garage taking up half the space. It offered some privacy from the homes behind it. I took the concrete stairs that led up to the back door. I tried to see in, but couldn't. I went back down the stairs and glanced up at the house. There was a window open about an inch, but it was eight feet off the ground. I dragged a metal trash can over. It just barely supported my weight, the top starting to cave in. I got a grip on the ledge, but the window wouldn't budge. I didn't stop to think, just pulled my shirt down over my hand and smashed the glass. It splintered, shards bouncing off my feet. I shoved the window open, hoisted myself up and in. The trash can fell over with a bang. If anyone was home I was making quite an entrance.

I landed heavy on my feet, rocked a few times to get my balance. I was in the kitchen. If Wright was home, he'd be coming for me. I felt an eerie presence, nothing I could explain, but I was chilled. I stood perfectly still; the only sound my breathing, then something else, a dripping sound.

I looked down and saw blood on the floor. *My blood.* I'd cut my hand pretty badly, though I hadn't felt it. *Great*, I thought, *leave more DNA*. But it no longer mattered.

I peered through an archway into the living room. It seemed quiet. Then a shadow slid across my vision. I sucked in a breath and raised my gun.

It was a moment before I realized it was Terri, outside the window, looking in.

I took a step closer to the archway. Was he hiding behind it? I held my breath and made my move, spun left, then right, gun straight out in front of me. There was no one there. But I still felt that eerie presence. My heart and lungs were meeting somewhere in my throat.

I made it across the living room and opened the two locks as quietly as possible.

Terri stepped into the room glaring, leaned into me, and whispered, "I swear to God, Rodriguez, if we get out of here alive I'm going to kill you."

She sounded like she meant it, but it was too late now, we were in and there was no turning back.

We inched our way around the living room, guns drawn, until we were certain it was clear, then headed up the staircase in slow motion, down a hallway, taking turns pivoting into rooms—master bedroom, a child's room, bath, all empty. The kid's room was way too neat, no toys on the floor, shelves that should have held books and games, bare.

"Looks deserted," Terri whispered, just barely audible.

"Maybe." I was trying to analyze why I was so sure we'd come to the right place. There was nothing to confirm it, but I could feel him in the air.

Where would I do my work in a house like this?

I pointed to the floor and Terri got it. We retraced our steps down the stairs, through the living and dining areas, looking for a basement door.

We found it just off the kitchen.

I nodded silently at Terri and she nodded back. I tried the door. It opened into a staircase that disappeared into darkness.

There was a light switch on the wall, but I didn't dare turn it on.

The presence was stronger here. *Could he be down there, waiting for us?*

I locked eyes with Terri, steadied my gun, took the first step. Then another. It felt like a long descent.

At the bottom there was the slight smell of mold and the chill of dampness, and it took a minute for my eyes to adjust to the dark.

The basement was unfinished, concrete-slab floor, half

the room taken up by an oil burner and hot water heater. And another door.

I leaned my ear against it and listened, looked back at Terri, her eyes wide in the dark, and wondered if she was thinking what I was: that if Tim Wright was anything like Carl Karff, he could have an arsenal behind this door and be ready to take us out.

I moved in front of her and tried the doorknob. It wouldn't budge. I ran my hand down the wood. It felt crude and cheap, the kind of prefab door you buy in a lumberyard and put up yourself. I dropped back and leveled a solid kick. The door cracked and splintered off its hinges, and I kept moving, propelled by the force of my own kick, stumbling forward into darkness, blind. And I felt it, that *algo malo* my *abuela* had spoken of.

There is a man in that room with you, Nato.

I managed to stay on my feet and when nothing happened I knew that I was okay, that he wasn't here, though somehow I knew I had found him.

Terri reached out to me, her shadowy form taking on detail. I fumbled along a wall and found the light switch.

I saw the presence I'd been feeling: this shrine to hate.

I recognized the swastikas, Nazi lightning bolts, insignia of the World Church of the Creator; the ones I didn't know were just more proof that a whole lot of people didn't like me. It was ugly stuff, chilling, but there was no time to process it.

The work table was neat: pencils lined up, drawings and folders in stacks. Pinned above it, newspaper articles about the Sketch Artist. It was true, he was proud of his work.

I'd found my proof and didn't have to say it.

"Is there a clue here to what he's planning next?" asked Terri.

I looked down at the stacks of drawings. I didn't know. There were too many.

Terri plucked gloves out of her pocket and we put them on. "We have to take them back to the station."

"Wait. Give me a minute." I needed to think like him. "What was it I said about him based on his drawings—that he was neat and compulsive, right? And his work table confirms it. Everything's in its place. So I'm guessing the top drawings would be the most recent ones, whatever he's planning next."

"But what is it exactly?" Terri tapped one of the drawings that topped a stack.

"A building? I'm not sure." That's when it hit me. It looked like my grandmother's last vision.

The other stacks had similar drawings on top, all variations of this same image, fairly abstract, but it was coming together for me. *But where?* I wondered. *And when?*

I swiped the top drawings off each stack and Terri gasped when we saw what was under them.

"My God, what is he planning, World War III?"

"It looks it," I said. "The question is, where?" I was trying

to stay calm, to think like him, to be organized and obsessive. Everything we needed to know was here, somewhere. I went through the stacks; more images of explosions and mayhem. I opened a folder and found a sketch similar to the one of the black man, Harrison Stone, who'd been shot in Brooklyn.

"This looks like a practice sketch, like

he must have drawn this vic over and over till he got it right."

There was a page of notes in the file too, dates and times, a stalker's journal.

I started riffling through other folders, opening one after another. More sketches with times and dates.

"They're all here," said Terri. "All his vics."

"It's like he's some sort of perverse perfectionist, drawing and redrawing his prey till he gets whatever it is he's after."

We kept looking, hoping to find something that related to those abstracted explosion drawings, but there was nothing.

We scanned the room—the walls covered with posters, the table, the floor—and that's when we found it: one more drawing, crumpled in a small trash can tucked under the table.

I smoothed it out on the table. It took only a few seconds for the image to register and set my body trembling.

"Oh my God."

"What?"

I explained it, stuttering, my fear kicking in, then we

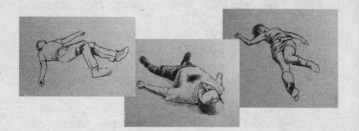

raced up the stairs and out the front door. It no longer mattered who saw us.

The Mercedes engine kicked over and I burned rubber down Twenty-third Avenue. I had one hand on the steering wheel, the other gripping my cell, hitting redial over and over. There was no answer. I pressed my foot to the accelerator and prayed I was not too late. I prayed to Jesus and Chango and every saint and *orisha* I could think of.

I prayed and prayed.

54

I was attempting to weave the Mercedes through a snarl of traffic we'd just hit on the FDR.

"Done," said Terri, snapping her cell shut. "NYPD has an APB out on Wright, Queens PD is sending a CS team to comb through his house, and I called the local PD and told them where to meet us."

"Did they say when they could get there?"

"They'll get there soon. It'll be okay."

I wanted to believe her, but couldn't stop worrying. I lay on my horn, but there was nowhere to go. "How about calling to get us an escort with a siren?"

"They'd have to fight this traffic to find us, and we're not far, are we?"

I noted the signs, the exit coming up. No, we weren't far, but every minute felt like an hour. I swerved the Mercedes onto the shoulder, reached the exit, and took the ramp a lot faster than the suggested thirty miles per hour.

"I've got to call Collins," said Terri. "It kills me to do it, but I'm not going to give the G cause to say I kept them out of this."

"While you're at it, remember to have them call the dogs off *me*."

* * *

Terri made her call, then sat back and stared out the window. She had not yet told Rodriguez about Cold Case opening his father's old murder book. Opening a Pandora's box was more like it. She had never imagined it would cause him more trouble, give the PD and feds further reason to suspect him. She had thought she was doing him a favor, hoping to get him some closure when she went to Tutsel and Perkowski, but it hadn't worked out that way.

She turned and looked at his profile, the square cut of his jaw set tighter than usual, the determined, almost frenzied, look in his eyes.

She'd been right about him. He'd broken the case for her.

And it was all going to be all right, wasn't it?

"Be quiet."

He slaps the tape across her mouth, sick of her whimpering, unmoved by the tears on her face. "And don't look at me!"

He cannot bear her stare, something about it unnerving. He would kill her right now if she were not so important.

He hears the footsteps above, the place filling up. He empties his gym bag, and sets to work.

55

There were two local uniforms hanging outside the apartment door, a big redheaded guy, the other black, both looked as if they were fresh out of the academy.

"You've just been *standing* here?" I was practically shrieking, ready to tear their heads off, fumbling to get the key in the lock.

"We just got here," said the redhead. "I knocked, but there was no answer."

"You call this fucking backup?" I said to Terri.

She steadied my hand on the lock, said, "Take it easy," and I almost took her head off too.

The young black cop said, "Our orders were to check out the premises, not to—"

I'd already drawn my gun and pushed the door open, so he didn't finish, just got his revolver out while his partner did the same.

I led them into the apartment, holding my breath. I called out, *"Uela!"*

There was no answer.

The big redhead cop spied the Eleggua by the door. "What's with the voodoo shit?"

I almost punched him.

Terri told him to go canvass the rest of the building, probably just to get him out of my face. Then we started down the narrow hallway I'd known all my life.

"Stay here," she said to the black cop. "And watch our backs."

He flinched. "You think the perp's still here?"

Terri didn't answer him and I had no idea, my usual radar buried under anxiety.

We checked everything. The front-hall closet was crowded with coats and scarves, impossible to hide in; the living room wide open; the *cuarto de los santos* produced raised brows from Terri, but she didn't say anything, and it was empty; so was the bathroom.

"Looks clean," she said. "Can you try calling her again?"

"This is her only phone."

"No cell?"

"My grandmother? You kidding? She hasn't even graduated to a cordless."

We went back to the kitchen, and I spread the drawing that I'd taken from Wright's trash onto the table.

"Did I read this wrong?"

The young uniform leaned over my shoulder. "What is it?"

"A drawing of this building, can't you see that?" I had no patience. All I could think was that Tim Wright had been here and taken my grandmother with him. But where?

"Looks it," he said. "But the number's wrong."

"What?" The guy was really working my nerves.

"This isn't 106. It's 301, according to the address we got on our orders—and that's what it says outside."

Jesus, he was right. I hadn't noticed until he said it. The minute I'd seen the sketch and recognized it as my grand-mother's building, I'd just reacted. Now I looked at the three sketches we'd taken from Wright's work table and tried to see if I'd missed anything else.

The cop Terri had sent out to canvass the building came back breathing heavy. "Fuckin' elevator is out."

"What about the neighbors?" she asked. "They see—hear—anything?"

"Place is practically deserted. Maybe 'cause it's Sunday," he said, "And because of the holiday."

"What holiday?" I asked.

"It ain't a biggie—unless you ask my wife, Maureen—Feast of the Annunciation. She's like an expert on every-thing Catholic. I don't know what it's about, the feast, I mean, but Mo, she doesn't miss a single—"

I stopped listening. "One-oh-six," I said aloud. Then it clicked, and I saw it: what Wright was planning to do. "Jesus Christ!"

"Yeah," said the redheaded cop. "I guess he had something to do with the feast."

I heard my grandmother's words when I'd kissed her good-bye. *Change my clothes and go to church.*

"A church!" I shouted, already moving, halfway out the door. "That's where Wright's headed. One-oh-six is 106th Street. My grandmother's church. Saint Cecilia's."

56

Terri was calling for more backup as I sped the Mercedes through the streets of Spanish Harlem. I'd told her what I thought was about to go down.

"You're sure about this?" she asked. "I just want to make sure before I call out the cavalry."

I nodded, eyes on the road, mind focused on getting there. "Yes," I said. I couldn't be certain, but that's what his drawings were telling me. I felt like I knew this guy—the way he thought, what made him tick. "He's been practicing, right? We saw that in his sketches. Three, four pictures of each vic till he gets it right. Maybe they were all practice—the murders, I mean, to build up his courage for something bigger, for *this*." My mind was flooding with images—going to the church with my grandmother; there with Julio as a kid, the two of us helping to paint a funky replica of the *Last Supper* in a small basement room; Wright's explosion sketches— past and present, bodegas and *botánicas* blurring past the car windows.

Terri was still on her cell when I made the turn onto 106th Street, tires screeching.

"There it is," I said. "Santa Cecilia."

* * *

Inside, the church was about half full. Not quite the standing-room-only Wright had probably expected and wanted, but enough to make a statement.

The priest was reading, switching between Spanish and English. Behind him a huge crucifix, garishly colored; Christ's flesh, pale yellow, striped with intense vermilion blood. Dozens of candles were burning and I could smell incense in the air. It brought to mind Maria Guerrero's *bótanica* on a grander scale.

I scanned the room, but couldn't find my grandmother. "I don't see her," I said, my panic escalating.

"We'll find her if she's here," said Terri.

And what if she wasn't? What then? I was no longer sure. Suppose Wright had made that drawing with the wrong number just to throw me off.

I started down the aisle looking for familiar faces, whispering the same question: *"¿Has visto á Dolores Rodriguez?"* I tried hard to keep the anxiety out of my voice. I didn't want to start a panic.

No one seemed to have seen her, a few people voicing objection to my disturbance. *"¡Silencio! ¡Silencio!"*

A friend of hers worked her way out of a pew. She said my grandmother had promised to meet her at church, but had never shown up.

The priest stopped the service and the congregation went silent, everyone staring at me and Terri. I didn't care. I got up on the altar and asked him if he'd seen my grandmother. He said no, told me I had to go, that I was ruining the service. I leaned toward him, and whispered, "You have to get everyone out of here."

He looked at me as if I were crazy. *"¿Por qué?"*

The congregation was getting agitated, whispers swelling, a few people muttering, pointing at me.

The priest took hold of my shoulders, and said, *"Debes ir,"* that I should go.

I heard the distant whine of sirens.

"Backup is arriving," said Terri. "I have to go out and

meet them." She turned to the priest and spoke very calmly. "In a few minutes there are going to be a lot of police here. I need you to ask your parishioners to leave. Do you understand?"

His face was filled with questions.

"Listen to her! *¡Escúchala!*" I said.

There were doors on either side of the altar that led to the sacristy. I chose the one closest to me.

By the time Terri got outside, the scene had taken on movielike proportions: a caravan of cop cars, EMT, ambulances, sirens blaring, beacons flashing; behind them the Bomb Squad, two vans with a SWAT team; two of her own men, O'Connell and Perez; detectives and uniforms emptying out of cars, heading her way.

She was going to have to handle this. It was her case until the feds got here. She still had no idea if Wright was inside. If he wasn't, she had just cost the NYPD a lot of money—and plenty of embarrassment. There was a TV news crew setting up across the street.

The local precinct captain reached her first, heavyset guy, face red, breathing heavily. "What's going on?"

"First off," she said, "get your men to cordon off the street—and get these people back." She gestured at the locals who were crowding the sidewalk in front of the church. "And see what you can do to shut down that damn news van."

The captain went into action and Terri felt the rush that accompanied power. She made her way to the SWAT team leader, a guy who looked like he'd stayed too long at the gym, overmuscled arms unable to lie flat against his sides. Behind him, his men were suiting up and Terri knew the sight of a dozen men carrying Mac-10 rifles would scare anyone. "I don't want a panic," she said. "But we have to get everyone out of the church. Give it a few minutes. The priest is asking everyone to leave quietly, and hopefully they will."

* * *

I heard the sirens. If Wright was in the church, he could hear them too.

My pulse was racing, blood pounding in my ears, but I had to stay calm, had to think. Where would he go if he wanted to be concealed and still do the most damage?

The basement.

The verbal part of my brain shut down and I was all visual instinct.

I saw a staircase and took it.

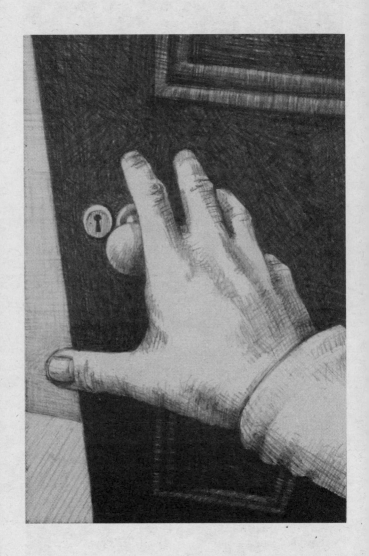

57

The minute my grandmother saw me she started struggling, but he got hold of her and knocked her to the floor.

I aimed my gun. I wanted to kill him on the spot, but didn't dare take a shot, not with explosives strapped to his chest and now a detonator in his hand.

Above her taped mouth my grandmother's eyes were wide with terror.

I didn't know if Wright had the guts to blow himself up but remembered Dr. Schteir's profile of zealots—*men who have no trouble flying airplanes into buildings and dying for what they believe in.*

I needed to see what he was thinking. Maybe I could talk to him. Maybe.

"You did a good job of imitating my drawing style. Of setting me up," I said. "The cops think it's *me*. Not you. You can walk out of here and they'll never know who you are. It will be me who goes down for the murders."

Nothing.

"You can be free. Do you understand?"

Another long moment passed. He said nothing.

"I'll help you get out of here, okay? Give me your mask. I can be you."

"It's too late." His words came out muffled, suffocating under the mask. "I have orders."

You know him. You've been inside his head. Think.

"Are you sure that's what He wants? What if you're wrong? What if you . . . make a mistake?"

"*He* makes no mistakes."

"No, but . . . mortals do. And you're mortal, aren't you? Or do you think you're a god?"

His body went rigid.

My grandmother's lips were moving beneath the tape and I knew she was praying.

We were only six feet apart. I could hear him breathing, almost feel him thinking. I pictured his basement hideout, the newspaper accounts he'd pinned to the wall, and remembered again that he was proud of what he'd done.

"Let me be a witness to what you are about to do. Let me see you, the man who is cleansing the race in the name of God."

He yanked the ski mask off so fast I flinched, my finger twitching on the trigger.

*   *   *

Everyone was out of the church. *Everyone but Rodriguez,* thought Terri. If he hadn't found Wright he'd have been out by now.

"Give me your two best shooters," she said to the SWAT team leader. "I don't want to freak him out with the whole battalion." Then she turned to Perez and O'Connell, and signaled them to follow.

I stared into the face I'd been drawing, come to life. Flesh stretched over muscle and bone, his eyes narrowed, staring back at me.

I wanted to understand what had made Tim Wright the man he'd become, but all I could see was the hatred in his features.

I saw the anger in his eyes and the touch of madness that drove him.

But then I saw something else, something that cut through the madness and hate and anger. For just a moment his eyes widened, muscles working in tandem to wrinkle his brows up, not down.

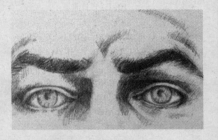

The risorius muscle stretched his lips, but the depressor labii parted them. Then the muscles drew his lips tight across his bared teeth.

And the mentallis muscle set his chin to quivering.

It was fear beneath the hate.

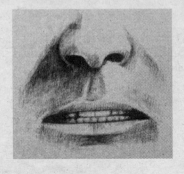

A quote resonated somewhere in the back of my mind: *We hate what we fear.*

I watched his facial anatomy shift between anger and anxiety, muscles convulsing and twitching. He was struggling to tamp down his fear, trying to set the tough-guy features back in place, but it was too late; I'd seen it, how truly scared he was under all his armor.

"You use God as an excuse," I said. "An excuse to hate—an excuse to kill. You want to justify the evil you do. But believe me, God is *not* on your side."

That hit a nerve, the line between his brows deepening, lips stretched taut across his teeth, anger and fear battling it out on his face.

I should have seen it coming but didn't: the lunge that knocked me off my feet.

My back hit the ground hard and the Smith & Wesson flew from my hand. He was coming at me again but I got my feet into his gut and sent him reeling, the detonator too. I held my breath, expecting the blast when it hit the floor, but nothing happened. Then he was on me and the room was spinning, his face inches from mine, a blur, the two of us kicking and punching, cries of pain and breath coming so close I didn't know if it was him or me. I felt a crack across my nose and tasted blood in my throat, elbowed him hard in the ribs, and when he pulled back punched him in the face harder than I'd hit anything or anybody in my life, my knuckles searing with pain.

He fell away from me and I used the moment to tear the tape from my grandmother's wrists and ankles. She was free, but she didn't move, frozen, not wanting to leave me.

"Nato—"

"Go!" I yelled. *"¡Vete!"*

He was coming at me again.

* * *

It was Nate's voice, Terri was sure of it. She signaled the cops and together they raced down the basement hallway and saw her, the old lady, coming toward them, shaking, unable to speak, pointing at the half-open door behind her.

Seconds later, Wright emerged, detonator in hand.

The two SWAT team cops dropped to firing position.

"Wait!" Terri raised her hands, displaying her gun, then very slowly placed it on the ground. "Easy now," she said. She nodded for the others to do the same. "Everything is going to be fine."

Perez and O'Connell put down their weapons and so did the SWAT team.

"On the floor," said Wright. "All of you. Or I blow this place up."

Terri took a minute to study his face. Was he going to do it? She couldn't judge. She needed Rodriguez to tell her—and where was he? There was blood trickling from Wright's nose and his lip was split. He'd been fighting.

Wright waved the detonator.

"Okay," she said, "okay. Everything's cool." She laid her hand on Nate's grandmother's shoulder. "It'll be all right," she said.

"Down! Now!" Wright screamed, his chin quivering, eyes wild, and Terri could see he was beyond reason.

When they were all on the floor, Wright marched over them and Terri watched his boots pass in front of her eyes. For a second she thought—*I can do this, I can grab him, knock him to the floor, and subdue him*—but she couldn't chance it.

When she dared lift her head, he was halfway up the stairs. He glanced back and shouted, "RAHOWA!" then disappeared.

Terri gave the signal and the two SWAT team cops charged after him. She got the old woman to her feet, then turned to O'Connell and Perez. "Get her out of here. Now."

"My grandson—"

"He'll be fine," said Terri.

"What about you?" asked Perez.

"I've got to find Rodriguez."

"I'll go with you," he said. "O'Connell, you take the woman."

They didn't have to look long. Seconds later Nate staggered out of the room, blood on his face, his shirt.

"My grandmother—"

"She's fine. O'Connell just took her out back. Your face—"

"Tell me about it later," said Nate. "Let's go."

The SWAT team was stalking Wright down the main aisle of the now empty church as Terri and I caught up to them.

Wright had turned to face the men, while inching backward slowly and deliberately. I didn't know if they were going to try to shoot him before he had a chance to blow himself up. It was a huge risk and impossible to call.

I was several yards away but close enough to see something had shifted in Wright's face, the muscles starting to relax, and it frightened me more than his anger.

"Don't crowd him!" I shouted to the SWAT team. They were closer to Wright than I was, rifles aimed.

I turned to Terri and whispered, "I think he's getting ready to blow."

She acknowledged me with a slight nod.

The main sanctuary of the church seemed bigger than it had only moments before, the emptiness oppressive, clanging heat pipes playing a discordant dirge, light from the clerestory windows picking out worn tiled floors and pockmarked wood, everything in surreal detail.

Terri laid her gun down on a pew and raised her hands as she walked into the main aisle, totally exposed. "Tim," she said softly. "You know me, Terri Russo, from the station. I can help you get out of here alive. Let me do that. Just put the detonator down." She took a few steps toward him and he seemed to be listening, his hand slightly lowered. Then one of the SWAT team, a young guy, sweat on his brow, lower lip trembling, raised his rifle just a fraction of an inch, and Wright stiffened, thumb quivering on the detonator as he backed out the church door.

58

Tim Wright held the detonator above his head, inched his way down the church steps, and onto the sidewalk. He was an easy target, but no one was going to take the chance; the explosives on his chest looked like they could take the church and half the crowd with him.

The Bomb Squad stood by while uniforms moved everyone down the block. The SWAT team got into firing position.

Collins had arrived with her agents and was conferring with a couple of the chiefs.

I was on the steps with Terri and Perez, and while Wright held everyone rapt I combed the crowd for my grandmother. When I saw O'Connell leading her into a patrol car, the big cop with his arm around her tiny frame, my eyes welled up. She looked so small and frail, this powerful woman who had saved my life and meant so much to me; the idea that I could have lost her unendurable.

"Tim Wright." Agent Collins's voice, amplified by a megaphone, crackled through the tension. "Don't do this."

Wright turned in her direction, then away, muttering something about heaven and God, and taking his place, and it sounded bad to me. His facial muscles had gone placid, jaw eased, brows evened out, anger replaced by resignation and calm.

"He's going to do it," I said to Terri.

She looked at the SWAT team commander and nodded so slightly there was almost no movement at all, but he caught it and relayed it to his men.

Collins called out again, "Wright. Don't do this. There's still time. What can I offer you to—"

I saw Wright's thumb twitch on the detonator, and I guess the SWAT team leader saw it too, because he yelled, "Fire!" and the crowd started screaming and running and the ensuing barrage of gunfire was lost in the blast of explosives as Tim Wright went up in a fireball of flames and smoke.

The blast knocked me backward, Terri along with me, my body hurtling against stone as if I'd been lifted and thrown; then noise and darkness, colors exploding behind my eyes, maybe in front of them too, but I'm pretty sure I had my eyes squeezed shut. I felt Terri's body hit mine, and I wrapped my arms around her, and then time slowed in a way that's hard to explain. There was the noise, of course, a blast that became a roar, carried in the wind along with the ashes and dust and blood, and when it settled there was a moment when it was so still, as if someone had thrown the OFF switch and everything just stopped, at least that's what it felt like; maybe it was simply the aftershock, my ears gone deaf, nerve endings numb.

I managed to get to my feet and helped Terri up as the blackened air around us began to clear.

The space where Tim Wright had been was hard to gauge. It appeared as if parts of the street, here and there, were on fire, thick gray smoke spiraling away from small smoldering masses, and I did not want to think what was burning.

"You okay?" Terri asked.

I nodded and asked her the same. "And my grandmother—?" I asked.

"With O'Connell."

"Right," I said, and remembered him putting her into a car just before the blast, which was when—hours, minutes ago?

And then the switch was thrown back to ON, the quiet erupting into an ear-splitting aria of sirens and screams, and people rushing about; Bomb Squad and SWAT team, Crime Scene and EMT everywhere, and the street pulsating under my feet.

Terri looked into my eyes, then touched my arm and went to join her men.

I stared at the dark clouds of smoke, coiling and swirling into the air like venomous snakes, could see the church was still standing and that no one other than Wright had been hurt, and I thanked God and Chango, and thought: *If only it could be this easy, one explosion to eradicate hate.*

Then Terri came back with Perez.

"Jesus, Rodriguez, you okay?" he asked. "You look like shit."

I touched my face and my fingers came away red.

"You're going to need stitches," said Terri, her face partially blackened but unmarked. We managed to exchange something that approximated a smile before I was lifted into an EMT van and got an ice pack against my jaw. A moment later I was floating on the sounds of sirens.

✶ DAILY JOURNAL ✶

25¢   Monday, March 27, 2006   www.ny.dailyjournal.com

BURN IN HELL!

SKETCH ARTIST FINDS SKETCH ARTIST

NEW YORK. One man died and several people were injured yesterday in an explosion that occurred outside Saint Cecilia's Church in Spanish Harlem at 106th Street. It happened during services being held for the Feast of the Annunciation.

At a joint press conference, FBI special agent Monica Collins and NYPD police chief Perry Denton described the discovery of Tim Wright in the basement of the church with explosives strapped to his chest. Police believe that Wright had planned an attempted murder and hate crime his a hostage situation ensued.

The hostage, Dolo003 Rodriguez, is the grandmother of police sketch artist Nathan Rodriguez. Clues left by the suspect led homicide detective Terri Romeo and Mr. Rodriguez to the basement of Saint Cecilia's, where they found Wright holding a detonator and Mrs. Rodriguez. Mrs. Rodriguez was uninjured. Romeo and Nate Rodriguez were able to help evacuate parishioners and prevent any further injuries. The NYPD cleared several streets and possibly saved hundreds of lives. The explosion blackened the front of Saint Cecilia but that was all. Police, EMTs, SWAT, and the bomb squad were summoned to the scene. Rodriguez suffered minor injuries and after receiving treatment was released from Bellevue Hospital.

Tim Wright was threatening to blow up Dolores Rodriguez and Saint Cecilia's—all in the name of racial purity. Wright is believed to be a part of an organization called the World Church and could be heard shouting "RaHoWa!" Ra for Racial, Ho for Holy, Wa for War before detonating the explosives and killing himself. A representative from the World Church agreed to speak with us and adamantly denied any previous knowledge of activities or crimes committed by Wright in the name of the World Church. Police are looking into Wright's involvement in four other murders involving interracial couples that happened earlier this year. What led police to Tim Wright were a series of sketches left by the suspect at the crime scenes of the murdered victims. Agent Collins and the bureau have uncovered numerous hate organizations across the United States and have been investigating several of them.

In the Queens neighborhood were Wright lived, people were shocked at the news. One neighbor described Wright as "a quiet man who always kept his lawn neat and trim"; others expressed disbelief that they could have been living next door to such a monster.

Wright's mother, a sixty-something retired secretary, appeared on Fox News to talk about the life of her son. Wright's wife, who was living with her sister in Yonkers, was reluctant to speak with reporters. But while leaving her small house, not unlike the one she lived in in Queens, she hugged her young daughter to her side and tried to get into her dented Ford Focus wagon and said she had nothing to do with her husband's crimes. She had begun to fear for her life due to her husband's "growing fanaticism" and had left him several months earlier, taking their daughter with her. "Was it my faith because I left him?" she said.

(Continued on page 6)

59

Tim Wright was famous. And, I guess, so was I.

Some reporter had gotten the story as well as my sketch and splashed it across the paper. No one had yet asked me *how* I'd made the sketch, which was a good thing because I didn't know how I was going to explain it.

The life and death of Tim Wright was the lead story of every local television station and headlined in the morning papers. Queens neighbors were interviewed, one who described Wright as "a quiet man who always kept his lawn neat and trim"; others expressed shock and dismay that they could have been living next door to such a monster.

They'd gotten to Wright's mother, a sixty-something retired secretary, who cried on Fox News.

TV reporters ferreted out Wright's wife, who was living with her sister in Yonkers. They caught her coming out of a small house, not unlike the one in Queens. She was a pretty woman, petite and blond. She hugged her young daughter to her side and tried to get into her side-dented Ford Focus wagon, but the reporters were on her like a pack of dogs. She said she had begun to fear for her life due to her husband's "growing fanaticism" and had left him several months earlier, taking their daughter with her. "Was it my fault because I left him?" she said, the camera zooming in for a close-up of her face, brow wrinkled, and eyes so sad it was almost embarrassing to watch, though I was rapt.

Denton and Collins held a joint press conference that made it look like the feds and the locals had played well together, each of them taking credit in their own way. Denton made much of the fact that only Wright had exploded, not the church, that no one had been injured, that the NYPD had managed to save hundreds of lives when the police had cleared the street, the explosives having blackened the front of Saint Cecilia but that was all. Collins took it from there, noting that the bureau had uncovered, and were examining, hate organizations across the States.

Terri had not participated in the press conference, but it was her name in every news article as the cop who had caught the Sketch Artist.

I'd spent nearly six hours in Bellevue's ER, having my nose reset and a three-inch gash on my chin stitched up, and Terri had been with me for most of it. Afterward, she told me to go home and sleep, but the calls wouldn't stop.

In the space of a few hours I turned down offers to appear on the *Today* show and *Charlie Rose,* but when a curator from the Whitney Museum called to offer me an exhibition of my forensic sketches, I debated, said no, then called back and said maybe.

I finally disconnected the phone and the media must have decided they could carry on without me.

I thought it was over until Terri called to say there was something she had to tell me. I expected she was excited about everything that had happened and her part in it and wanted to celebrate. But the minute I set foot in her office, I knew that wasn't it.

"I was just looking to get you some closure," she said.

"About what?"

Terri started pacing. It brought me back to the first day I'd been in her office.

"What is it? What's going on?"

She stopped fidgeting and sat down across from me. "I never meant this to happen. Not like this. But it's okay now."

"Didn't mean *what* to happen? Jesus, Terri, tell me already."

"I opened your father's case, his murder book."

"*What?* Why?"

"Like I said, I wanted to get you some closure. I thought if you knew what happened, you could—"

"You opened my father's case?" I didn't know what to say; I was still processing it, what she'd done, everything I knew about the case.

"When you told me about your father I could see how it was eating you up inside, the guilt and all, so I thought . . . I just wanted to help, but it backfired. It made the cops and feds more suspicious of you, but it's okay now. I mean, now that you're in the clear."

"Made them more suspicious of me—*how*?"

"Well, they're not. Not anymore."

"Terri." I locked eyes with her. "Just tell me what's been going on."

She took a deep breath. "I'm sorry, Nate. I didn't mean to cause you any shit. It was the furthest thing from—"

"Jesus, Terri, if you don't tell me what this is all about—"

"Okay," she said. "I called you because I didn't want you to hear it from someone else, that the case had been reopened—by me—and what's been discovered." She put her hand up before I could ask another question. "What they found were three distinct samples of DNA taken from the murder weapon, the gun that killed your father."

"Three?" I was trying to make sense of it, but the pictures I had always imagined about that night were flashing in my brain.

"It means there were two other people on the scene other than your father, two other people who deposited their DNA on the gun. One left saliva, the other a tissue sample, flesh caught in the firing pin. It must have pinched his hand when he pulled the trigger. They couldn't test DNA back then, but the DOJ kept the samples on ice. Cold Case just had them tested, sent the results out to data banks, and scored a hit. Actually, two hits."

When I didn't say anything, she slid a report over to me. "Does the name Willie Pedriera mean anything to you?"

There was something familiar about the name, but I couldn't place it.

"His DNA is one of the samples, the tissue sample. He's serving life up in Green Haven for homicide. Don't know how long that will be. According to Cold Case, he's sick."

"What about the other one?"

"It was a juvey case, sealed. That is, until Cold Case got the DOJ to open it about five minutes ago. Now they'll arrest him." She turned a paper around and I read the name.

It took me a minute to process the information and recover from the shock. When I did, I begged her to get Cold Case and anyone else to hold off.

Terri sucked on her bottom lip, thinking about it.

"Trust me one more time. Can you do that?"

She nodded.

"Thanks," I said. "I need to be the one to do this."

Ten minutes later I was in a cab heading down Broadway, a twenty-year-old memory coming back to me in a rush: My father finding the drugs and heading off in search of the dealer; and me, a scared kid who wasn't thinking straight, calling Julio, telling him to warn the dealer, then to meet me uptown. For twenty years that was how I'd imagined it: The drug dealer had killed my father because I'd sent a warning. But now I was seeing it differently.

60

"He's with a client."

I walked past Julio's secretary, into his office. He looked up, then at his client, a man in a chalk-striped suit.

"I need to talk to you," I said.

"Not now." Julio smiled at his client and frowned at me.

"*Now,*" I said. "It's important."

The suit left and I handed Julio the results of the DNA test.

"Hey, that was an important client. This is my job, Nate. Are you out of your mind?"

"Read it." I tapped the report. "It's a DNA test. Twenty years old. *Your* DNA, Julio. On the gun that killed my father."

I was back in El Barrio twenty years ago, remembering how Julio had been stoned by the time I'd met up with him, edgy, and hardly talking. After I'd left, he'd taken the ill-fated joy ride that had landed him in Spofford, wrapped a stolen car around a lamppost, high as a kite, weed in his pocket. He'd called me from the station, used up his one call. He had something to tell me, he said, but I wouldn't let him. My father had just died, and I'd killed him; it was all

I could think about. Julio was sent to Spofford, and I wished it were me, a way to pay for what I'd done. I couldn't face my mother, or my life. For a year I lost myself in drugs: stoned on grass, high on meth; anything to mask the pain and guilt. I was trying to kill myself and might have succeeded had it not been for Julio, who came out of Spofford a new person and helped me get clean. He stayed by my side when I was jumping out of my skin, and held my head when I was sick. We never spoke again about the night my father died. I knew what I'd done and I thought Julio was sharing my secret. I didn't know he had one too.

I stared at Julio, waiting. He didn't say anything, but his face did, surprise mixing with sadness and pain. "You have to believe me, *pana,* I was trying to stop it." He sighed and sagged into a chair.

Then he told me how he'd been with the dealer, Willie Pedriera, when my father showed up; how my father had threatened Pedreira, who produced a gun; how he and Pedriera had struggled and fought; and then how he'd watched, helpless, as Pedriera shot my father. Pedreira threatened to kill him, and me, if he ever told anyone what had gone down.

"Pedreira's cousin was with me in Spofford," he said. "He told me Willie was watching, that he would *always* be watching, and that he would kill me."

"And you believed him?"

"Nato, I saw him shoot your father. I knew what he was capable of." Julio pinched the bridge of his nose. "He would call me every few months and remind me. And then . . ." He took a deep breath. ". . . time passed. And I just, I just couldn't tell you. It had been too long."

"Pedreira's in prison," I said. "And they're going to arrest you because your DNA was on the gun."

"We fought, like I said. My hand was on the gun, my sweat; it's possible."

"More than possible, Julio."

He nodded. "I wondered if this would ever happen. I used to have nightmares about it, but now . . . You believe me, don't you?"

My friend looked up at me, his features clear, no ambiguity in the muscles of his face. I could see he was telling the truth.

"Yes, I believe you. But they know I'm here, Julio, the cops. And I have to call them. I have to bring you in."

He nodded, resigned. "I'll go to them."

I called Terri, told her Julio would turn himself in, and asked if she would personally meet him. Then I asked him if I could borrow his car again.

"Hey, *pana* . . ." Julio managed a smile. "You might end up keeping it."

"No," I said. "*Confia en mil.* Trust me."

I called in every favor I had, even got Perez to do one for me, then got directions, borrowed an NYPD magnetic beacon, planted it on the hood of Julio's Mercedes, and raced up the Taconic State Parkway.

The Green Haven Correctional Facility was in upstate New York's Dutchess County, in a town called Stormville, eighty miles from the city. I made it there in just over an hour.

I parked the car in the lot and stared up at the thirty-foot-high wall and guard towers. It was like something out of *Birdman* of *Alcatraz* or *The Shawshank Redemption.*

Green Haven was a maximum-security prison, most of the inmates serving long stretches, all of them for violent crimes.

I showed my ID and a guard sent me through. They were expecting me, thanks to Perez, who had called the warden, a longtime buddy.

I went through three checkpoints before a guard named Marshall, which struck me as ironic, met me. "Inmate you want is in UPD."

"UPD?"

"Unit for the Physically Disabled. It's over in C-Block, ground floor, 'cause of the wheelchairs." Marshall was a large black man, affable, who kept up a running monologue as we headed over. He was proud of the jail, the dairy that was managed by the prisoners, and the profitable upholstery shop. He was full of information.

"Green Haven is New York's only execution facility. Used to have the electric chair, but they exchanged it for lethal injection. Lot better, if you ask me."

Neither option sounded good to me, but I nodded.

UPD looked more like a hospital than a prison: nurses' station, doctors walking the hallways with clipboards.

Marshall stopped in front of a door, knocked, unlocked it, and waved me in.

"I'll be right outside." He closed the door behind me.

There was a man sitting in a wheelchair by a barred window; cheeks hollow, eyes sunken into sockets, skull visible beneath pale skin. I had seen Pedriera's arrest sheet; he was only a few years older than me. But this guy looked about eighty. I thought Marshall must have made a mistake, but when I asked if he was Willie Pedriera he managed a nod. There was an IV in his arm, bruised and purplish welts on his skin. I recognized the illness.

"I'm Nate Rodriguez," I said.

He turned his head toward me like a lazy lizard. "So . . . you're the son." His Barrio accent was strong. His eyes were rheumy and slightly unfocused; he was obviously doped on pain meds. "They told me you was coming." He took a long, hard look at me. "You don't look familiar."

Now I remembered him. Julio had always bought the drugs, but there was one time I'd been with him. I reminded Pedriera, and he shrugged. "That why you're here? To buy some weed?" He laughed and coughed, the veins in his forehead swelling. He wiped spit off his chin, and reached for a small one-legged figurine he had propped beside a wooden cross on the windowsill.

"You know Aroni, the midget healer?" he asked. "Has his work cut out for him with me, eh?"

"You should have Inle too, for healing," I said. "And Babalu-Aye, who governs the sphere of illness. And Lubbe Bara Lubbe, who will take care of your past—and your future too."

"I have no future," he said, then squinted at me. "So, you are a believer?"

I didn't have time to consider my answer. "Yes," I said, and it seemed right to me.

He nodded, and closed his eyes, a faint smile on his lips.

"My friend, Julio Sanchez, you remember him?" I asked.

He took a minute. "Yeah . . . I remember."

"He was with you that night."

Pedriera sharpened. "Which night was that?"

"The night you killed my father."

He shook his head slowly. "Not me."

Even with his facial muscles in decline I could see he was lying, the corners of his mouth ticking up one second, down the next, zygomatic muscles tugging at his flaccid cheeks, but failing, the contradictions playing out on his face.

"That's what I told those cops. *I. Wasn't. There.* You hear me? Now . . . leave me alone. Can't you see I'm dying?"

"Yes, I see that," I said. "So why lie?"

"You think I should help those bastards?" His lip curled up in disgust. "I was eighteen the first time they locked me up. I sold some drugs, so what? They put me in with rapists and murderers."

Because you are one.

"You see what they do to me?" He flicked a bony finger at his IV. "Why should I help them?"

"It's not about helping *them*."

He waved a hand and it seemed to exhaust him. "Why should I help anyone? No one ever helped me. Never! *Nunca!*" He laid his head back against the wheelchair and took a strangled breath, the chords in his neck like thick ropes.

"But this is your chance, Willie. Your last chance. To save your soul, your *ori*."

He closed his eyes and turned away, but I kept going.

"If you believe in Iku, then you know this is fate," I said, and realized that I believed it too. "This is what was prescribed, the number of days you had written. My father's number was cut short. *You* did that. You offended Ellegua and Chango and Oshun. All of them. Do you want your *ori* searching for a resting place forever? Don't you want the gods to forgive you?"

He didn't say anything for a minute and I didn't either. I watched him struggle for breath and with something less tangible, perhaps his past. Then he leaned forward, reached out and gripped my hand. "Will you do something for me?"

I nodded, waiting.

"Bring me a *madrina* or a *padrino*." He drew in a breath and swallowed hard. "No, an *espiritista,* one with real powers, no fakes." He locked his eyes on mine. "You can do that?"

"Yes."

"Prometeme," he said, his bony fingers tightening around mine.

I promised. I would drive Maria Guerrero here myself. I would pay her whatever she asked. I hoped the warden was as good a friend as Perez said he was and would allow it. I didn't think they would deny a dying man his last wish, particularly in exchange for his testimony.

Then I got the guard, Marshall, to be a witness. He stood and listened while Pedriera told his story: how he'd sold drugs to the neighborhood kids, me and Julio included; and how my father had come to find him that night. It took a long time for him to get it out, coughing fits and gasps for breath interrupting him, and once, even tears. I transcribed every word, leading up to him firing the fatal shots that had killed my father.

"And what about Julio Sanchez?" I asked.

"He tried to stop me," Pedriera said. "*Mas nada*. He didn't do nothing to your father."

I made him say it again, and when he was finished he signed it and Marshall did too.

I promised again that I would bring the *espiritista*, and he told me to hurry.

61

The next day I drove Maria Guerrero to Green Haven. She stayed in Pedriera's room for two hours and when she came out said that she did her best to cleanse him, but he would soon be dead. Then she returned my money.

Two days later Willie Pedriera was dead.

On the way back to Manhattan she told me she'd had a dream that I would find a man on fire. It reawakened the unsettling vision I'd had that day at the station when Denton dared me to look inside his head. It sent shivers down my spine and I told her about it. She told me not to worry, that I was still protected, but I should come to the *bótanica* for candles and herbs. I promised I would.

That night, inspired by her dream, I made a drawing of my vision.

It was different from the original. I hadn't remembered seeing the valley when I'd first had the vision, but it had come to me while I was drawing. I even got out my red ink and added the blood I'd seen on his chest. It didn't make sense—a burning man in a valley—but I thought I'd take it uptown and show it to my *abuela* and to Maria Guerrero to see what they'd make of it.

* * *

The next morning I got an unexpected call from Mickey Rauder, and went to his office.

The chief of operations patted me on the back and offered congratulations on a job well done. He asked how I was doing and I said fine. Then he asked if I was interested in working another case.

It took me by surprise. I hadn't thought about it. But when I did, I said yes, as long as I didn't have to give up my forensic artwork.

"Oh, no. That's a big part of why I'm asking you," said Rauder. "Bill Guthrie, in the fortieth, up in the Bronx, has a real strange case. A fire. Looks like arson. A man burned to death in a tenement. Fire department put out the blaze, but the guy was a goner, burned beyond recognition. No ID on him. No nothing."

The minute he said it—*a man burned to death*—I thought of my vision, the drawing I'd just made, and shuddered. "And the landlord can't identify him?" I asked.

"No, it's some slumlord real estate operation. They don't know him. Say he paid cash every month. But here's the strange part. The only thing that survived was a five-thousand-dollar Rolex watch on the guy's wrist. Half the gold melted, but the lab could still ID it. Odd, isn't it? I mean, here's some guy living in some crap hole and he's wearing a watch like that."

"So it wasn't a robbery-arson or whoever killed him would have taken the watch?"

"Right." Rauder winked at me. "Plus, the ME pulled two slugs out of what was left of his body. The arson was to cover a murder. The guy's teeth were kicked in so there's no way to check dentals. Guthrie's guessing it was a murder for hire. Somebody had this guy snuffed and I'd like to know who—and why." Rauder's eyes narrowed. "So here's my question: You ever do one of those facial reconstructions?"

"You mean build a face based on a skeleton?"

"That's it."

One time, at Quantico, an instructor brought us to a morgue to draw a corpse who'd had half the flesh on his face torn off in a car crash. We were supposed to reconstruct it based on the bone structure. Later, we were shown a picture of what he had looked like and my drawing was dead-on. No pun intended. After that, we had to do the whole thing over, in clay and plaster.

"Yeah," I said. "I made one. It's been a long time, but it was part of my training. I guess I wouldn't mind getting my hands in some clay and trying again."

"Great. They've got the remains at the morgue, and you can nose around a little with some of Guthrie's men, like you did for Russo. It's always good to have a new pair of eyes on a case that's going cold too fast. And you won't get any resentment from Guthrie's men. They're happy to have anyone that's willing to come up to the Bronx. Plus you proved your worth." He smiled.

I thought again about the first time I'd had the vision of the burning man, and I didn't know why, but I started to feel something weird about the case, and about Denton.

"Chief Denton have any interest in this case?"

Rauder's brows knit. "Why do you ask that?"

"No reason. I just wondered."

"Maybe what Russo says about you is true, kid, that you're a bit of a psychic."

"Me? No . . . not really."

"No? Because Chief Denton *did* take an interest in the case, which is odd. I mean, the chief doesn't take much interest unless it's a big story. Don't get me wrong, I'm not saying anything about the chief. It's not his job. But this morning we're having a meeting, one of our regular ones where the chiefs report to me and I report to Denton, and when I tell him about the burning man in the Bronx he starts asking a whole lot of questions. Even asks to see the case file, the CS pics, autopsy report. Odd, because, like I said, the chief doesn't usually get involved, or care. But I figure if the chief cares about this case so much I'd better make sure Guthrie gets some help. This kind of John Doe usually ends up cold, but maybe not this time—and maybe not with your help."

I didn't say what immediately came to mind—that Rauder might have gotten Denton's reaction backward—because I wasn't sure I was right, but I told him I'd help.

"Thanks," he said. "Your dad would have been real proud of you."

I didn't want him to get started on my father, but it was too late.

"You know what I remember most about your dad? His locker. What a sight that was. Most of the guys had the usual pin-up girls and crap, but not him. The inside of his locker door was a shrine to your artwork. Every other day he was taping a new picture in there. He'd bring me or one of the guys over and say, 'Look at what my boy did.' It sounds like he was showing off, but frankly Juan Rodriguez didn't give a rat's ass what me or anyone else thought when it came to you. It was just what *he* thought. And I can tell you there was no one, no one on this earth more proud of what you could do with a pencil than your dad. He was proud of you then and he'd be proud of you now."

I swallowed, tried to blink away the threat of tears, and said I'd get over to the morgue and start that reconstruction right away. Then I got the hell out of Mickey Rauder's office as fast as I could.

I hadn't spoken to Terri since she'd told me about opening my father's Cold Case because I wasn't sure what I wanted to say. My emotions were mixed, but I knew I wanted to see her.

We met at a bar near her place and she looked really pretty, though I could see she was tense—furrowed brow, mouth tight.

We didn't kiss hello and we were way past shaking hands, so it was awkward, a nod, a quick "Hi," then we ordered drinks and sat at a small table by the bar not talking. After the waiter delivered our beers, Terri started the conversation with an apology. "It was a mistake to open your father's case, and I'm sorry. I'm really sorry. I hope you believed what I said, that I was trying to get you some closure."

"Are you sure that's what you were trying to do?" The question had come from my subconscious, nothing I'd planned to ask.

Terri took her time before she answered.

"You know, I honestly can't say. Maybe at the time I was kidding myself. Maybe . . . I just wanted to find out more about you. It's possible. But I'll tell you what I feel now." She looked into my eyes. "Whatever suspicions I had about you, any motives I may have had for bringing you on the case, that's in the past. It's not about that anymore. You broke the case for me, and I'm grateful, but I'm talking about something else, something that happened just before that, when I stopped wondering and I started . . ." She shrugged and went for her beer.

"Yeah," I said. "Me too."

"You too, *what?*"

I didn't want to say what I thought she'd been about to say: that she had decided to trust me and had started to care, because then I'd have to say it too, so I went back to my father's case. "I know what you were trying to do, and it's okay. It got me some answers I never would have gotten."

"So you're okay? You're not mad at me?"

"No."

"So how come you look it?"

"I'm not angry," I said. "It's just that I was thinking about what happened between me and my father. It was the worst thing that ever happened, and . . . I have to live with that. But it's the past and I can't change it. There are some things you don't get over because you're not supposed to."

Terri nodded, and touched my hand. After a moment, she asked, "How's your friend doing?"

"Julio? He's good." I thought about the long night we'd had, me and Julio, talking and talking, and even letting our machismo down, and crying a little too. At first it had stung, that he hadn't been able to tell me, but now I understood. There were things one didn't ever want to say. I had never told my mother what had happened, and after a night of debating whether or not I'd get on a plane to Virginia Beach and confess, I realized that was about *my* need, not hers. It would open an old wound and only add to her pain. She didn't need it, and it wouldn't change anything.

"Maybe I've been looking for absolution or redemption," I said, "but I know now that's never going to happen. Knowing the truth about what happened that night hasn't changed the facts. I still feel responsible, but . . . I was a kid. I don't know, but . . . maybe now I can let that kid off the hook. Just a little." I thought about the cartoon I had of myself, the one I'd been carrying around for a long time: the little boy looking for his dad. It wasn't that it had completely changed, but the cartoon had morphed into a fuller portrait of a man and his father.

"Good idea," she said, and I thought I saw some tears gathering in her eyes.

"Hey, tough-cop Terri Russo isn't going all soft on me now, is she?"

Terri wiped her eyes and put on a really great fake smile. "Fuck, no. It's just the damn smoke in this place."

I didn't bother to point out that no one was smoking because she knew that. I clicked my beer bottle against hers. "Is it okay if we don't talk about this anymore?"

"You kidding me, Rodriguez? I thought you'd never stop."

I laughed, then got serious. "You took a chance on me, put everything on the line—your job, your reputation; I know that, and I appreciate it. I probably wouldn't be sitting here if it weren't for you."

"Damn right. You'd be in an Attica cell with Montel calling you *honey*."

"Nice," I said. "I open my heart and what do I get, a knife."

"Just telling it like it is, Rodriguez." She smiled and tilted her head and I could see she wanted to ask me something.

"What?"

"I'm wondering . . . Am I wasting my time on you?"

"No way. I'm your man."

"I'm serious, Rodriguez." She took a swig of her beer, put it down, and looked at me, one eyebrow cocked. "I just don't want to spend six months on some goon who is never going to commit."

"Wow," I said.

"That's your response: *Wow?* What the fuck does that mean?"

"Hey, give me a minute to think about it, okay?"

"What's there to think about? I didn't ask for your hand in marriage. Hell, I don't think I ever want to get married. Just that I'd like to—"

"I heard you." I tried to collect my feelings, but she didn't give me a chance.

"What a cliché you are, Rodriguez. And so am I. Here we are, the thirty-something man who can't commit to anything past dinner and the thirty-something woman who is on her way toward bitter." She waved a hand. "Never mind. Let's just enjoy our beers and forget I ever said anything."

"I swear I can make plans past dinner," I said. "You want to set up brunch next Sunday, I'm there."

"Ha-ha."

"Oh, come on, Terri."

"No, forget it, seriously. I'm sorry. I made a mistake. Not my first and probably not my last."

"How about we have dinner and see where it leads."

"I know where it will lead, Rodriguez. Into your bed."

"Is that so bad?"

She sighed. "I don't know about you, Rodriguez, but Terri Russo is starting to want more out of her life than a good lay on Saturday night."

I chewed a cuticle and studied the damage. I thought about the apartment I hadn't turned into a home and probably never would; I thought about Julio and Jess and how they were always trying to fix me up and would probably not stop; I thought about their kid growing up and me playing "Uncle Nate"; I thought about dinners once a week with my *abuela,* whom I loved, but how three years from now she'd still be asking me why I didn't have a girlfriend. Then I thought about my father taking me to ball games and reading me bedtime stories, and I started to feel so bad I didn't know what to say.

"Jesus, I'm sorry," she said.

"Do I look that bad?"

"Yes. And it's not the bruises or the stitches on your chin, which, to be perfectly honest, I find sexy as hell. But you look like I just punched you in the gut." She laughed a little. "I didn't mean to."

"Go ahead," I said. "Take your best shot."

"Think I already did."

I looked at Terri and tried to figure out what I wanted to say, but I was feeling too many things at once and couldn't come up with the words.

"I'm not going to beg you, Rodriguez. My life is fine the way it is. I didn't ask for you to come into it, and if you don't want to stay in it, that's fine too." She stood up. "Maybe it's better if we just called it a night."

I got up and pulled her toward me, but she pushed me away.

"If you want me to stay—and I don't mean here, now—I mean, if you want me to stay in your life, you're going to have to say it, Rodriguez."

She only took a few steps back, but it suddenly looked as if she were disappearing. I grabbed hold of her and held on. "Don't go. Let's see if we can make this work." I said it fast so I wouldn't check myself and stop.

"Hey, that was pretty good, Rodriguez."

"Are you going to call me Rodriguez *forever*?"

Terri smiled. "I can't believe you just used the f-word. I'm speechless."

"Now that's a first, *you* speechless." I smiled back. "But you should know better than to listen to my words. You want to know what I'm really thinking, look at my face." I gave Terri a look that I hoped conveyed the warmth I was feeling.

"I think I'm getting it," she said, then gave me the look she'd had so many times over the course of the case—brows knit, eyes narrowed, as if she were trying to see into my brain.

"It's not that hard," I said. "I *want* you to see me."

ACKNOWLEDGMENTS

My thanks to the following people for their help with this book: The brilliant Suzanne Gluck; my superb editor, David Highfill; Janice Deaner, invaluable reader and friend; Ryan Ernst, who lent his computer expertise and his face; Gabe Robinson, Dan Conaway, Elaina Richardson and the Corporation of Yaddo, Reiner Leist, and SJ Rozan; Anthony Romero, Manuel Marinas, and Saraivy Orench-Reinat, who corrected my Spanish without complaint or derision; the William Morrow/HarperCollins family, who continue to support me—Jane Friedman, Lisa Gallagher, Michael Morrison, Debbie Stier, Danielle Bartlett, Carla Parker, Lynn Grady, Carl Lennertz, Tavia Kowalchuk, Sharyn Rosenblum, Mike Spradlin, Christine Tanigawa, Brian McSharry, Juliette Shapland, and everyone else who has helped behind the scenes. For their creative effort beyond the call of duty, Betty Lew, Richard Aquan, and Jimmy Iacobelli deserve medals.

More thanks to my sister Roberta; my mother, Edith; my daughter, Doria; and always my wife, Joy.

To the many booksellers and readers I have met in my travels who have supported my work: *Where would I be without you?*

One final note: To truly comprehend the work of face-reading expert Paul Ekman, Ph.D., I recommend reading one or more of his fascinating books, among them *Unmasking the Face: A Guide to Recognizing Emotions from Facial Clues, The Facial Action Coding System,* and *What the Face Reveals: Basic and Applied Studies of Spontaneous Expression Using the Facial Action Coding System (FACS).*

Don't miss

THE MURDER NOTEBOOK

**The new Nate Rodriguez thriller
From Jonathan Santlofer
In hardcover June 2008
from William Morrow**

NYPD sketch artist Nate Rodriguez can't shake his nightmarish visions, so he comes to grips with them the only way he knows— by putting them down on paper. When he realizes that these sketches have an uncanny resemblance to actual murders from the past *and* the present, he knows he has to do something about it. His search for answers will push his talents— and his sanity—to the limit.